People Pleaser

NON-FICTION BOOKS BY BRYONY GORDON

The Wrong Knickers
Mad Girl
Eat, Drink, Run
Glorious Rock Bottom
No Such Thing As Normal
Mad Woman

YOUNG ADULT BOOKS BY BRYONY GORDON

You Got This
Let Down Your Hair

People Pleaser

BRYONY GORDON

PENGUIN
VIKING

VIKING

UK | USA | Canada | Ireland | Australia
India | New Zealand | South Africa

Viking is part of the Penguin Random House group of companies
whose addresses can be found at global.penguinrandomhouse.com

Penguin Random House UK,
One Embassy Gardens, 8 Viaduct Gardens, London SW11 7BW

penguin.co.uk

First published 2026

001

Copyright © Bryony Gordon, 2026

The moral right of the author has been asserted

Penguin Random House values and supports copyright.
Copyright fuels creativity, encourages diverse voices, promotes freedom
of expression and supports a vibrant culture. Thank you for purchasing
an authorized edition of this book and for respecting intellectual property
laws by not reproducing, scanning or distributing any part of it by any
means without permission. You are supporting authors and enabling
Penguin Random House to continue to publish books for everyone.
No part of this book may be used or reproduced in any manner for the
purpose of training artificial intelligence technologies or systems. In accordance
with Article 4(3) of the DSM Directive 2019/790, Penguin Random House
expressly reserves this work from the text and data mining exception

Set in 13.2/16 pt Garamond Premier Pro
Typeset by Six Red Marbles UK, Thetford, Norfolk
Printed and bound in Great Britain by Clays Ltd, Elcograf S.p.A.

The authorized representative in the EEA is Penguin Random House Ireland,
Morrison Chambers, 32 Nassau Street, Dublin D02 YH68

A CIP catalogue record for this book is available from the British Library

HARDBACK ISBN: 978-0-241-74743-8

TRADE PAPERBACK ISBN: 978-0-241-75283-8

Penguin Random House is committed to a sustainable future
for our business, our readers and our planet. This book is made from
Forest Stewardship Council® certified paper.

For you. Just in case it's been a while since you had anything for yourself

Prologue

Olivia Greenwood is focusing on the lollipop. She is being torn alive from the inside, but she is mostly focusing on the lollipop. The pale pink plastic over the cola-flavoured sweet, which her mother will lovingly unwrap as a reward for Olivia not making a fuss. The smile as dazzling as the stars that Olivia will be shown for not ruining things, for not making it all about her.

Lollipop. Smile. Good girl.

Even so, it is getting increasingly hard for Olivia to ignore the fact that there is something living in her stomach, and it is trying to get out. The teacher is talking about photosynthesis, and how plants use the sun to create life, and as Olivia shifts uncomfortably in her flimsy plastic chair, she wishes that she could pull off this trick too, and turn the milky grey light streaming in through the classroom window into some sort of life support machine that might sustain her through whatever terrible thing is happening inside her body.

But no. She is human, and she has something alien in her, and because of that alien thing, she is about to die. She's sure of it. In forty-eight days, she is supposed to turn nine. Just yesterday she had spent hours trying to work out how she could subtly mention this to her parents, in the hope that they might plan a birthday party a little ahead of time, as opposed to twenty-four hours before, as normal. How cruel it seems to Olivia then that she is now battling a pain in her abdomen so sharp she is sure she won't make it to break time, let alone her next birthday. She twists in her seat, tries to stretch out her middle.

'Olivia!' snaps Ms Smith, who makes the class pronounce it Mizz, so they know for sure she is a serious teacher, and not a silly little Miss. 'You are to sit still and concentrate. Your parents don't pay all this money for your education for you to throw it all away by spending lessons fidgeting.'

Olivia feels a hot stab of shame, though it could also be the talons of the creature currently trying to disembowel her. The pain is unbearable, but then so is the alternative: interrupting the class to tell the teacher she feels unwell, that a monster is about to burst out of her chest, the ensuing eye rolls and huffs, the long, silent walk as she's escorted to the school office, where phone calls will be made to her parents, and important work meetings will have to be abandoned, and Olivia will prove yet again that she is an attention-seeker and a drama queen, all of which feels impossible to manage when she has this animal clawing at her . . . bladder?

Oh god.

'Sorry, Mizz,' Olivia says meekly to the teacher, clenching her body so the monster will stay inside it, at least until break time.

Olivia's brain tries another tack, which is usually quite successful at keeping things inside: shame. She lands on the conversation she had with her mum that morning, over the breakfast table. Olivia pictures her little sister Lily, adorable and easy, eating neatly, quietly, smiling broadly at their mother. Then she pictures herself, pain glowing in her stomach, unable to contemplate the bowl of cornflakes her mum had placed in front of her.

'What's wrong?' asks her mother, juggling a steaming cup of black coffee with a stack of important work papers.

'Nothing,' says Olivia. She is already so good at lying that she genuinely believes it to be the truth.

'So why aren't you eating?' Her mother places her mug down on the table. It says WORLD'S BEST DAD in cutesy baby-blue writing. Her mum growls at the mug, a gift to Olivia's father that the sisters had given him before he took off on yet another business trip a few days ago. Olivia has no idea what her dad does, other than that it involves being away from home an awful lot of the time, and when she spotted the mug on a weekend shopping trip, she had begged her mother to let her get it. 'Maybe then Daddy would be happier?' she had reasoned, not adding that maybe this would have the knock-on effect of Mummy being happier as well. But now the mug sat on the table, forgotten by her dad, a source of annoyance for her mum, and Olivia could see that this was her fault too.

'Can we not just have one morning where everything goes smoothly?' Her mum points her manicured nails at the pitifully empty wall chart on the fridge, the one that is supposed to be filled with a gold star every time Olivia and Lily manage to get out of the house and to school without causing any trouble.

'Sorry, Mum.' Olivia attempts to spoon some cornflakes into her mouth, and visibly winces at the discomfort this produces.

'Jesus, Olivia, they're cornflakes, not a bowl of nails.'

'I've just got a bit of a stomach ache, that's all.' Olivia forces herself to swallow the soggy cornflakes which do, actually, feel like nails.

'Of course you have.' Her mother sighs, sips her coffee while gathering her purse, keys, a corner of toast. 'Listen, Olivia, let me get something straight: you are not faking a stomach ache to get the day off school, OK? Not today. It's an important day at work, one that I cannot afford to miss.'

'Could Dad come home?' It seems both entirely reasonable and absurd, all at the same time.

'Ha!' Her mother spills some coffee on her shirt, swears. 'Right, upstairs, get dressed. If you go to school and get through the day without a fuss, I will give you a medal for your troubles.'

'I don't want a medal.' She wants a cuddle.

Her mum sighs, rolls her eyes. 'OK, a lollipop. You can have a lollipop, Olivia. Ah, I thought that would make you smile. Now chop-chop!' She claps her hands together, then scoops Lily into her arms and kisses her head. 'Come on, angel, let's go brush your teeth.'

Oh, that does it. That gives Olivia the motivation to get through the next seventeen minutes of the science class. If she can just hold everything inside for a little bit longer, if she can just hang on . . . lollipop, smile, good g—

'Ohhhh,' groans Olivia, as a wave of pain floods her body, and her body floods her thighs, which in turn floods the floor below her desk. Many things are happening at once. The other children are looking at Olivia, and half of them seem to be laughing, while the other half seem to be squealing in horror. Ms Smith is turning and stabbing a piece of chalk in the air in Olivia's general direction. Olivia is trying to stand up, to get out of the classroom and to the nearest bathroom, where she can hopefully flush herself and the monster down the toilet.

'Olivia Greenwood!' shouts Ms Smith. 'Will you SIT DOWN?'

Olivia tries to do as she is told. She wants to do as she is told. She wishes she could be the kind of child for whom it is easy to follow instructions, like her little sister, instead of the kind of child she actually is.

Olivia attempts to sit back down, but she misses the chair. She lands hard on the floor, into the puddle she's just created, her damp school uniform riding up to reveal the knickers she's just wet.

She passes out.

Olivia Greenwood doesn't get a lollipop, or a smile, for her troubles. She just gets peritonitis and two weeks in hospital, as her appendix bursts and infects the abdomen around it.

'I came as quickly as I could,' Olivia hears her father say to her mother, as the general anaesthetic wears off and she groggily comes round on the children's ward.

'Aren't you a hero?' her mother mutters. Olivia opens her eyes and sees her mum's giant red shoulder pads rise up and down in one almighty sigh.

'Really, Tina?' her father replies, loosening his tie. 'Even now? Can't you have a day off, especially when our firstborn is lying in a hospital bed after a major operation?'

'No, I can't have a day off,' she hisses, 'because we have a mortgage to pay and not all of us get to spend our time wining and dining people for a living.'

'I didn't mean from work,' snaps her father. 'I meant from the bitchiness.'

'I might be a bit more inclined to be nice to you if you were less of a self-centred arsehole.'

Olivia senses her parents turning back towards her. She quickly flickers her eyes closed, wills herself to drift into a beautiful, dream-free sleep. One where she is not in hospital, or the object of her mother's ire, but back at home, enjoying a lollipop with her sister, a reward for being a good girl, an easy child, a delightful one.

A world where she has made everyone around her feel so . . . pleased.

1

First week of summer term

Like most humans who are very good at making other people happy, Olivia Greenwood is beginning to realize that she is thoroughly miserable. Not dramatically miserable, in any way that could be seen or noticed or commented on and made a fuss of, but quietly miserable, in a polite manner that won't make anyone else uncomfortable. Not making anyone else uncomfortable is the key, really. To do that would only make her anxious as well as miserable, and that is a combination Olivia strives to avoid at all costs, like Negronis on an empty stomach.

Today, as Olivia rises to the sound of her children fighting to the death over the last bagel in the house, she decides she won't do this any more.

'I'm not doing this any more,' she says, sitting up straight in bed. 'Today is the day that everything changes!' As ever, she is talking to herself. The conversations she has in her head are some of the punchiest, pithiest and – most fundamentally – improbable she ever takes part in. If in her mind she is Shiv from *Succession*, in reality she is more like Cousin Greg.

Her husband Nick is asleep, or is pretending to be. What's the difference, really, given that as a couple, their interactions have almost entirely dwindled to 'hmm', 'Is that right?', and 'Is it OK if I go to CrossFit?', the latter coming exclusively from him and particularly common on days when they already have plans she has reminded him about weeks in advance – plans such as his mother's birthday, or a six-hour drive to the greyest, windiest parts of the country for some of the Easter holidays.

'How was I supposed to know that we were going to Cornwall?' he had actually protested, when they all woke last Saturday morning, bags packed, and Nick had cheerily announced he was off to do a competition that involved rowing the length of the Nile over a weekend, in teams of three, on a stationary machine positioned nowhere more exotic than an industrial estate near Haywards Heath.

'Because I told you we were,' replied Olivia, standing in the hallway, incredulous. 'Because it's been in our diary for four months.'

'I didn't know we had a diary,' snapped Nick. He stood at the top of the stairs, dressed in his workout gear, looking like a Sainsbury's version of one of those middle-aged ex-SAS soldiers turned TV presenters. There was once a time when they had worked out together, every sit-up and squat and sprint on the treadmill a sexy step towards being naked and alone in bed later on. But now it seemed to Olivia that Nick worked out to get away from her.

'It's one of those old-fashioned diaries that tends to exist entirely in your own head. What happens is people you are exceptionally close to, your wife for example, tell you some important information about plans, and then you store that information in your brain for future reference.' These days she felt more like his assistant than his wife.

'There's no need to be passive-aggressive,' countered her husband, heading back towards their bedroom to change out of his Special Forces cosplay outfit.

The horrendous traffic on the journey home yesterday had

tipped her over into being aggressive-aggressive, with Nick missing two exits in a row while Olivia tried to catch Jack's car-induced sickness in an empty crisp packet.

She clutches wildly around the bed for her glasses and discovers that they have somehow ended up under her pillow. She places them on her face, notices that after a night of being crushed under the weight of her head they are now really lopsided as opposed to just vaguely lopsided, grabs her phone from the bedside table and then swings her legs on to the floor. While she pees, she continues the never-ending conversation she has with herself about how, as a woman born in 1980, she is still playing out the same dull gender dynamics that destroyed her own parents' marriage and led to her dad living in her garden shed, and her sister camping on the sofa bed in the living room two nights a week, as a sort of part-time nanny/children's entertainer/live-in therapist.

Olivia would like to describe the small structure in the garden next to the dead flower bed as an annexe, but she knows deep down that not even the most deluded estate agent in the world would try to get away with this characterization, nor Nick's insistence on describing the tiny shower room she sits in now as an en suite. For a start, it's off the landing, accessible not just to her and Nick but any one of the increasing number of family members staying with them. And secondly, the lock is broken, meaning it provides about as much privacy as the concourse at Euston station during the morning rush hour.

Olivia hates that Nick still hasn't got round to fixing the lock in the non-suite, but not as much as she hates the thought of being seen as a nag, so she has taken to pulling the overflowing washing basket in front of the door as a way of maintaining some dignity as she showers.

She washes the ruins of her body, trying to remember when

Nick last looked at it. When will her life resemble the kind she is served up all the time on her Instagram 'For You' page? Reels featuring perfect light-filled houses with pastel-coloured kitchen units and tastefully chosen knick-knacks that look like art as opposed to clutter entrance her.

Today, perhaps?

Yes, today is surely the day, the one where everything is going to change. For almost two decades now she has been waiting for this moment, since she began at *The Morning* fresh from the exams, judgement and paralysing perfectionism of her journalism degree. It was all she knew. It was all any woman her age knew. But today, all the hard work, all the graft, all the patronizing from mediocre men with half her talent and triple her entitlement, is finally going to pay off. After years of being the journalistic equivalent of a nodding dog – *of course I will bash out 1,200 words on the latest craze sweeping Hollywood that promises to remove five inches from your waist and a decade from your face* – she is going to be given her first column.

Today, she will become OLIVIA GREENWOOD with a strapline that reads FRANK, FEARLESS, FUNNY.

Probably. Most likely. This is almost certainly the 'exciting news' that the editor wants to discuss with her after conference. It has to be, right?

Right?

Just to be sure, Olivia decides she must reanalyse the email that Stephen sent two days ago and make sure there isn't anything she might have missed in her previous 5,942 readings of it. It was a fairly nuanced message, after all.

Liv. Need to see you after conference on Friday, have some exciting news. S

Back in their bedroom, Olivia finds Nick fumbling with himself under the covers. He freezes as he hears the door, pretends first that he is asleep then a split second later that he is stirring from a deep slumber – though unfortunately not the one that has become a metaphor for their fourteen-year marriage. 'Morning,' he says, with all the embarrassed innocence of a schoolboy who has just been caught wanking by his mother.

She has become his mother.

Or, even worse, her *own* mother.

She decides not to dwell on that right now, as the man she once thought of as the great love of her life continues in his attempt to play the innocent, wiping sleep theatrically from his eyes and stretching his arms above his head in an exaggerated yawn before picking up his phone from the bedside table and checking his email. For whose benefit this performance is she isn't sure. She does know he doesn't put as much energy into attempting to seduce her as he does pretending he's OK with their non-existent sex life. Strangely, it is in these moments – where he seems as terrified of being seen for his real self as she does – that she feels closest to him nowadays. It's something they still seem to have in common, after all this time.

'Morning!' she beams, trying to ignore the ruckus that continues downstairs. She is OLIVIA GREENWOOD: FRANK, FEARLESS, FUNNY, not Olivia Greenwood: cross, cranky, cantankerous. She breezes over to her wardrobe, or at least she likes to imagine that she breezes over to her wardrobe, which she also likes to imagine is a walk-in, filled with colour-coordinated, neatly catalogued outfits that could be pulled out at any moment to form a capsule collection she could easily throw into a chic limited-edition carry-on when she is called at a moment's notice to spend a couple of nights in New York for work. In reality, her job had last taken her to Swansea on an assignment about an assistance guinea pig, and even that had seen her in and out in a day, a stain of milky white guinea pig urine on her jeans accompanying her all the way back on the train.

'FOR FUCK'S SAKE!' she shouts, as she trips over a yoga block, a remnant of her half-arsed attempts at Bikram before breakfast from eight months ago. It had not made her a better person or even stretched out her creaky hips all that much, just added more useless tat to a house already crammed full of it.

'You know, strength training is especially important for women as they enter perimenopause,' Nick says, grinning as he finally gets out of bed. 'Maybe you should think of doing one of the Olympic Weightlifting classes they have at CrossFit at the weekend.'

'I stubbed my toe, it's fine,' says Olivia, poking around in her cornea as she swaps her wonky glasses for her contact lenses. 'Also, who would transport the kids around to their varied and rich social lives if we were both fannying about with a load of dumb-bells every Saturday morning?'

'That's no way to talk about my friends.' Nick kisses the top of her head, springs around the room with far more energy than Olivia thinks is fair for a 44-year-old, and does not stumble over one of her yoga blocks. She sighs at the sight of his shoulders, broad now not from picking her up and fucking her against the wall, but from bench pressing at the gym. RIP, hot shower sex. 'Could we pay Lily to come an extra night?'

'Why don't we just invite her to move in with us as well? And bring in Mum too, while we're at it. Then we can really meet the full madhouse brief.'

'I just think you'd feel better about yourself if you were

able to invest in your health more,' says Nick. His skin looks particularly glowing today. Is he taking a multivitamin or something?

Olivia suddenly feels like one of those washed-out, decrepit 'before' photos that people post on their social media. She knows her husband is genuinely trying to be supportive, but she wants to leap on him and claw out his peppery dark hair in rage. How come he gets to improve with age, transforming into some sort of McDreamy style heart-throb, while she feels like a *Grey's Anatomy* surgery gone terribly wrong?

Is this why she and Nick have drifted so far apart? Because her husband is able to prioritize his wellbeing and his needs without the world falling apart, while she seems to be stuck in a perpetual loop of self-sacrifice and *still* everything always feels like it's about to go to shit?

Every day, Olivia pretends she has dreams, dreams that her mother and Instagram and society at large would approve of. Dreams such as: living a life true to herself; standing in her own power; dancing like nobody is watching. Et cetera, et cetera. Olivia has become very good at pitter-pattering these dreams into conversations with Nina and the other young women she has been mentoring at *The Morning* under their Women Rising scheme. Initially she was sceptical about it: a corporate initiative set up to pinkwash the fact that the majority of senior staff are men. Not to mention it involved an extra eight to ten hours a month, for no additional pay. Olivia would like to dream big, but the constant threat of cut budgets and redundancies keeps her in a perpetual low-level nightmare. But it turns out she loves the scheme, loves being able to breathe confidence and certainty into the young women who actually have a shot at breaking free from the stifling patriarchal bullshit she's become numb to – even *entertains* sometimes so as not to rock the boat, in a kind of never-ending bad dream she hasn't quite worked out how to wake up from.

But perhaps today? Perhaps today.

She stares at her tired reflection in the mirror on the back of the wardrobe door. She's learned to mask her exhaustion with various helpful props: a teeth-whitened smile; a biannual injection of botox that she can neither afford nor admit to; and a make-up palette that consists entirely of inoffensive nudes that will make her look fresh and pretty but not too threatening. She sets to work now, grateful for the almost meditative ease with which she has perfected her morning routine.

Make-up done, Olivia attempts to make sense of the jumble of clothes that she has shoved haphazardly in her side of the wardrobe, stuffed there in stark contrast to her husband's beautifully folded workwear and military cosplay uniform. That a man so fastidious about folding and functional fitness could also be so incapable of remembering holiday dates is one of life's great mysteries to her.

Today, Olivia carefully selects an outfit that she believes to be stylish yet businesslike. The look of a woman who knows her own mind, as dictated to her by the Instagram stories of the latest popular midlife fashion influencer everyone is following. A pair of Boden trousers, a white shirt and a selection of faux-gold jewellery from Zara that will show she's serious but fun. She teams the outfit with a simple pair of ballet flats that are back in fashion according to said influencer, who saw them on the runway at all the shows last season, a knock-off version of which Olivia found on Boohoo.com.

If anyone asks – and frankly, Olivia flatters herself by imagining that they will – she will say that they are vintage, i.e. from 2002, when they were last popular and Olivia's mum bought her a pair of £100 Pretty Ballerinas because 'it's the kind of shoe that I can imagine on a young lady Prince William would go out with'.

She checks her phone: 8.12 a.m. She needs to get a move on. Suddenly a scream pierces the house, the kind that Olivia recognizes as sibling warfare, but that a neighbour might reasonably misidentify as homicide. She bounds down the stairs at a speed she wishes she could emulate on the imaginary 5K she runs regularly in her fantasies, but has yet to attempt in real life.

'Kids!' She comes to a halt in the kitchen, where her younger sister is holding a bagel in the air like a prize, a triumphant look on her face, as Jack and Saskia attempt to snatch it from her hands. There is a Marmite moustache above her lip, and Olivia would not be surprised if her sister had put it there on purpose, as some way of distracting the kids while bargaining with them to get out of bed and ready for school.

'Don't mind me while I avert a small diplomatic crisis in the style of Emmanuel Mac-a-ron.' Lily pronounces it like the French pastry, rather than the French president. She is dressed in a bright pink kimono from one of her many jaunts around the world to find herself. Jaunts financed, conveniently, by their mother. Lily throws the bagel to Olivia but she fumbles the catch and fails to prevent Jack immediately snatching it from her grasp.

'Mum, that's MY KETO BAGEL!' Saskia appears close to tears, in a way that Olivia finds both entirely disproportionate and incredibly relatable.

'Isn't there toast, cornflakes, any number of other things in the vastness of the cupboards me and Dad are forever stocking with food?' Olivia places her arm around one of her daughter's bony shoulders.

'You know I don't like toast or cornflakes, Mum, and that they're basically nutritionally bankrupt items of food that taste of cardboard.' Saskia shrugs her mother's hand away, repulsed and annoyed in equal measure. 'And Jack knows that those bagels are specially formulated so they are vegan and keto-friendly and have more protein than carbohydrate in them, which I need if I'm ever going to progress into the next level of the football squad, because unlike Jack, I actually have a life and do sport with my friends, as opposed to just sitting around at home staring at a poster of Erling Haaland.'

Jack wrinkles his freckled nose in dismay. 'I have friends, you just don't know them because you're too busy thinking about yourself. And I don't just sit and stare at posters of Erling Haaland!'

'You mean Ian Harland,' says Lily, sitting down at the kitchen table to eat her toast, licking the Marmite from above her lip.

'*Erling* Haaland,' correct Jack and Saskia together, in a rare show of unity.

'Whatever his name is,' sighs Lily, quietly triumphant. 'We're all talking about the blond bloke who looks like a thumb with a face, right?'

'I've always thought he has more of a vibe of Legolas from *Lord of the Rings*,' says Olivia, grabbing the bagel back out of her ten-year-old's hand, passing it to Saskia, then reaching in a cupboard for a hidden packet of non-keto bagels that she bought on her lunch break yesterday to head off this exact emergency. She is OLIVIA GREENWOOD: CALM, COOL, COLLECTED. If she had a moment, she might reflect on how many roles she is able to flip between, and all before 8.15 a.m.

Instead, she robotically heads over to the ancient Nutribullet to make her morning elixir: a dollop of yogurt, some frozen spinach, a banana, a handful of blueberries, a thimble of chia seeds, a whole heap of midlife crisis. 'Now if you could eat your breakfast without resorting to violence,' she says, placing the lid on the machine, 'that would be much appreciated. I've got a big day ahead of me, work-wise.'

'Oh wow, you really have turned into Mum,' sniggers Lily, shoving a piece of toast in her mouth.

'That is NOT funny,' Olivia snaps.

'I know, mate, I was being deadly serious.'

Olivia presses the button on the Nutribullet, hears the deafening clatter of the machine's motor, and allows her shoulders to relax as she enjoys one of the few screech-free moments of the morning.

'Football kit!' Olivia shouts into the ether, as soon as the machine has stopped its incredible racket.

'Smoothie machine? Toaster? Television? School bag?' Lily runs a hand through a wild and wonderful thicket of golden curls, the type that Olivia had longed for since childhood, signifying as they did a sort of carefree joie de vivre that had always seemed slightly out of reach. 'Are we just naming random things for fun or is "football kit" code for something?'

'Sorry, it suddenly popped into my head that it's football kits today, for both kids. Why is it that these things only come to me when something's making a sound similar to a pneumatic drill?'

'You'd probably be able to answer that question, sis, if you'd ever taken my advice and got some therapy.'

'Not all of us have time for therapy, Lil. I'm too busy trying to remember the football kits.'

Lily breathes the sigh of a woman who has become used to being roundly patronized. 'Well, luckily for you, I'm not too busy to remember the football kits. They're already in their PE bags by the door. I think I've been doing this long enough to know that Friday is football day,' she titters, tightening her kimono round her waist. 'I can't believe you're still taking Dad a cup of tea in the morning.'

Olivia hears the click of the kettle announce that it has boiled. 'How do you know that's what I'm doing?' she says, grabbing a mug from a cupboard.

'Because it's what you always do, and it's kind of tragic. It's enabling him, babes.'

'If you weren't taking my kids to school for me, I might point out the hypocrisy of telling me off for enabling Dad.'

'I don't know what you mean.' Lily says it in a sing-song way that suggests she knows exactly what it means.

'Oh I dunno, just how me coddling Dad isn't all that different to you allowing Mum to treat you like a baby.'

'I am her baby, Olivia.' Lily puts on the condescending voice of a parent talking to their toddler. 'I'm her baby girl.'

'You're about to turn forty!'

'Imagine how insufferable she'd be if I didn't allow her to perform this vital function of still being loved and needed by a member of her family. She might start bothering you. I'm being of service to us all. Taking one for the team.' Lily approaches Olivia at the kitchen counter, takes a sip of her smoothie, and sticks her tongue out in horror. 'Urggh, still gross. Oh, speaking of the parents, Mum asked me to remind you to RSVP to my party.'

Olivia pours the hot water on to the teabag and feels her blood run cold. Her mother's judgement is always there, even if the same cannot be said for her actual mum, who still seems to see Olivia as a sort of annoying adjunct to Lily, a kind of pointless vice president you are forced to invite along to things out of formality rather than any actual desire to be with them. She is the JD Vance to Lily's kimono-clad Trump.

'Ah, yeah,' Olivia murmurs as she adds milk to her dad's tea. 'I'll get back to her once I've got today out of the way.'

'I'm excited for you,' smiles Lily, heading towards her makeshift bedroom in the living room. 'Mum's going to lose her shit getting to tell everyone that her daughter's the next Selina Martin.'

'I feel like . . .' Olivia gazes into the middle distance in a sort of reverie. 'Like after all this time playing the game, I'm going to get my prize. Finally.'

'Go get 'em!' Lily blows her sister a kiss, grabs her bag from the living room, where she sleeps without complaint, and heads upstairs to the dribbling shower. Olivia squishes her toes into the ballerina shoes, and ventures into the patio area she likes to describe as a garden, to knock on the door of the shed she would like to be able to describe as an annexe.

There is no answer.

There never is.

She clears her throat, thinks about the man who once returned from a work trip to Dunstable with a mini-pinball machine he'd somehow won on a night out. It was always this memory that had stuck with Olivia, for its pure comi-tragedy, its crisp, neat ability to sum up their childhood. The innocence of youth had allowed her to paint their father as a Disney Dad, a man who returned from glamorous business trips away laden with gifts and hugs and declarations that he had missed his girls with all his heart. It was only in adulthood that Olivia and Lily had come to realize that their Disney Dad had also been a pretty Half-Arsed Husband (at best), a man who made up for his absences with gifts he couldn't really afford, given that their mother had actually been the main breadwinner, a successful marketing executive to his travelling salesman, a role that he had vastly exaggerated so as not to upset the traditional eighties status quo of the man being the master of the house. It was at uni that Olivia had clocked on to the fact that Dunstable was a dreary market town in Middle England, and not the centre of the universe.

She coughs theatrically, or pathetically – she's never sure which. Still nothing. She waits, admiring the large pile of fag ends that sit at the bottom of a vodka bottle he has hidden badly by the plant pot.

'Lily,' she calls, hoping that if she shouts into the house it might wake up her father without causing a scene. 'Can you make sure that Jack and Saskia are ready to go in three minutes?'

There's a mish-mash of noise from the house, but nothing from the shed.

She knocks again, feels her right big toe already throbbing in the faux-ballerina pump.

'Dad?' She tries to bat away the ever-present anxiety that exists like the low thrum of her heartbeat, the worry that one day, he simply won't be able to answer.

'I've made you a delicious cup of tea to counteract all the delicious vodka you seem to have enjoyed last night!'

If she is passive-aggressive and cheery and speaks like a Matalan Mary Poppins, then everything will be OK. Everyone will think they are a normal family. A normal family who keep their elderly stashed in the back of the garden.

'Leave it on the step,' her father finally croaks from within. 'I'll come and get it before I start my chores.'

Olivia places the cup down, aware that when she returns in twelve hours' time, there's every chance that the tea will still be there, and that the chores – whatever they might be – will still not have been started.

'OK, well have a good day, Dad. Maybe take it easy so you don't burn out.'

She wonders if she has veered from passive-aggressive into aggressive-aggressive territory, waits a moment or two for him to respond. Then she notices the time on her Apple watch, an accessory that she mostly uses to berate herself for not exercising, and realizes she is going to be late for work. She heads back into the house, scoops up the heaving stack of post from the hallway table and shoves it in the Waitrose tote bag that seems to be doubling as a handbag.

Then Olivia Greenwood strides headfirst into the first day of the rest of her life.

2

Olivia doesn't mind the 35-minute train journey from the suburbs into central London. Like the calamitous whirring of the Nutribullet, it might be one of the few parts of the day that she actively looks forward to. She's even fairly laid-back about the fact she rarely gets a seat, and the frequent delays that leave her and her fellow passengers stranded on the tracks somewhere outside Redhill, staring into the back gardens of people who don't appear to have anything more peculiar than a lawnmower in their sheds. It gives her time to collect her thoughts, which is midlife code for 'do all the shit nobody else bothers to'.

Today, it's tackling the fortnight's worth of post she has allowed to accumulate, much like the coarse hairs that seem to keep sprouting out of her chin with increasing regularity. She hopes that dealing with the mail, if not the hairs, will give her a sense of achievement before her life-changing meeting with Stephen. It will enable her to go into his office with goddess energy, which is something she's heard about (on Instagram) and that she feels she should probably be exuding now that she's about to be made Queen of *The Morning*. She pulls the post out of her tote bag, notes the grey footprints which have been stepped into the various envelopes over the last few days, the effort of picking up the post clearly too much for a single one of the Greenwoods, herself included.

There is a phone bill she can ignore, a message from the

DVLA she can't, some vouchers for Pets at Home that might have been useful if Jack's guinea pigs hadn't shuffled off their mortal coil six months ago, and then, there is the thick, gold-lined envelope bearing the unmistakable cursive handwriting of her mother, addressed to Mr and Mrs Nick Greenwood. It embarrasses Olivia, the formality of it all: the fact her own mother refers to her by her husband's name, the fact she still writes in the ridiculously pompous script she taught herself as a teenager, via a library book called *Classic Calligraphy Techniques for the Modern Twentieth Century* (lol) and a fountain pen complete with actual ink pot that a distant, sympathetic uncle had gifted her. Olivia had heard this story on a number of occasions, usually to underline how lucky she had been to have an expensive education that both her parents (but mostly her mother) had grafted hard for, but also sometimes to hammer home the fact that Tina had managed to lift herself up and out of the grime of her terrible childhood, scrubbing it off her person so that, in public at least, she could pretend it had never been there in the first place. What did the Greenwood girls (but mostly Olivia) have to complain about, given the life of relative luxury that their parents (but again, mostly their mother) had created for them? Could they (but mostly Olivia, because Lily had always been sweetness and light) not see how lucky they were?

Tina was well into her sixties now, but still she couldn't drop the sob story about her impoverished childhood in Essex, her neglectful parents who had basically abandoned her so they could drink themselves to an early death. It was sad, Olivia got that, but the woman now lived in a sprawling five-bedroom Georgian house with views of the South Downs while her estranged husband squatted in Olivia's shed, drinking himself to an early death on his daughter's watch instead of Tina's. Olivia wondered why her mum couldn't at least have offered her dad 'the Coach House', the grandly titled actual annexe at the end of the grounds, where Lily now essentially lived, surrounded by her crystals and her incense sticks and the 'supplements' that Tina believed were vital to her youngest daughter's health. It was one way of explaining the mushrooms, Olivia supposed.

As Olivia stares down at the gilded envelope, her heart sinks at the thought of her mother sitting in judgement on her, complaining to her new alt-right boyfriend Clive about Olivia's jealousy, her inability to put petty sibling rivalry to one side and RSVP like a grown-up.

Is that why Olivia hasn't, as of yet, managed to open the invitation to her sister's fortieth birthday party? Some sort of childish strop at Tina pulling out all the stops for Lily, while all she got for her fortieth was a WhatsApp. Olivia hates how this still rankles, even though she knows logically that her fortieth happened during the height of one of the lockdowns, when Tina could hardly take over the local Italian restaurant for a huge knees-up, as she is doing now with Lily, and when she was still with their dad, and probably didn't much fancy throwing him, a public event and plenty of booze into the mix together. As the train rumbles on, Olivia folds herself into the luggage rack like a buggy and wonders why, at the age of forty-four, she still can't let this stuff go? Why does she have to make everything so difficult?

Olivia has a variety of tactics she uses to stop herself from appearing difficult – including, but not limited to, nodding along to opinions that are diametrically opposed to her own, saying yes when she actually means no, and staying silent when she feels the need to speak up. At work, her boss Stephen once joked that she was like the human equivalent of a chaise longue, forever bending herself into impossible shapes in order to make everyone else more comfortable. Incredibly, Olivia took this as a compliment – for being a human chaise longue, she was certain that today she was finally going to be given her own throne.

Let's get this out of the way, she thinks, as the suited men sitting comfortably tap away at their laptops. Olivia tears at the envelope and feels something twist inside her as she reads its contents. Something very primal and very childish, like that feeling you had as a kid at Christmas when you decided your brother or sister had been given a bigger present than you.

Mrs Tina Fryer
cordially invites the Greenwood family (and Peter)
to celebrate the fortieth birthday of Ms Lily Fryer
RSVP essential by 10th April

Olivia looks at her watch, sees it is the 12th. She begins to berate herself, in the style of her mother. Why couldn't she get her shit together? Could she not do this one little simple thing? Would Saskia be less controlling about protein bagels if Olivia wasn't so thoughtless and chaotic? Would Jack have a stronger sense of self? Unexpectedly, she feels her eyes sting with tears. She shakes the thoughts from her brain and searches for the WhatsApp group she is in with her mother and sister. 'Fabulous Fryer Ladies 💃' last saw action several months ago, a series of perfunctory messages confirming that both Tina and Lily would be coming to Jack's tenth birthday party.

Double digits, wouldn't miss it for the world! ♥ Lily had written.

It's very kind of you to extend an invitation, her mother had written. *Clive sends his apologies as he has a council meeting. I will of course be there.*

Of course.

Olivia starts typing a suitably contrite message to try and make up for the inexcusable act of RSVPing late.

> I am so unused to invitations to anything other than smear tests that it took me a while to recover from the shock of this one. Please forgive me. The Greenwoods (and Peter) would love to come to Lily's party xxxx.

Send. She feels suitably confident in answering on behalf of her dad (Peter) owing to the fact that his social life, much like Olivia's, seems to largely take place entirely in her living room.

Olivia puts the invitation back in her bag and shakes her hands as if ridding herself of her mother's energy. Once she's got this new job, the late RSVP will all be forgotten about and Olivia can set about offering her mother her favourite thing: good news, the type that shows how stunningly successful Tina is as a parent. To be fair, delivering good news is also Olivia's favourite thing. A delicious sweet treat that makes up for all the 'nonsense' Olivia has put everyone through over the years, like the time she would only eat food that had an even number of letters in its name, or that was orange in colour, two pretty specific neuroses that she still hasn't got to the bottom of all these many years later, but has at least got over.

The thought of doing something right, of achieving something important . . . it's all Olivia has ever really wanted. To impress, rather than disappoint. To lift people up, as opposed to dragging them down. When she thinks back to the endless troubles she seemed to cause as a child, the upsets she was always at the sharp end of, no matter how hard she tried not to be, she feels a sort of desolate darkness that she would do anything to avoid. Becoming a journalist at a national newspaper may not mean much to anyone of Saskia or Jack's generation now, but back in the late nineties and early noughties, when everyone rushed to the newsagent on a Sunday morning to learn who had been diddling who, journalism had felt important. Working for a broadsheet was honourable, cultured. It was the kind of thing that her parents could be proud of. She worked hard, because to be lazy – even if this translated into being burnt out and exhausted – was unforgivable. Her mother's values dictated that a lack of professional success was every bit as indefensible as the abandonment that Tina had gone through as a child. Tina had decided that her firstborn was going to be academic, and that the second one would be a free-spirited creative, and both girls had gone out of their way to play these roles for their mother, Lily with far more success than Olivia. How thrilling, how terrifying, that today could be the day when all her hard graft finally paid off.

High on hope, Olivia rummages for her AirPods, pops them in her ears, and indulges in her favourite form of disassociation: listening to a playlist of nineties power ballads and fantasizing about a life where she is universally loved and admired, and not a grown adult who feels constantly sick with worry that people are cross with her. This thrumming bassline of anxiety was so familiar to her that she had ceased to notice it any more – she simply accepted that it was the necessary soundtrack to her life, a kind of payment she had to make each day in order to inch closer to success. 'You can achieve all your dreams,' her mother had told her throughout her childhood. 'A girl as dynamic as you will have no problem smashing the glass ceiling, but you'll want to tone it down around men so they don't get too intimidated by you. You don't want anyone to think you're too much, Olivia.'

Olivia had arrived on the graduate scheme at *The Morning* all those years ago ready to take over the world, to become a daring war reporter or a fearless political commentator, a woman to be taken seriously in the media. Instead, she had quickly been siloed to the features department with every other woman who had arrived at the newspaper, where their journalistic remit encompassed diets, clothes and spurious celebrity trends. The male news reporters called it 'The Cotswolds', a place where nothing particularly interesting ever happened but everything looked very nice. Meanwhile, they rather grandly referred to their own department as 'Baghdad', which amused Olivia, not just because it dated so many of the reporters to the year 2003 where they firmly belonged, but also because the furthest most of them ventured was the bar of the Red Lion.

The women in the Cotswolds took their work seriously, even if the men in Baghdad didn't. They knew that a good news organization required light as well as shade, that the pages they dealt with were every bit as important as the commentary on the Middle East. Olivia believed this with all her soul, even if some of her female colleagues were less generous in their assessments of the work they had to do. It was what made her the perfect person to head up Women Rising, a cheery, positive presence who could rally the more cynical colleagues, such as Nina. 'You're delulu if you think any of the blokes who run this paper actually care about our careers,' Olivia's young protégée had once complained, during one of the compulsory mentoring sessions that always seemed to have been scheduled by HR at the busiest point of the day.

But Olivia had genuinely seen it as an honour and a privilege when she was asked to head the group up five years ago. In her mind, it showed how central she was to the organization's success. Now, she was sure all those extra hours of work that Nick had baulked at were finally going to pay off.

The editor, Stephen, was at the top of the patriarchal pile, a man Olivia had long tolerated for her own professional gain. She allows herself a small moment of pride, that she has taken all that unfortunate business from the beginning of her career, and somehow managed to nurture it so that it's now going to work to her advantage. She imagines the look on Nina's face when the younger woman learns of her promotion – the excitement and respect that she will express when she sees what is possible if you doggedly stick at it, as Olivia has done.

Lured back into her imagination, Olivia goes to her phone and selects Celine Dion's 'It's All Coming Back to Me Now'. Olivia likes to see these little fantasy sessions as more of a premonition, an opportunity to manifest, allow in abundance, et cetera, et cetera. In today's fantasy – sorry, premonition – she is at her desk, writing a banal story about a 55-year-old actress deciding to cut her hair short, when an email arrives from the editor's PA asking her to come to his office immediately.

'I, I . . .' She shakes her head at her screen. 'Guys, I've been called to see Stephen.'

Her colleagues all stop what they are doing.

'Hope I'm not in any trouble,' she whispers to Joe, who has been her desk mate since they started together on the graduate programme all those years ago, the only man ever placed in the Cotswolds, on account of the fact he is gay.

'You, Olivia Greenwood, in trouble?' he says, with a roll of his bright blue eyes. 'There's more chance of the comment desk writing a balanced editorial about immigration.'

As Celine begins to sing about the nights when the wind was so cold, Olivia stands up and makes her way towards Stephen's glass office. One by one, journalists turn their heads as she passes to her destiny. The office falls silent as people put everything on pause to witness this era-defining moment in *The Morning*'s history. Stephen stands at his door, awaiting Olivia. She turns round and gives her colleagues one last nervous smile before she walks into the next, long-deserved phase of her career: she is the new Selina Martin, the legendary Fleet Street columnist who has recently retired (translation: been sacked because she kept refusing to get a social media account, of any description, or file her copy on a laptop, via email, instead of dictating it drunk at 5 p.m. down the phone to whichever junior had drawn the short straw).

After weeks of speculation, the shocked smile on our heroine's face confirms what everyone has long suspected: that after years of loyalty to both Stephen and *The Morning*, having turned down numerous exciting opportunities from other media outlets because in a world of flighty, fickle journalists who are only really interested in where their next pay cheque comes from, our heroine has principles . . . Olivia Greenwood is to be rewarded with the biggest newspaper-column slot in Britain.

Which, given that nobody really reads newspapers any more, isn't really saying anything.

But come on, this is Olivia's fantasy. The whole point is to depart from reality.

Olivia thanks Stephen profusely for the privilege of making her a columnist during *The Morning*'s centenary year. The editor opens his office door, and beckons her out to the editorial floor, which has risen to its feet as one, everyone applauding as our heroine bashfully shakes her head and pretends to be embarrassed by the attention. Nina rushes past desks to embrace her friend, Joe not far behind. 'I'm so proud of you,' Nina whispers in Olivia's ear. 'You're going to be great!'

Just as Celine Dion reaches her crescendo . . . Olivia realizes she is still on the 8.27 to Victoria being hollered at by a woman in her seventies who looks a bit like Paddington Bear, if Paddington Bear shopped at Phase Eight.

'Will you turn that down!' cries the woman, hitting Olivia on the shoulder. Olivia removes her AirPods, startled. Somehow they have disconnected from her phone, which is now playing the climax of the seven-minute-forty-second Celine Dion track across the whole carriage. Olivia scrambles to press 'stop' as the men at the tables begin to snicker. 'Your music was loud enough even before you took the headphones out. I'd be surprised if they couldn't hear it all the way down the line in Victoria.'

'I'm so sorry,' says Olivia, breathlessly. 'I do apologize.' Her face turns red, as she feels the oh-so-familiar burn of shame that comes from upsetting someone without meaning to. If she can just be smaller, quieter, nicer, just make herself more poised, polite, pliable, just until she's seen Stephen . . . everything will be OK.

3

Olivia enters the office reminding herself that she is OLIVIA GREENWOOD: FRANK, FEARLESS, FUNNY, even if she feels more Olivia Greenwood: harangued, humiliated, and horrifically blistered. (Her cheap ballerina shoes are eating her feet alive.) She decides to send a quick WhatsApp to Stephen to let him know she's ready whenever he is, although by 'quick' what she actually means is 'constructing, agonizingly slowly, a perfectly bright, breezy and slightly bootlicking message that will give absolutely no hint of the deep detestation she feels for this man from the very bottom of her soul, nor the desperation she feels for him to acknowledge and validate her'.

> *Hey Stephen, just to say I'm free if you still wanted to have that chat. Hope you're having a good morning! X*

It's the kiss that makes her wince the most. It's a terrible throwback to when she first arrived in the Cotswolds during the noughties, and genuinely thought that an X at the end of a message made you look kind and trustworthy. Over the years it's become her thing, her trademark, the sign-off which marks her out as the nicest, most loyal person in the office. She can hardly stop using it now. People might think her rude, and she doesn't want that.

'Look what the cat dragged in,' says Joe, as Olivia sits down and immediately removes her ballet pumps under the desk, the air a balm for her soles.

'You're in early,' sighs Olivia, turning on her computer.

'Yeah, well I didn't want to miss any of the drama from your meeting. It's not just middle-aged women from Bromley who like to get in early, you know?'

'I don't live in Bromley,' corrects Olivia. 'That's in Kent. I live in Sussex.'

'Kent, Sussex, outer space, it's all the same to a guy who lives in Lower Clapton, babes. Wherever it is, it doesn't change the fact that since you moved out to the sticks, the most interesting thing that ever happens to you is managing to claim compensation from the Fat Controller for all the time you spend standing on packed platforms, waiting for the delayed 18.57 to turn up. It's like a really dull version of your twenties, but at least then a clapped-out service would occasionally pull into the station.'

'Is "clapped-out service" a metaphor for Nick,' replies Olivia, rubbing the back of her heels as her computer takes an age to power up, 'and "station" a euphemism for my vagina?'

'Liv, just the person!' She hears Stephen's voice, closes her eyes, hopes that by the time she has turned her chair around and opened them again, she will magically be the kind of person who is able to brazen out saying 'vagina' in front of her boss.

'Here I am!' She smiles her sweetest smile. 'All the way from the suburbs.'

'I've heard great things about Bromley,' says Stephen, looking at his watch.

'Yeah, it's a really wonderful place to live.'

'Got your message,' he says, suddenly less interested in the delights of market towns. 'Shall we get that chat out of the way? Won't take a minute.' He uses his arms to motion away from the slums of her desk.

'Sure,' says Olivia, slipping her ballet shoes back on before standing up, wincing at the pain on her heel. She follows Stephen towards the water cooler, where he stops, grabs a paper cup, and fills it up.

'Would you like one?' he says, offering the cup to her. Olivia hopes that cost-cutting hasn't led to the end of the executive cold filtered water provided to all people important enough to have their own office, even if it's absolutely ruined tap water for her.

'I'm fine, thanks,' smiles Olivia, ready to follow him on to his office. Instead, he leans on the water cooler as he drinks from the cup, before placing it back under the tap and refilling it.

'So, Liv,' he says, using the machine as a prop to lean on. 'As you may well know, there's some exciting changes taking place at *The Morning* in our centenary year.' Olivia wonders if, by choosing to stay at the water cooler instead of going on to his office, he is trying to signal to his staff that he is one of them. That, together, he and Olivia are about to mark the start of a new, more egalitarian news organization, where the editor and senior columnist catch up at the water cooler, *just like everyone else*. She imagines how cool she must look, just standing there shooting the breeze, the boss about to reward her many years of loyalty.

'Big year for *The Morning*, big year for you, Liv.' She feels her heart soar, while also trying to rub at the speck of smoothie she has just noticed on the left leg of her trousers. 'The good ship *Morning* is sailing into the future, and I want you to be up on the captain's deck with me for every moment of the journey.'

She tries not to look too excited. 'You've got what it takes to go really far at this paper,' Stephen always said to her, every time she agreed to write a feature nobody else would go near because they had actual principles, or it would mean working overtime and they'd been very boundaried that they needed to be home by 6.30 p.m. to relieve the childcare. Olivia had never let her position as a mother get in the way of her career. That was what being a feminist meant, right? She was a role model of ambition and hard work and dogged reliability. And if her children were occasionally displaying the same signs of obsessive dysfunction that she herself had as a teenager, like a full-blown freak-out over a bagel, well that was normal, wasn't it.

When her waters broke three weeks early with Saskia – catching her unawares as she hadn't quite got round to writing up several months' worth of interviews with celebrities about their day in diet form, which she had promised to get done ahead of going on maternity leave so that the department wouldn't be inconvenienced by her having a baby – Olivia had sat in the living room on her birthing ball, Nick holding the Dictaphone whenever a contraction made it too tricky to copy down the life-altering news that the runner-up of *Celebrity Ironman* season four began each day with a squeeze of lemon in hot water and four small prunes ('You don't want any more than that unless you want to spend the day on the loo,' transcribed Olivia, between waves of pain and nausea).

When Jack was three weeks old, she had agreed to write a piece about hypnobirthing, because apparently Kate Middleton had been bang into it and the features editor had heard Olivia talking about it once, in passing, during her pregnancy. 'You're *The Morning*'s very own Princess Kate!' her boss had explained on the phone, Olivia swallowing back the tears caused by hormones and mastitis and her freshly stinging emergency C-section scar so that she could accept the commission. Her desire to be affable and easy-going outweighed anything as ridiculous as her need to lie on the sofa with her left tit ensconced in a frozen cabbage leaf; she had simply assumed that if they were asking her to do it, then it must have been reasonable. Other people's requirements always, always took precedence over her own clearly skewed judgement. After all, she was forever hearing about that one woman who worked in the City and had managed to birth nine children while building her way to the top of the major FTSE 100 company, so surely Olivia could take a day out to write about the importance of golden-thread breathing while you were being torn apart from the inside? A not-so-small, not-so-insignificant part of Olivia also liked the fact that she was needed, that the office clearly couldn't do without her. It made her feel valuable in a way that breastfeeding just didn't, no matter how hard she tried to convince herself otherwise.

'Anyway,' says Stephen, loosening his tie. She tries not to look too excited. Was he going to give her her own office? Would there be a photo shoot to launch her, perhaps some sort of advertising campaign? She'd have to go shopping. Given she was about to get a significant raise at *The Morning*, she might be able to finance this dream. In fact, once she's a columnist, she will only have to write once a week, so she'll finally have more time and money to spend with Nick and the kids. She'll have to research her column if she wants to push the boundaries a bit, move it on a bit, but she won't have to rely on Lily quite so much. She loves seeing her sister, but she'd rather Lily came round just because she wants to.

'There's nobody like you when it comes to steering a boat through choppy waters.' Olivia hopes he won't make some sort of *Titanic* analogy. Too late. 'You've always been a cheerful, solid presence when the good ship *Morning* has occasionally hit an iceberg, if you get what I'm saying.' He refills his cup for the third time. 'You're like the head of the orchestra on the *Titanic*, refusing to leave the deck while all around you, everyone is acting like a bit of a dickhead. Do you get what I'm saying, Olivia?' He downs the contents of the paper cup again, crushes it in his fist before throwing it in the bin next to the water cooler.

Olivia smiles at Stephen, who she still loyally emails to congratulate every time the paper publishes an exclusive. Joe had once described such gestures as 'arse-licking' but Joe wasn't the one standing at the water cooler with the editor of *The Morning* now, was he. Neither was Nina, who refused to say more than two words to Stephen because she thought he was a 'misogynistic psychopath with all the morals of a ferret'. Olivia almost admired this younger generation, and how entitled they all felt to a glittering career without ever having to put any of the unglamorous legwork in. But as she had told Nina and all her other Women Rising mentees time and time again: if you wanted to get ahead, you sometimes had to swallow your pride and remember where you came from.

Well, at least Olivia was about to be rewarded for her arse-licking. Would Joe think her 'suburban' when she came back to her desk as a star columnist? Would Nina finally understand that principles counted for nothing until you actually had somewhere to voice them publicly? All those years of being the good girl were finally going to pay off, in the most spectacular style.

'So listen, an exciting new role has opened up in the organization, Liv, and I think you're absolutely perfect for it.' Her heart hammers under her carefully curated Zara shirt. She continues to nod, hoping that the motion will steady her. It would be mortifying to burst into tears, here at the water cooler, when he breaks the news.

'I'm so excited for you, Olivia, I can't even begin to tell you how great I think this is going to be for you. It's such an important role for *The Morning*.'

When is he going to get to the point? She tuts herself. She has waited this long, it won't harm her to wait a little bit more and humour him as he delivers his big news. After all, it's probably a pretty big moment for him too, replacing Selina Martin after thirty years.

'So, it is with a huge amount of excitement that I want to offer you the role of . . .' He drums his stubby fingers on the top of the water cooler. Olivia beams, her gratitude shining out of her face so brightly that it could probably power the whole office, not to mention the printing presses too. 'Anniversary Architect!'

Stephen claps and cheers.

Olivia's mouth drops open in shock.

'I knew you wouldn't believe it, Liv.' Stephen pats her on the shoulder as he laughs. 'If you could see your face right now, my god. I knew this would be a big moment for you, but I didn't know you'd be quite this blown away.'

Olivia feels a little like she did all those years ago in hospital, when she inadvertently heard her parents arguing about what a pain in the arse it was that her appendix had ruptured – like she's somehow overheard something she wasn't supposed to, a half-baked, impulsive thought that wasn't really meant for her ears. She needs to employ the cool, calm and collected version of herself to stave off the tears that are now taunting her contact lenses. But all she feels is hot, liquid humiliation.

'Anniversary Architect?' chokes Olivia.

'Fucking great title, don't you think? Only the best for you, Liv.'

'It's . . . brilliant,' lies Olivia. She's pushing down all the sensations she doesn't like, zoning out so that she can leave her body and the office and the whole entire universe.

'It's better than brilliant, Liv. You're only in charge of our whole centenary celebration. I'm thinking, massive fucking party, loads of celebrities, incredible venue. Bubbles. A chocolate fountain. Fairground rides! Brilliant pull-out, special edition, with all the best writers. And who better to put it all together than our ANNIVERSARY ARCHITECT, LIV GREENWOOD!'

Stephen raises his voice so that around them, various departments fall quiet.

'So does that mean . . . I won't be . . .' What is happening to her?

'Having to write any more?' finishes Stephen. 'Yep, no need to roll your sleeves up and get your hands dirty, Liv. You'll be part of senior management, getting to boss everyone around.'

Olivia has wanted this job ever since she heard her mum wax lyrical about the ball-breaking writer Selina Martin as if she were a hero. Olivia remembers one moment so clearly, just after the whole appendicitis debacle, her mother moodily reading the papers one morning, unable to go to work because Olivia had just come out of hospital and needed to be looked after. 'I wish I could be as outspoken and articulate as Selina Martin,' her mum moaned, the paper spread out before her on the kitchen table. 'Imagine being a woman who just said what she thought without giving a hoot what anybody thinks!' Olivia had watched her mum's face light up at the very idea of it.

'But I enjoy writing. I've covered a lot of stories lately while we've been understaffed.' She starts chewing the inside of her mouth and scratching one of her thumbs with the other.

'Writing is a mug's game, Liv,' Stephen waves her comment away. He lowers his voice and leans in to her conspiratorially. 'You only have to look at Selina to see that. Phoning in her copy, pissed, once a week, as if she was Barbara fucking Cartland? Her engagement was terrible, you know. It's terrifying doing her job.

If you're not talking directly to the people, to their hearts, they abandon you. Your head is permanently on the fucking chopping block. Nah, you don't want to be writing any more, Liv. Any old chatbot can write. Writers will be extinct in a couple of years.' He lets out a laugh. 'If you want to continue the *Titanic* analogy, writers are basically Leonardo DiCaprio, teeth chattering in the Atlantic, clinging on for dear life to a piece of old wood while knowing that, inevitably, they are going to sink into the water and drown, while you, Liv, are Kate fucking Winslet, rescued by the *Carpathia* so you can continue on your journey to, if not exactly greatness, then a comfortable life that gets turned into an Oscar-winning movie by James Cameron.'

She doesn't remind him that a moment ago, she was the conductor of the orchestra, ready to play on and go down with the ship.

'God, Anniversary Architect,' she nods, rearranging her face into something she hopes expresses gratitude. At the mention of job security, she does feel a weird relief wash over her, and he's right that she won't be opening herself up to all that potential for criticism, all the trolling that columnists were increasingly reliant on because it meant they were keeping people on the website, even if it was just to tell them how shit they were. 'I mean, thanks. That's, that's just incredible, Stephen. I'm honoured. And, umm, does it come with, like, a pay bump at all?'

'Ha,' Stephen laughs. 'I like your gall, Liv. Always good to ask, of course, but right now we're on a hiring and salary freeze so that won't be possible. I'm sure you understand.' Olivia does recognize, somewhere deep down in her soul, that this is a complete and utter cop-out, but it's a place she can't quite bear to go right now. 'But if the party comes off we can definitely have another look at your package.'

'Thanks, Stephen. No worries. I won't let you down.'

Stephen pats her on the shoulder. 'I know you won't, Liv,' he says, tipping his forehead to her as he walks off to his office. 'I know you won't.'

Olivia smiles sweetly at his back. She wants to throw something at it, something hard and sharp. She stares down at her own bloody feet and her eyes shimmer. She is surprised by her rage. She takes a deep breath, swallows it down.

Olivia knows from experience that nothing good happens when you make a fuss.

4

Olivia heads back to her desk and is immediately greeted by the sight of Nina in a full-on embrace with Joe. The rage flares back up her body, this sensation understanding what Olivia is seeing before even she has. She turns on herself. Why didn't she push for more details, like whether or not it would involve any perks, before blithely accepting it? Why didn't she stand her ground and insist on a more private meeting, instead of one next to a water cooler, so that she could take notes and have more of a discussion? And why is she so insistent about working in an industry where even the executives compare themselves to one of the biggest maritime disasters of the twentieth century?

But before she can answer any of these questions, Joe breaks off from his hug with Nina and starts waving for Olivia to come over.

'Liv,' he bounces up and down on the spot. 'Get your arse back to the Cotswolds for a debrief!'

Olivia closes her eyes in the hope that when she opens them, it will all have been a dream, and Leonardo DiCaprio – aka her career – won't have slipped off his door to the bottom of the icy-cold Atlantic.

Instead, Olivia's eyelids flicker open to the sound of Nina asking what has happened to her feet.

'There's blood all over your shoes,' Nina says, pointing down at the cheap footwear Olivia would like to rip from her person and shove in her colleague's pretty, red mouth. Olivia shudders at the rage, begins flicking her thumbs with her index fingers in the hope of batting all her anger away.

'Oh, you know, new shoes,' smiles Olivia. 'But more importantly, I've got a new job!' It's out of her before she even realizes, as if saying it will somehow silence the fury building inside her.

'This is so exciting,' claps Joe. 'So has Nina!'

Nina giggles coyly, and Olivia now starts clicking her middle fingers and thumbs together, the snap of the motion an increasingly deranged attempt at diffusing the rage.

'Are you OK?' asks Nina, looking at Olivia's fidgety fingers.

'Oh I'm fine,' says Olivia, folding her hands across her chest to stop them from moving, the motion spreading to her right foot, which starts tapping up and down wildly instead. 'Tell me about your job.'

'OK,' says Nina, starting to smile bashfully. 'So you're looking at *The Morning*'s new Saturday columnist!'

'Exciting!' shrieks Joe, jumping up and down on the spot.

'Wooooow,' squeaks Olivia, just about remembering to breathe. She begins to walk the well-trodden tightrope of processing her own feelings whilst simultaneously not showing them – she is something of an Olympic gymnast when it comes to this discipline. 'That's amazing, Nina.' She looks down and sees that her hands are now coming together in something that looks like applause, but that is actually more of a nervous clap.

'Thanks, Liv,' says Nina, coming in for a hug. 'That means so much coming from you. I couldn't have got here without all your incredible guidance and support.' She embraces Olivia then pulls back, her long, toned arms on display as she holds her shoulders. 'So tell us your exciting news.'

Before Olivia can open her mouth, Nina is swarmed by more colleagues from the Cotswolds, plus a few who have made the perilous journey over from Baghdad. Realizing that Joe is the only person still paying her any attention, she turns to tell him her news. 'So I'm going to be *The Morning*'s Anniversary . . .' Olivia searches through her brain for her new title. 'Erm, Anniversary . . .'

'Anniversary?' repeats Joe, nonplussed.

'Architect!' Olivia perks up. 'I'm going to be *The Morning*'s Anniversary Architect, in charge of all the centenary celebrations later this year.'

'That's so great,' says Joe, rubbing her arm, a little pityingly. 'What a cool title. God, when we started way back when, who'd have thought that you'd end up being an architect!'

'I mean, I don't think I'm actually an architect,' explains Olivia, her foot bouncing manically again. 'Like, I don't think it means I will be able to build houses or anything like that.'

'Well, no,' nods Joe. 'Obviously not. But it's great, right? Well done, you!'

'What's great?' says Nina, reinserting herself back into the conversation.

'Olivia is going to be *The Morning*'s Anniversary Architect,' explains Joe. 'It means she's in charge of all the celebrations.'

'Like the party?' asks Nina. 'That's so cool. Architect, wow. Does that mean you still get to be a . . .' Nina looks awkwardly at Olivia's bruised and bloodied feet. 'Journalist?'

'I mean, what even is the definition of a journalist nowadays?' shrugs Olivia. She exhales theatrically. 'I'm Everywoman, always have been! I guess this was a natural progression after heading up the Women Rising project.'

'Oh god, yeah, this company would be nothing without you and that project, I'm so glad they're recognizing that.' Nina sounds genuine, which somehow makes it all worse.

'Bit of party planning here,' blathers Olivia. 'Bit of commissioning the centenary magazine there. Important to keep evolving, I like to think!'

She knows she is speaking fluent bullshit, but what else can she do? Actually say what she's feeling? Explain how betrayed she is in this moment? How absolutely fucking livid she is? Once she starts down that road she may never be able to stop, and what would happen then? What would they think of her that she didn't already think about herself? Only then, she would be able to see it, visibly, on their faces, and she . . . Cannot. See. That. Not today.

'Ooh, speaking of parties,' interrupts Joe, excitedly, 'we should totally all go out and celebrate these new roles tonight.'

'Yes!' exclaims Nina. 'That would be so amazing. Let's get the department together and sink some bubbles. I'm in the mood to celebrate my first column and the incredible Anniversary Architect who made it all possible!'

'That would be epic,' lies Olivia, giving Nina's arm a squeeze. 'After all that mentoring, I'm just so happy for you!'

In this most disingenuous of moments, Olivia recognizes the taste in her mouth as self-loathing. She hates herself. She really, really hates herself.

'Aww thanks, babe,' smiles Nina. 'You're the best. Right, better go and get writing. They've even given me my own office so I can concentrate on column day!' Nina struts off to the glass box next to Stephen's and turns back to blow a kiss. Then, with all the force of a woman who actually knows her value instead of letting other people decide it for her, she slams the door.

5

Olivia will stay for two drinks. One would look rude, three would risk her not being back in time to put Jack to bed and make sure Saskia has actually eaten something. She tells herself she can do this. She can keep up the pretence of happiness for an hour or so. After all, she's managed it pretty successfully for the last forty-four years.

Going to celebrate new role with a few drinks, she had texted Nick earlier. *Won't be late!* It isn't exactly a lie, but it's not exactly the truth either. Since he quit his job in PR to retrain as an English teacher, Olivia has been praying for a bigger salary, and now she's not going to get it, she feels panicky and anxious, not to mention left behind. He has spent the last year doing something he's always wanted to, and now it turns out she's spent the last year working towards something she's never going to get to do. She isn't sure she's ready to unpack it all with him just yet. Certainly not over WhatsApp.

Proud of you, he had replied. *Already booking the builder for our celebratory en suite!*

The WhatsApp tab is punctuated by a glaring red dot, full of unread messages she's swerved reading all day. Olivia's heart sinks as she opens her mother's reply in the group chat. *While I appreciate that you have finally let us know whether or not you will be coming, please could you be so kind as to reply via the RSVP card*

I went to the trouble of producing? It won't take you a minute and I have already paid for the postage.

Any news on the job? says Lily, mentioning the thing her mother didn't deem important enough to. Olivia feels both wounded by her mother's lack of interest in her professional life, and relieved that she doesn't have to go into the more pathetic details of it right now.

At the Red Lion, Olivia makes her way to the bar, where she hopes to down a glass of passable red wine before ordering another one and heading over to her colleagues. And yet every time a bartender seems to approach to ask for her order, they are distracted by some other, younger specimen who manages to cut in first. She seethes silently as the minutes go past and she remains, desperately, without alcohol. Joe arrives at the other end of the bar and is immediately served. He raises his glass in the air with a smug smile at Olivia then sidles over. 'Do you think Anniversary Architect is slang for "shave down staff numbers to a level that makes *The Morning* viable enough to move into its next centenary"?' asks Joe, his lips loosened by the gin and tonic in his hand.

'I think it means I get to plan an awesome party, Joe,' says Olivia, staring hard at the barman, in the hope that it will stop her voice from cracking and giving her real feelings away. Better to swallow them down. She focuses on the bottles behind the bar, thinks how good it will feel once the contents of them hit her throat and extinguish the awful feelings inside her.

'Right. Can't imagine anyone putting you in charge of firing people,' continues Joe, suppressing a chuckle, before wandering back to the table.

'Oh, I don't know,' says a young woman in a pale pink suit,

sliding in at the bar next to Olivia. 'It's the innocent ones you always want to look out for. Never heard the phrase "baby-faced assassin"?' Like Joe, the girl immediately catches the attention of a bartender. 'A pint of Hells,' she says as Olivia swears under her breath, 'and whatever this woman is having.'

'A glass of house red,' says Olivia, stunned. She hands the barman her card and looks at this brazen young woman next to her. 'Thank you. I've been waiting for bloody ages to get served.'

'Rose,' says the girl. She reaches out a bangled arm and shakes Olivia's hand. She is twenty-four, twenty-five tops, but has a steely look about her that terrifies Olivia. 'I'm a new PA at *The Morning*.'

'I'm Olivia.' She leans against the bar and takes her glass of red gratefully from the barman.

Rose pulls some tobacco out of her suit pocket and begins to roll a cigarette. 'And which department do you work in, Olivia?'

'Oh,' says Olivia, her sense of self deflating ever more. 'I work on the features department. Although actually, my boss has just given me a new job as Anniversary Architect.'

'What the fuck does that mean?' laughs Rose, looking up from her Rizla so she doesn't blow the tobacco across the bar.

Olivia blinks. Who is this woman? 'It means I need another drink.'

'Come for a smoke with me,' says Rose, handing Olivia her freshly created cigarette and beginning to roll another one.

'I don't smoke,' says Olivia, holding it awkwardly.

Rose looks at her, puzzled.

'Why not?'

'My mum told me not to,' she mutters, realizing how pathetic this sounds. 'It's, erm, bad for you.'

'Lots of things are bad for you, Olivia.' Rose stands up, and nods in the direction of the door. 'But the baddest thing of all is not being willing to live a little.'

Olivia clears her throat. 'Well,' she says, rising to her feet. 'I'd better not get off to a bad start with you, if you're new.'

'And what would happen if we did get off to a bad start?' asks Rose, turning on her bright-white Nike Air Force 1's.

'Well, I mean, it would just be . . . suboptimal.' Olivia winces as Rose throws her a pitying eye roll. She meekly follows the younger woman out of the door and into the smoking area. 'If we've got to work together, that is,' says Olivia, watching Rose light her cigarette. 'It would be terrible if we started off on the wrong foot.'

Rose exhales, then goes to pass her lighter to Olivia. Olivia fumbles with it awkwardly. She hasn't smoked since her last birthday party pre-pandemic, but she figures the odd one won't do her any harm. After a day like today, it might actually do her some good.

'People get off on the wrong foot all the time,' Rose says, surveying Olivia as she lights the rollie. 'The world wouldn't stop spinning on its axis.'

'Well, I prefer smooth sailing,' coughs Olivia.

Rose gazes at her, blowing smoke out the side of her mouth. 'How's that working out for you?'

'Great!' beams Olivia, trying not to choke. 'Just been promoted, get to work with you, have a wonderful family waiting for me at home. It's all working out great.' She coughs out a load of smoke, just as she notices Stephen and Nina walking up the street towards her.

'Hmmm,' says Rose, as Nina and Stephen pass behind her into the pub, without giving either of them a second look. Olivia watches as the pub erupts in celebration at the arrival of *The*

Morning's editor and his new star columnist. 'The frown that spread across your face as you watched those two would suggest that everything is working out far from great.'

'Yeah well, he just gave her the job I'd been promised. I guess I'm still working through my disappointment.' Olivia sucks furiously on her cigarette.

'Who are they?'

'Hang on, don't you know who he is if you've started working here?'

'I'm still settling in.' Rose coolly drags on her rollie. 'Just at the beginning. I'm looking forward to getting going in this thrilling industry.'

'Well, I'm looking forward to working with you. I should probably go inside and—'

Rose flicks some ash on to the ground. 'No, you're not.'

'Not . . . what?'

'Looking forward to working with me. There's no need to lie.'

Olivia splutters. 'I'm not lying. I don't lie.'

'So far in this conversation, all you've done is lie,' Rose says casually, as she drops the butt of her rollie on to the pavement and crushes it with an Air Force 1. In the pub, Olivia watches Stephen handing over his credit card to the barman, who hands him several bottles of champagne in return.

'I beg your pardon?' Olivia feels her phone vibrating in her pocket, and rummages to retrieve it.

Before Olivia has even realized what is happening, Rose has plucked the phone from her hands.

'What the hell are you doing?!' It's the closest that Olivia has allowed herself to a visible expression of fury since she last saw her mother.

Mum, when are you going to be home? We're out of gluten-free pasta. Rose's face is uplit from the glow of Olivia's phone. It makes her seem like an avenging angel. She starts tapping out a response. 'I'm just telling your daughter that you're having a well-earned night out with your friends, and you're not available for requests at this time.'

Olivia stares at Rose uncomprehendingly as she hands her back her phone.

'Oh,' she manages, her brain unable to form anything coherent from sheer shock. Behind Rose's head, Stephen is pouring out glasses of champagne and gathering their colleagues round the table. 'Right.'

'Shall we get the fuck out of this miserable shithole?' says Rose, looking over her shoulder to the scene taking place inside. 'And have some actual fun, instead of pretending to celebrate a position with the worst job title since someone came up with the idea of Chief Happiness Officers.'

'It is kind of shit, isn't it?' agrees Olivia, saying the first true thing she has felt all day. She watches as Stephen throws one arm around Nina and raises the other into the air as he makes a toast. Inside, she feels something fracture just a little.

'Let's go,' says Rose, a mischievous smile breaking out on her face, and she leads Olivia towards the Tube.

6

Olivia Greenwood is in a galaxy far, far away. She has a pint of Kronenbourg in one hand and a packet of Marlboro Golds in the other. She can't quite explain how she went from meaning to have a couple of drinks at the pub near the office to necking her fourth pint while chain-smoking in the garden of this dive bar somewhere in east London, but here she is, feeling young again, putting the world to rights with her new friend Rose.

'It's like I'm Doctor Who,' laughs Olivia, lighting her seventh cigarette in twenty minutes. 'Do Gen Z watch *Doctor Who*? God, you're probably too young to know what I'm even talking about.'

'Don't confuse being young with being stupid,' bites Rose with a confidence of contempt Olivia finds equally terrifying and admirable.

Olivia has really let rip this evening, away from the Red Lion. She feels that in this new environment, with this new young companion, she is safe to say what she really thinks. She gets the impression that saying what she really thinks is going to endear her to Rose, if 'endear' is even a word that might apply to this forthright young woman who has just walked into her life, seemingly out of nowhere.

And so it is that in the last hour or so, Olivia has told Rose everything. About how upset she is with Nina, how disappointed she is not to have been made a columnist, how hard she has worked to please Stephen, how much the family finances depend on her, how worried she is about Saskia's obsession with keto bagels and Jack's obsession with strange-looking football players. How annoyed she is that she has ended up having to house her alcoholic father, and that her mother mollycoddles her sister while being constantly disgruntled with her. She imagines that with each fresh revelation, with each confidence, Rose will like her a little bit more. She will see Olivia's openness as a kind of gift, an intimacy that she doesn't extend to just anybody.

Instead, Rose listens with about the same amount of interest Saskia showed her mother when she tried to talk to her about the birds and the bees.

Olivia is worried that her new colleague is bored, or even worse, that she thinks her self-obsessed. She changes tack. 'Enough about me,' she says, brightening. 'So how long have you wanted to work in journalism?'

'Oh fuck that, I don't want to work in journalism, Olivia,' sniggers Rose. 'Nobody wants to work in journalism any more, because journalism barely exists. Look at *The Morning*. Stephen thinks he's the editor but really he's just turning the computers on. It's an algorithm that's in charge. It's data. All he does is look at the data, see what everybody is clicking on, and asks for more of it. A monkey could do his job. You could do his job, if you didn't have such a tragically low opinion of yourself.'

All Olivia hears is the sweet sound of Rose not thinking she's up herself.

'It's the most fascinating thing, Olivia, seeing how your generation does things. You're just that little bit too old to be considered a Millennial, but too young to be a member of Generation X. You're part of Generation Neither-Here-Nor-There, and it shows.'

Olivia tries to raise her eyebrows in indignation, battles against the botox, gives up.

'I mean, you're what, only twenty years older than me?' continues Rose. 'That's not a vast amount of time. It's nothing in the grand scheme of things. It's barely the blink of an eye in evolutionary terms. And *yet*.' Rose laughs to herself. 'Look at you all. You've spent your whole lives being told you could have it all, and yet now you're discovering that you don't actually want any of it, because guess what, "having it all" was simply a steaming pile of shit that the patriarchy managed to wrap up and pass off as some sort of gift. And despite the stench, you fell for it. You all fucking fell for it.'

Olivia shifts uncomfortably on the garden bench she is perched on. She should make a counterargument, but she can't find one. Because the truth is, this woman she didn't know a couple of hours ago has hit the nail on the head. She's managed, somehow, to encapsulate the exact reason for the crushing disappointment that Olivia is currently trying to drink and smoke away into oblivion. How has she done this? How does she know Olivia better than Olivia knows herself?

'And now you're aware of the steaming pile of shit you've been handed, and the worst thing of all is that despite seeing the flies coming off it, and the disease in it, you're too terrified to hand it back! To say: "No thanks, this doesn't work for me at present. It stopped working for me a long time ago. Actually, it never worked for me, and I can't believe that it's taken me this long to work out that the sandwich you've been making me eat is actually filled with SHIT."' Rose raises her voice, unconcerned about the people around them. 'Instead, you're playing with the shit and seeing how you can make the best of it, because you don't want to offend the blokes that handed it to you. Blokes like that wanker Stephen. You're actually smearing yourself in the shit, because you'd rather do that than upset that arsehole. "Here's a shit job, Olivia, that's massively below your pay grade and your abilities and one I absolutely know you won't like."' Rose mimics a cockney wide boy. 'And instead of standing up for yourself, you've just accepted it, without even checking the finer details. Without even asking for a pay rise, or if you're going to have anyone to help you.'

'I did ask if I'm getting a pay rise, actually.'

'And are you?'

'No.'

Rose takes a cigarette from the packet she made Olivia buy. 'Christ. Look, babes, I can see from your face that you're in shock that I'm actually spitting facts at you, but you need to know that I'm coming from a good place here. You're clearly a decent person who doesn't mean anyone any harm, so believe me when I say: YOU DESERVE BETTER THAN THIS!' Rose points her cigarette directly in Olivia's face. 'From the moment I walked into the Red Lion this evening, you've done everything I've asked of you without once questioning it.' She lights the cigarette, drains her drink, and then takes a sip from Olivia's pint. 'Look at you. You're a 44-year-old woman with a mortgage and a family and a first from Cambridge and yet here you are, hanging out on a Friday night with someone you've never even met before and confiding all sorts of secrets in me that you really should have kept to yourself, by the way. You could have done with going home and grounding yourself with some bath salts or Bougie overpriced candles or whatever it is you middle-aged people do, and yet as soon as I say, "Come and smoke with me, Olivia, come and drink with me, Olivia," you jump to attention like a bullied dog eager to please. They've ground you down to such a level that even a stranger can get you to abandon your needs for theirs.'

Olivia nods along, dumbstruck.

'You're all "yes, Rose, three bags full, Rose".' Rose now switches to mimicking a posh girl. 'You followed me out the door of the Red Lion like a toddler following a man with some lollipops into the back of a van.'

Olivia gasps. 'That's a bit dark.'

Rose sighs. 'Life is dark, Olivia, life is dark. It's darkness, it's light, it's a million shades in between, and yet all you're interested in is the view from the sunny uplands. You're so desperate to make everybody else happy that you've forgotten what makes *you* happy. You've not just forgotten it, you've abandoned it, on a bonfire full of all your other hopes and dreams. A bonfire you're too scared to light in case the neighbours report you to the council.'

She takes another pointed sip of Olivia's pint. Of course, Olivia does not stop her. Rose shakes her head with disappointment.

'And let's talk about this bullshit job you've so gratefully received today, and your seething resentment about Nina taking your dream gig, as if she has some personal vendetta against you. Why do you think it has anything to do with you, Olivia? Why is it so difficult for you to comprehend that maybe, just maybe, Nina was making decisions based on her own wellbeing, as opposed to yours? That it has absolutely fuck all to do with you? Nina doesn't wake up thinking about you, because Nina is too busy looking after herself. And good for Nina, I say. I'd even suggest you be more Nina, but then you might take that literally and set about furiously channelling her so that you become more likeable and successful, while completely forgetting who you are in the first place. And as of today, it turns out that you are not a viable replacement for Selina Martin.'

'But Stephen told m—'

'Stephen is not a trustworthy man,' snaps Rose, closing over Olivia's voice with frightening ease. 'Stephen will say anything if it helps him get what he wants. Whereas you will say anything if it helps someone else get what they want. You're not so dissimilar in that respect, in that you're disingenuous, just for totally different reasons.'

Rose downs the rest of Olivia's drink, stands up, motions for Olivia to do the same, and then marches to the bar. Olivia follows, half-stunned, half-grateful to be able to get more alcohol to numb herself with.

'I'll have two more pints of Kronenbourg,' says Rose, 'and my friend here will pay.' Olivia watches in stunned silence as the barman pulls their drinks, and then wordlessly hands him her card.

'The amazing thing,' begins Rose, as she marches back into the garden and sits down at the table, 'is that you really thought Stephen was going to give you a column in the first place. Because from where I'm standing, sorry sitting, you don't seem capable of expressing an opinion publicly. What were you going to write this column about? How nice the Princess of Wales is? How wonderful the prime minister's new policies are? How we can all put our warring beliefs aside and be there for one another in Kumbaya bullshit happy land? How you're sure that the Israelis and the Palestinians can get together and put all their differences to one side? Hate to break it to you, Olivia, but being a national newspaper columnist means developing beliefs, making judgements, and then having the courage of your convictions when everyone on social media calls you a bigoted arsehole or a left-wing arse-wipe. I reckon you'd faint if someone so much as criticized your parking.'

'I'm not sure that's fair—'

'I haven't finished, Olivia,' says Rose, holding up a commanding hand. How is she so self-assured so young? When Olivia was this age, she could barely choose an outfit to wear to work without first canvassing fifteen different people's opinions.

'You're so desperate to make other people happy that you've forgotten what it is to be anything other than sad. Let's take that loser Stephen. You've spent a decade or so doing everything he asks of you, simply because he's said he might one day give you a half-decent writing job. Stephen tells you he wants you to one day be a columnist, and you tell him you're dedicated to *The Morning*, and you all keep living in cloud cuckoo land until the sad day that one of you shatters the illusion. And the key, Olivia, is to be the one who shatters the illusion. But sadly, you haven't had the guts to, so here we are, sitting in a pub garden in Stoke Newington, as you try to come to terms with the fact that you've not just been working with a bunch of arseholes for your entire adult life, but that you've actually been colluding with them. And what's incredible is that instead of being fucking furious with him, or fucking furious with yourself, frankly, for being naive enough to believe him, you turn your anger on Nina. Nina, who has done nothing wrong. It's the oldest trick in the patriarchal book.'

Not for the first time in her life, or even today, Olivia feels a hot stab of shame in her stomach.

'You're so scared of upsetting people you can't even decide on a hair colour. Do you actually pay someone to dye your hair that specific shade of mousy blonde?'

'It's caramel!' exclaims Olivia.

'It's a cop-out is what it is,' says Rose. 'It's neither one thing nor the other. You're so desperate for other people's validation that you appear to have lost the capacity for independent thought. And the most tragic thing of all, is that you're better than this.' Rose takes Olivia by the shoulders and stares deeply into her eyes. 'You're so much better than this. You are capable of so much more than being a dreary old people pleaser.'

'I don't see what's so wrong with wanting to make other people happy.' Olivia thinks she might cry. She feels a tear prickling her cornea. 'It's better than inviting someone for a drink and then spending the evening insulting them.'

Rose, still gripping her left shoulder with one hand now, says more gently, 'Am I insulting you, though, Olivia? Or just speaking some truths you need to hear? Honestly, the time has come for you to step into your own power, babe. To realize that you're the boss of your life. Own your sovereignty. Be the awesome human the universe knows you can be, not the cut-price version knobs like Stephen want you to be. If you knew your unique and immeasurable value to the world, you'd never have ended up in this situation in the first place.'

Olivia's mouth drops open in shock. Nobody has ever bothered to speak to her like this, never taken her aside and given her a pep talk about what she might be capable of. She heard plenty from her mother about what she *should* be capable of – in her exams, in her romantic life, in her career. She feels some tectonic plates she didn't even know were inside her begin to shift. The wind has been knocked out of her, and put back in, all at the same time.

Under the table, Olivia feels Rose hand her something that has the texture of a wine gum. She looks down and sees a blue sweet, shaped like a football.

'It's an edible,' says Rose into her ear.

Olivia continues to look blankly at the sweet.

'Shit-strong drugs in delicious sweet form,' explains Rose, patiently.

'I don't do drugs,' says Olivia, in a tone which suggests that while she can take a character assassination, she draws the line at any suggestion she might partake in illegal substances.

'Of course you don't,' sighs Rose. 'Anyway, we call that one the Erling Haaland, because it's so damn good at what it does.'

'Did you say Erling Haaland?' asks Olivia, just as she realizes, with a surprise, that she is putting the football-shaped gummy in her mouth.

'Yep,' smiles Rose. 'Are you a fan?'

7

Olivia Greenwood comes round to find the bed next to her empty, the windows wide open, and absolute silence in the house. Even more intriguingly, she is able to see. Her vision, usually that of a geriatric mole, is now perfect, even if her eyes feel somewhat crusty and dry. She blinks a few times and realizes she has fallen asleep with her contact lenses in.

The disappointment is swiftly dissolved by a rush of panic. Has she overslept? What day is it? She grabs for her phone on the bedside table but it isn't there.

She sits up in bed, rubs her eyes, and feels the subtle sting of one of her contact lenses tearing. She swears, the words rough against the sandpaper texture of her throat and the shallowness in her chest, and remembers all the cigarettes she smoked. And beer she drank. And . . . drugs she took? She groans, horror battling with nausea. She fishes her contact lenses out, drops them in the vague direction of the bin and makes her way to the non-suite, bumping into various things as she goes: washing baskets, doors, flashbacks of the night before.

Sitting on the toilet, she realizes she is wearing only her pants, bra, and her shirt, now unbuttoned, creased and looking more Rab C. Nesbitt than Zara, the dark hues of a red wine stain down one side and a fag burn on the other.

Various words swim through her frontal lobe as she does

the longest wee in history: Anniversary Architect, Rose, Erling Haaland.

The biscuity, dehydrated stench of her pee hits her as she goes to flush the toilet. She's glad she can't see how dark it is, because then she might have to go straight to the nearest A&E and ask to be put on a drip to stop herself from dying of kidney failure. She washes her hands, splashes her face, feels the burning desire to peel off the top layer of her skin and start again, like a snake. She will settle for scrubbing her face with a flannel and some cleanser, and then brushing her teeth. Back in the bedroom, she locates her packet of fresh contact lenses on the dressing table, is able to squint at the packet so that she places the right prescription in each eye, and then appraises herself in the mirror in the same way a mortuary clerk might a cadaver.

'Fuck, you look rancid, Olivia,' she says to herself, shivering in self-loathing.

She shrugs off the shirt and removes her bra, putting her index fingers in the big welts that have developed from lying for a long period, semi-conscious, with the straps digging into her armpits. She thinks that if her mother could see her now, she would have a conniption fit, and considers snapping a picture and sending it to the Fabulous Fryer Ladies WhatsApp group, with a caption that reads: *Shove your RSVP card up your arse.*

If only she could find her phone.

'Nick!' she shouts downstairs. 'NICK!' There is no reply. 'Children? Anyone?'

She grabs her dressing gown from the back of the bedroom door and makes her way downstairs, where she is greeted with a scene as chaotic as her head. Jam is smeared across the kitchen worktop, mixing with spilled coffee, an upended carton of Oatly, and the uneaten crusts of six or seven pieces of toast. On the side, a half-empty bottle of red wine stands uncorked, a glass containing the dregs next to it. She supposes that she could describe them as half full, but she's beginning to see that it's not going to be that kind of day.

Next to the wine lies a fruit bowl full of blackened bananas, and under the blackened bananas she sees her phone. It makes sense, in as much as anything does right now. She grabs it, locates a pot of coffee left on the stove, realizes that it is cold, and then that she doesn't care. She rinses out a dirty mug in the sink, which will have to do because the dishwasher doesn't appear to have been put on at any point since she left the house yesterday morning. She pours the cold coffee into the dirty mug, and then sits down at the kitchen table to go through her phone for clues.

She opens WhatsApp and clicks into her chat with Nick, only to find a slew of messages she sent last night, all of which are startlingly rude. *I'm not taking the kids to their clubs just so that you can do CrossFit*, she had written, at 11.33 p.m. *Will be having a lie-in, so fuck you.*

And later:

I find it so predictably tedious that you would channel your midlife crisis into fitness rather than fucking me.

And even later:

Why do you never go down on me any more?

She hadn't even put kisses on it. Which was very unlike her.

She is relieved to see that she didn't reply to her mother's message about the RSVP – that, she supposes, is one good thing to have happened today. She scrolls through the phone book, hoping to find a number for Rose, but there is nothing. She opens her email, wondering if there might be something there, but all she sees is a missive from Stephen, sent at six o'clock this morning.

Liv – need at least ten great ideas for centenary supplement on my desk by Monday morning. Have a good weekend.

She lets out a grunt and begins typing a reply.

Stephen – how am I supposed to have a good weekend if I spend it working to meet a ridiculous deadline that you are not even legally entitled to set, given that it is written into my contract that I have Saturdays and Sundays off? You'll get the ideas when I'm ready to give them to you, and you can rest assured that they will be great, because I'm the person coming up with them.

She presses 'send', and then realizes there is no button to un-send.

'Shit,' she says, trying to empty the remainder of the cold coffee pot into her mug. She waits to feel the anxiety rising inside her, knows that the coffee will do nothing to quell it, but reasons she needs the caffeine to wake her up from this bad dream. It doesn't come.

Olivia looks through the work email address system for a Rose, but realizes that without a surname, her search is completely futile. She takes a deep breath and her tummy rumbles. She hasn't eaten since yesterday. Lunchtime. Everything will feel better with food in her stomach. She goes to the fridge, is appalled by the assortment of fibre-rich, meat-free food that she would normally, painstakingly build together into a healthy, nutritious meal, and heads instead to one of the cupboards, where she finds a Twix bar and a packet of pickled onion Monster Munch, the remnants of some party bag that Olivia had hidden in the event of an apocalypse. It is here.

In the living room, she throws herself on the sofa, peels open the Twix bar, and starts to weep, great big wailing sobs. She can't remember crying like this since childhood, when she would become inconsolable over issues as varied and multiple as the hole in the ozone layer and its effects on baby seals in the Antarctic, and her best friend Katie's decision to stop taking their beloved after-school tap-dance classes. Olivia had spent her early years being called a *sensitive* soul, and not in a complimentary way. It was to her detriment that she felt things so very deeply; she was causing a fuss over nothing, making mountains out of molehills, and so on and so forth, until she came up with a variety of ways to mask that sensitivity. She smiled, she joked, she complimented, she flattered, she was amenable and she was, above all, likeable. But this morning it's as if all the masks have been pulled off by whatever it was that happened yesterday, a gushing wave of terrible *feelings* tumbling out in the process.

As she lies there, both eating the Twix and crying over it, she feels absolutely everything. The truth of what has happened begins to surge over her pitifully. She is reduced once more to the little girl she has spent so long trying to run away from, the one who felt too much, and spoke too much, and couldn't live within the lines society had drawn for her. The one who wallowed in self-pity and served no useful purpose to anyone, draining people rather than lighting them up like Lily always did. She means nothing to anyone at work, she's wasted decades trying to impress people who barely register her existence, and worst of all, she's somehow managed to delude herself into believing that the complete opposite is true. It's as if she's come round from a dream into a waking nightmare, only to realize that she was the person who willingly drugged herself into the fitful, foolish fantasy in the first place. It's taken a complete stranger to snap her out of it. With drugs, ironically. Olivia cries and she cries and she cries, the tears mixing stickily with the Twix so that it becomes a strange, sugary-salty mess, and she only stops when she hears a hoarse cough from the kitchen.

'Dad?' she says, annoyed at the interruption. 'Is that you?'

'Yes, dear,' he whimpers back.

She stands up and makes her way down the hall to find her father, who is hunched in front of the kettle wearing a sarong and a Roy Orbison T-shirt. 'Sorry, dear,' he says, a mug in hand. 'Was just making myself a cup of tea. Are you OK? You seem a bit...' Her father looks as uncomfortable as her head feels.

'Upset?' Olivia shrugs, heading towards the half-empty bottle of wine and the half-drunk glass next to it. She downs the rancid glass of wine, winces, and then refills it. 'Tell you what, Dad, why don't we forget about tea today and just go straight for a drink.' She grabs another glass from a shelf, places it on the worktop next to him, and then fills it with the remainder of the bottle. 'We may as well start as we mean to go on, eh?'

Olivia hands the glass to her bemused-looking father and starts to drink. 'And while we're at it, can I have one of your fags?'

'My what?' Her father is almost as dishevelled as she is, though Olivia hopes she has less facial hair than him. She runs a finger over her chin to check, makes a mental note to crawl back into bed with her tweezers later.

'Your cigarettes. The ones you pretend you don't smoke by hiding the butts, badly, behind the hydrangea pot, where you think I can't see them. I'd like one of them, please.'

'Well, OK,' he concedes, putting down the mug of tea, swigging from the wine glass, and heading back into the garden.

Olivia slips her battered feet into a pair of Jack's Crocs that have been left by the door and walks out to the rotten garden table, where she plonks her wine down, stretches her arms out, and sticks her middle finger up at the neighbour who is watching from a first-floor window.

'Olivia!' scolds her father, throwing a lighter and a packet of Benson and Hedges down on the table.

'Dad!' replies Olivia, looking at the packet in horror. 'How could you smoke such shit?' She lights one anyway, takes a deep drag before chugging back another swig of wine, hoping her dressing gown doesn't fly open in the breeze.

'Cheers!' She raises her glass into the air. Her father meekly does the same. 'Here's to Nick taking responsibility for the kids this weekend, instead of trying to up his deadlift!'

'They're good kids,' says her father.

'All kids are good, Dad.' Olivia tightens her dressing gown around her, then inhales deeply on one of the Benson and Hedges. 'They don't become "troubled" out of a clear blue sky. It's not gangs or social media or drugs that make them that way. It's usually the shit they're having to put up with at home.'

She flicks the cigarette on to the patio, watches as it burns itself down. 'Like, looking back, I was the difficult child, wouldn't you say, Dad?'

He stares at his glass of wine, looking for the answer at the bottom of it. As ever.

'The whole world revolved around me! Do you remember she said that, when I had my appendix out and didn't want to go back to school after a week? Like, I know she was having to juggle an awful amount of stuff because you were living it up in Darlington or Ditchfield or wherever, but fuck, can you imagine what that made me feel like?' Olivia chugs some more wine, lights another cigarette. 'I guess you can, because you got it in the neck as well. But at least you were an adult and kind of deserved it. You could cope with it. Though fuck knows why, as a grown-up, you put up with it for quite so long. I guess that's where I get it from.'

Peter lights a B&H in solidarity. 'Your mum has her own reasons for her little midlife crisis, we just have to bear with her for a bit.'

'She's nearly seventy, I'd hardly call it midlife. Or at least I hope not, or we're all in for a long old slog.'

'Olivia, you can't wish death on your mother!'

'Oh my god, Dad, you think you'd get in on the joke a bit more, given that she literally evicted you from the house in which you made a life together for almost forty-five years.'

'Listen, I'm sure once she's got all this, all this . . .' He waves his cigarette around in the air hopelessly. 'All this silly business out of her system, everything will go back to normal.'

'Good of you to be so magnanimous when she's not exactly extended you the same kindness over the last few months. Tell me, Dad, why are you being so nice about her when you're having to live in my shed?'

'As I said, I'm sure it's all a phase. I'm just grateful that you're being so kind to an old man down on his luck.'

'It's the least I could do, considering you've always at least been nice to me. Maybe you haven't always been there, but when you were, you went out of your way to show us that you loved us.'

'Ach, it was nothing. Your mother did the lion's share. I know she didn't always get it right, but she tried.' He looks morosely at the hundreds of butts behind the dead hydrangea, as if pondering the life he's also thrown away.

'Cheer up, Dad.' Olivia rolls her eyes. Today is not the day to dwell on the ruins of her parents' marriage, not when so much of her own life lies smouldering in flames. 'We've got Lily's fortieth to look forward to. Mum's pulling out all the stops for her resident chakra reader.'

'Her what?'

'It's Mum's latest wheeze to excuse bankrolling Lily. She's got her reading all her friends' chakras and is paying her for it.'

Olivia's father looks at her blankly.

'Chakras, Dad. Energy points in the body, or some such guff that Lily learned about when she went to India last year. She swears that after a life-changing spiritual experience in the Himalayas, she can now unblock people's chakras through the healing power of her hands.'

'What a load of old bollocks,' says her father.

Olivia feels a smile creep across her face. She's forgotten what it's like to actually laugh with her dad, after all this time.

'Anyway, back to the party, which Mum is approaching as if it's a state banquet. Apparently, despite being family, we have to provide a formal RSVP to announce that we will be attending.'

'Do you know if that Colin is going to be there?'

'Clive, Dad. His name is Clive.'

'Colin, Clive, Nigel, you know what I mean.'

'I imagine that Mum won't miss a chance to hijack Lily's special evening and introduce us to her new beau, if that's what you mean.'

'He's a Tory, you know,' announces Peter.

'Didn't you vote for them at the last election?' Olivia looks momentarily confused.

'Yes but I wouldn't disclose that information in public,' Peter says, his cheeks reddening. 'Whereas he proudly *admits* to it!'

'Well, you know what they say, Dad?' Olivia tries to look philosophical while dragging deeply on her cigarette. 'Rejection is the universe's protection!'

'Who says that?'

'Wise people.' Olivia drains more wine. 'It means that when something isn't for you, it's because the universe wants you to do other, better things. Like . . .' She takes another drag of her cigarette, thinks for a moment. 'Being Anniversary Architect for *The Morning*.'

'Being what?'

'Never you mind, Dad.' She wishes she could have been this facetious with Stephen yesterday. 'What I'm saying, Dad, is that maybe you should be seeing this whole divorce thing as a lucky escape. Maybe instead of it being the worst thing that ever happened to you, you could see it as a second chance at life.'

'But I'm living in your shed, Olivia.'

'It could be worse. You could be living in *her* shed.'

'Actually, until we're officially divorced and the papers are signed, it's our shed.'

'Dad, you've got Stockholm syndrome. She's always blamed you for everything going wrong in that marriage. Even when we were kids, everything was your fault.'

'That's because it was,' he shrugs.

Olivia can't be sure, but she thinks she sees tears in her father's eyes. She almost reaches across the table and comforts him – she's always had this painful sense of feeling sorry for him, which is why she took him in so readily – but a small, childish stab of revulsion stops her.

'No need to be maudlin,' Olivia says, draining more of her drink. She realizes, with a shock, that she sounds a bit like . . . her mother.

'Mum!' Jack is standing in the kitchen door, a look of horror on his face. 'What are you doing?'

'Ohmygod this is hilarious,' says Saskia, joining him. 'Mum has completely lost the plot.'

The good girl in Olivia – the one who has controlled her for most of her life – thinks this is probably true, and yet the Erling Haaland gummy in her seems to think she's never been more sane.

'Peter,' says Nick to his father-in-law, as he appears behind his children. 'Would you care to explain what you're doing out here?'

'Oh that's it, address my dad instead of speaking directly to me!' Olivia throws another cigarette on the ground and uses the Crocs to stub it out. 'What is this, the Republic of Gilead?' She puts on a high voice and starts shivering meekly. 'I hope you don't mind, kind sir, if I put aside my duties to accompany this gentleman as he partakes in an ale and a pipe.'

'Mum, you're wearing my Crocs?' Jack stares at the Man City Jibbitz on her feet, as if trying to make sense of the scene before him.

'Can't a mother wear her son's Crocs while having a fag and a glass of wine outside at eleven o'clock on a Saturday morning?'

'Erm, no, not really?' Jack tugs nervously at some of the curls on his head.

'Olivia, I think you need to come inside,' says Nick, trying to reach for his ten-year-old son.

'Olivia,' parrots Olivia, in a baby voice, 'I think you need to come inside.'

'I just want to say that this was all her idea,' says Peter, weakly.

'Oh god, Dad, take some fucking responsibility for yourself

for once in your life,' she spits. The good girl gasps internally, but Erling Haaland appears to be mentally punching the air in joy.

'We shouldn't be swearing in front of the children,' says Nick through gritted teeth.

'I know, we should just be minding our Ps and Qs and pretending we're a nice, normal family.' Olivia laughs to herself, and in the process spits some wine down her dressing gown. 'That worked so well for my parents.' She drains the last of her glass, kisses a clearly appalled Jack on the head, and then heads back into the kitchen.

'I am loving this version of you, Mum,' sniggers Saskia.

'Olivia, what is going on?' Nick looks equally furious and worried.

'I'll tell you what is going on, darling,' she says, looking in the fridge for another bottle of wine. 'I didn't get the job I'd been led to believe I was going to get by my lying, manipulative boss. Instead, he gave it to Nina, the woman I have lovingly mentored for the last three years.' She shuts the fridge and waves a bottle of Sauvignon Blanc triumphantly in the air. 'Despite all my hard work, and the many years spent doing EXACTLY what that sociopath has asked of me, he has essentially demoted me, stripping me of my ability to write a single word, and giving me a nonsense title which basically involves ordering some cheesy Wotsits for a party and putting together a "celebratory" magazine that will mostly be used to line cat litter trays.'

'Oh Olivia.' Nick softens, moving towards his wife as if to give her a hug. 'You should have said.'

'Well, pardon me if I didn't want to say. Pardon me if I wanted to go out and shake out some of my rage. And I'm continuing to shake out the rage, because it turns out there's a hell of a lot of it bottled up.' Olivia cracks the top of the bottle and grabs a clean glass. 'Now if you don't mind, I want to go upstairs for a bit of me time. And yes, that is a euphemism for exactly what you think it is, Nick.'

'That is so gross,' sneers Saskia.

'You can't wear shoes upstairs,' says Jack, sensibly. 'You always say that.'

Olivia's inner good girl, not to mention her husband and children, watches in amazement as she kicks the Crocs off her feet and into the air, so that they land on the floor with a smack.

'I'm storing this one in my bank for the next time she tells us off for being messy,' says Jack, nervously twirling his hair round his finger. Saskia sniggers. Olivia storms up to her bedroom, with only the wine bottle for company, and the voice of her inner good girl pleading with her to sleep whatever this is off.

8

Olivia spends the rest of the weekend in bed, emerging only to go to the non-suite to throw up, and, once she has sobered up, to apologize profusely to her family. She's still feeling weirdly liberated for letting rip, when it is usually the last thing she would do, but she also knows that she needs to toe the line between being an arsehole and speaking-her-truth, and flinging her son's Man City Crocs into the air is *probably crossing it*.

'I think Mummy has had a bit of a bug or something,' she says to Jack, slumping next to him on the sofa on Sunday morning. 'I'm really sorry that I was so rude to you all. And if I frightened you by drinking wine in my dressing gown. I really love you and you didn't deserve to have me take all my frustrations out on you.'

'It's OK, Mum,' says Jack, who is playing Football Manager. 'Dad says that all kids should expect to see their mothers drinking wine in their dressing gowns at least once in their childhood.'

'Does he now,' winces Olivia, whose husband is upstairs having a long bath, after spending two hours at CrossFit that morning. 'Have you noticed how fit he's got doing all this gym stuff? I mean, fit as in PHWOAAAAAAAARR? He's definitely getting at least a two-pack, I'd say.'

'Mum, do you mind? I'm trying to revise and I need to practise this section to stay on track for an A. Plus, you sound a bit pervy,' huffs Saskia from across the room.

'He's my husband, babes!' Olivia gets up and goes to sit next to Saskia. 'It's good for you to see me model a healthy romantic relationship where I fancy the pants off your dad, as opposed to one where I barely tolerate him.' She throws her arms around her daughter, who cringes, as is her teenage right. Olivia might have taken this personally a day or so ago, but today she's just grateful to be here, alone with her kids, in their own cosy space, with no sports clubs to ferry them to. She holds on to Saskia a few moments longer and feels her soften just a little.

'Are you feeling OK?' Saskia looks up from her homework with barely concealed contempt. 'You do know that I'm your teenage daughter and I really don't want to hear you talking about fancying my father? It's completely gross.'

'Yeah, yeah, I get the message. Right, well, I'm still feeling a bit ropy.' Olivia gets to her feet, very slowly, groaning slightly, and makes her way towards the door. 'Your father will be manning the fort this evening. If there are any problems, please don't let me know, because I'm going to be too busy lying in the dark, trying to get over a two-day hangover.'

'Mum!' Saskia laughs in shock. Jack shakes his head, his gaze never once diverting from the screen.

Upstairs, Olivia slumps into bed and stares at the ceiling in a sort of wide-eyed wonder, not quite believing how easy it has been to ask for what she wants from her husband. It hasn't felt too terrifying, and he hasn't (yet) asked for a divorce. It certainly beats seething in silent resentment about the apparent stalemate in their marriage.

She gets under the duvet and reaches for her phone to see if Stephen has replied to her message. She keeps wondering whether she should send an apologetic email to try and mitigate her first response, but try as she might, she can't do it. It's as if there's a sort of force field preventing her from cleaning up the mess she has made since she went on that Friday-night bender. Normally, she'd be the first person to apologize for even the slightest misstep – and quite often, for simply existing – but today, she just can't find it in herself to give a damn, at least not when it comes to people who don't give a damn about her. She has been running around, trying to pander to everybody else's needs, for years. Perhaps it's time she stopped? Isn't it a good thing for Nick to know that she needs more foreplay? And what's so wrong about putting a boundary down with her boss, especially when he's just screwed her over so royally? She thinks Rose would be impressed with her, if only she could track Rose down.

But Olivia has spent two hours checking out every Rose, Rosemary, Rosie and Rosalie that exists on *The Morning*'s email database, and not a single one of them checks out as the person she met on Friday night. Maybe pink-suited Rose is so new that she doesn't yet have an email. Tomorrow, Olivia is going back to the office so she can track down this new assistant and ask what the hell it was she gave her the other night. An edible, or a *lobotomy*?

Because ever since she came to yesterday morning, Olivia has found herself saying absolutely everything that comes into her head. Every sarcastic thought, every unkind opinion, every unwarranted judgement . . . they've all come tumbling out of her mouth, and Olivia has been powerless to stop them. This morning, when Nick asked for an apology for the way she had behaved yesterday, she told him to fuck off and stop being so righteous. This was unlike her, to put it mildly. Then, when he said he was going to CrossFit as her little bender had kept him from attending yesterday, she launched into a twelve-minute diatribe about how she was forced to spend her free time doing laundry instead of exercising, and that she was not exactly thrilled that millennia of human evolution had boiled down to them having the same, tedious argument that their ancestors had probably hashed out in caves. But other things were coming out too: wants and needs, desires even. When Nick was putting his Lycra on, she asked if he could perhaps start spending a bit of extra time working on her body as well as his, if he knew what she meant? (He did not, so she had told him, very loudly, that she wanted him to tweak her nipples and then eat her out before taking her hard from behind. Bewildered after a period of sexual abstinence that had gone on more or less since her dad moved in six months ago, bringing a general put-upon vibe that seemed to have filled his wife with lethargy and self-loathing, Nick had left for the gym in a horny state of confusion.)

And when the Laura Kuenssberg show had been left on in the living room earlier she had started hurling insults such as 'tedious windbag', 'absolute asshat' and 'sanctimonious tossbag' at the various politicians who made their way on to the screen, until Jack had suggested he commandeer the TV so he could play Football Manager and she could 'calm down'.

'If it stops you from talking incessantly about Erling Haaland, then I'm all for it, darling,' said Olivia, wincing as she spoke. 'Sorry, I didn't mean that. Or I did, but I meant it lovingly, in a way that you shouldn't take too personally.'

Why couldn't she just be nice, like she normally was?

She finds she has no filter, no social graces, no ability to massage reality and tell the little fibs that usually cushion her days like clouds. All attempts to protect other people's feelings seem to have been abandoned in a furious race to express hers. Where was it all coming from? Olivia has always baulked at gobby right-wingers who defend their nastiness with the words 'I was only saying what everyone was thinking', but now she gets it.

She texts her sister, to see if she knows of any drugs with side effects that include inducing a state of truth-telling psychosis in the user. Lily is exactly the kind of person who would know about this stuff – while their mother believes that her youngest daughter likes to travel for reasons of cultural enrichment, 'sampling global art and cuisine', as Tina likes to put it, Olivia is aware that, more often than not, the cuisine Lily is sampling is narcotic-based and usually of the psychedelic type.

> *Lily – went on the lash on Friday and a young person gave me something dodgy. I think I did some of that microdosing, or whatever it's called??? I need your help, please don't tell Mum!!!!!!*

> *What did you microdose? Acid? Or Ozempic, like all the other yummy mummies? Are you shitting the bed?*

> *No, I'm TRUTH-TELLING and I just wondered if this was a side effect of some drugs? I need the antidote pronto*

> *You're going to need to explain to me what the hell it is you took, because you sound utterly mental*

> *It was like a Haribo. But not a Haribo. Shaped like a football, called the Haaland because it's so damn good at what it is, according to the girl who gave it to me. Haaland as in IAN HARLAND, the thumb with a face*

> *Lol, you took a weed gummy. Calm down, Doris. You're just experiencing a comedown. Like a hangover, but with drugs. Have a banana and some broccoli and an early night and I'm sure you'll be fine. See you Tuesday xxx*

'I think I'm experiencing the opposite of a Yes Day,' she explains to Nick later that night, when he gingerly dares to venture into the bedroom to communicate with this woman who claims to be his wife. 'Like a No Day, or something. An absolutely No-Fucking-Way Day.'

'You're definitely being more . . . spirited?' He closes the door behind him, tentative and – yep, she can see it in the way his eyes are crinkling – terrified. 'Maybe you're just having an extreme reaction to what happened at work on Friday?' He nervously sits at the end of the bed.

'Or maybe I'm having a perfectly normal reaction to everything that's happened at work for the last twenty or so years that I've been there? Maybe tomorrow I will wake up and feel a bit more like myself. But today, I would just like it to be known that Stephen can go fuck himself.'

BRYONY GORDON

'Who are you?' Nick says, completely stunned. 'And what the hell have you done with my wife?'

Olivia manages to keep her mouth shut. Neither of them are prepared to consider the possibility that, far from his wife disappearing somewhere, she was only just beginning to come back.

9

Olivia has taken a later-than-usual train to work – not out of any fear, or to put off the inevitable, but because she is still quite tired from Friday's escapades and wants to take a service where she might actually get a seat. She's embarrassed by the thought of the fawning version of herself who would always arrive half an hour before anyone else. Nobody was paying her for that extra time – extra time that could have been spent in bed. Hours and hours, entire days, she had wasted sitting at her desk, hoping someone would notice and give her a big shiny medal.

As she plonks herself down next to a suited man in his sixties, she feels remarkably . . . relaxed. She knows that she should be anxious about going to work. That she should be ruminating wildly over what she will face when she gets there: the judgement from Stephen about the message she sent him on Saturday morning, the embarrassment of having taken drugs with a new colleague who is, after all, young enough to be her daughter, and the shit new role that she's supposed to be grateful for. She knows that she should be bargaining with some punishing higher power in the sky, promising that if she can just get through this day without getting sacked, then she will devote her life to prayer and service and good deeds.

But she's starting to realize that life could be a bit different. That the things she spends her time on could be about what *she* wants.

Like eating pickled onion Monster Munch in bed, for example. Day drinking in the garden to let off steam. Giving yourself multiple orgasms, the type that can go on and on until you get bored, or tired, and decide you need to have a little nap. She'd forgotten that this was a thing she could do to herself, and now she didn't want to stop. Just as she had forgotten that she could wear comfortable clothes to work: jeans, and trainers that don't hurt her blistered feet. She has never allowed herself to dress in anything like this for the office, but she figures that in her new role as a glorified party planner, she can be a bit more casual.

As the train passes East Croydon, Olivia decides that there are so many things she could be doing with her one precious life other than worrying. It's truly bizarre how absolutely clear she feels on this: *que sera sera*, whatever will be will be. She plugs in her AirPods and turns up the volume on a 'Celine Dion Classics' playlist she found this morning on Spotify.

She feels a tap on her shoulder, and turns to the man sitting next to her, removing an AirPod as she does so. 'Excuse me,' he says, spittle flying everywhere, 'but will you turn that racket down? Some of us are trying to think.'

Olivia sighs deeply and screws up her face. 'Not *again*,' she says, putting the AirPod back in. 'This is no racket. It's CELINE FUCKING DION.'

Then she turns the volume up so high that she gets an alert on her phone, telling her that she is in danger of damaging her ears. She waves the screen in the man's face while cackling wildly. He gets up and moves to another part of the train, and Olivia spreads her tote bag over the vacated seat.

At work, she realizes she hasn't got her pass – most unlike Olivia, given that in 2019, the security team for the building handed her the title of 'Employee Least Likely to Annoy the

Front Desk by Forgetting Their Lanyard', the small plastic trophy still somewhere on her desk – but is saved by Joe who signs her in. 'You're in late,' he says, surveying her outfit with a barely concealed sneer on his face.

'And you're rather rudely looking me up and down as if I'm auditioning for *The Morning*'s Next Top Model,' snaps Olivia. 'Which is not OK, in this day and age. So could you stop?'

'Wow, Olivia!' He pretends to lick his finger, and makes a sizzling sound to dampen down an imaginary fire. 'What a zinger, I love it. Fair enough. So can I say that you're looking fresh today. No make-up?'

As they step on to the escalator up to their floor, Olivia tries to remember putting on foundation, blusher, mascara, brow gel. She can't. But she has no interest in discussing her beauty routine – or lack of one – with Joe; she is far more eager to mine him for information.

'Hey, you know everyone round these parts,' she says, changing the subject. 'Have you met one of the new assistants, a girl called Rose?'

'Hmmm?' says Joe, looking up at her.

'Rose?' Suddenly, as if from nowhere, she feels pressure building in her stomach. She lets out a loud trumpet of a fart to relieve it.

'What the hell!' Joe tries not to fall backwards down the escalator. 'Are you OK, Liv? You are *not* your usual suburban self today.'

'Why are you always so rude?' asks Olivia, her face entirely straight. 'You think you're being funny, or arch, but really you're just a bit disrespectful. All I did was let out a bit of hot air from my, frankly, hot arse. It's better it comes out that way than on to the page, as is so often the case in this place.'

'Oooh, Olivia,' Joe shivers, looking excited. 'I am here for this mood on a Monday morning.'

'Right, so can you answer my question. Do you know anyone called Rose?'

'No idea who you're talking about.' Joe shakes his head and follows her off the top of the escalator into the canteen at the entrance of the office.

'Fat fucking lot of use you are to me,' sighs Olivia, storming off to the bathroom.

To Olivia's immense surprise, she doesn't head immediately to the cubicle furthest away from the door, where she has always gone, fearful of anyone hearing her urinate or – even worse – defecate. Instead, she locks herself inside the nearest available cubicle, pulls down the toilet seat, and relieves her pickled onion Monster Munch bowels with a loud sigh of relief. As she wipes her behind, she is suddenly plunged back to Friday night, going to a grotty loo with Rose and singing the Haaland song to her as she peed, the one Jack insists on playing over Alexa at every given opportunity.

'Haaland, Haaland/Yorkshire born, Norwegian lad/Roy Keane tried to kill his dad.' She had hollered this at Rose, as her young colleague kindly used the sole of her Air Force 1 to hold shut the broken door in the ladies' loos of . . . a nightclub?

When did she last go to one of those?

Olivia finds herself singing it now as she sits on the toilet seat. She is interrupted by a cough from outside.

'Olivia?' comes the unmistakable voice of Nina from the other side of the door. 'Are you OK?'

'I'm fine, thanks,' she says with absolutely zero shame, another stunning revelation. 'Just had a bit of bowel trouble after a heavy weekend of Monster Munch.'

'I've been sent in here to check on you. Joe said you were . . .' Nina pauses, and Olivia hopes this is because she is giving up and going away. 'He said you weren't yourself.'

'Is that because I wasn't wearing make-up?' Olivia pulls up her trousers and flushes the loo, then goes to exit the cubicle. Nina moves out of her way as she washes her hands and admires the surprising clarity of her foundation-free skin, given the amount of ultra-processed food she's consumed over the weekend.

'I think he was just maybe concerned that you were, err . . .' Nina starts nervously doing her hair in the mirror. 'That maybe you were, I dunno, struggling with the changes?'

Olivia turns and looks at Nina, her young, immaculately put-together protégée who has made senior columnist at *The Morning* before she's even hit thirty-two. She smiles at her, and lets out a small, impressed laugh.

'Oh my love, I'm not struggling with the changes. If anything, they seem to have woken me out of a sort of stupor. The only thing I'm struggling with is the realization of what an absolute doormat I've allowed myself to be for the last, oooh, four decades or so.'

Nina begins squirming. 'I think it's really important to say that Stephen only told me on Friday morning, and I never meant to treat you like a doorma—'

'Not you, you pillock. All you did was ask my advice and then, thankfully, ignore it. I mean what the fuck did I know? I should have been listening to you all along. All those hours I spent patronizing you by telling you to be humble and grateful for the opportunities afforded to you, all those fucking Women Rising sessions where I was essentially a woman falling into the cliché that is female martyrdom.' She breaks into a childish, squeaky voice. 'Oh if I just do everything everyone asks of me and never put a foot wrong, then surely I'll be rewarded for being a good girl! Give me a lollipop, someone, for being nice!' Olivia shakes her head, notes the look of alarm on Nina's face. 'Whereas you, Nina, knew to do the right thing. You knew that simpering to cockwombles was a terrible abandonment of yourself. And well done you, for standing by your morals and values. I'm just disappointed that I didn't have the guts to do it sooner.'

'Well, I was not expecting that,' says Nina, unsure what to do with herself.

'To tell you the truth, because it's all I seem to be able to tell anyone at the moment, neither was I. But here we are. Anyway, I'm fine thanks, especially now I've got that out of my system.' Olivia pauses, realizes what she has said. 'The rant, that is, not the pickled onion Monster Munch.'

'Yeah, I got that.' Nina shuffles towards the door.

'OK, so I'm going to freshen up and see you back out there. Toodle-pip!'

Talking like that with Nina was one thing, but Olivia needs to pull herself together. How can she go back to something more akin to her normal style, where she's a little less . . . *forthcoming*? It's all well and good having an epiphany, but does she need to share the results of it with everyone before she's worked out what to do with them? So far, she hasn't got herself into too much trouble, but she knows that if she doesn't rein herself in, her head is going to be on the block by lunchtime.

She surveys her bare face in the mirror. A couple of days ago, turning up to work without make-up on would have felt a bit like going into the office naked, but today she feels completely ambivalent towards her reflection. It's just a face, no more, no less, and given none of the blokes around her feel they have to pretty themselves up with an eyeshadow palette and some tubing mascara, why the hell should she? Olivia splashes some water on her skin and pulls up her jumper to dry it. Then she removes the jumper, shoving it in her tote bag, straightens the old blue T-shirt she threw on without thinking – the one bearing the slogan SORRY I'M LATE, I DIDN'T WANT TO COME – and shrugs as she makes for the exit.

'There she is,' says Stephen, who is hovering in the corridor, rubbing his hands together in glee.

'Here I am,' replies Olivia. 'Not at all freaked out by the fact that you're hanging around outside the ladies' loos waiting for me with a sort of shit-eating grin on your face.'

Olivia winces at the words that have just fallen out of her mouth, wonders how long she will remain employed. Fifteen seconds? Twenty? A minute, tops?

'Liv, you are on fire today!' claps Stephen, putting his arm around her as he walks her back towards the main office.

'Thanks, Ste,' she says, shrugging it off.

'It's Stephen.' He suddenly looks very serious, like a shiny balloon that has just been popped.

'I know it's Stephen, Stephen.' Olivia rolls her eyes, very visibly, as opposed to only inwardly, as she normally does. A new theory enters her head: what if aliens abducted her on Friday night and took control of her body, implanting fake memories of a Gen Z-er in a pink suit doling out drugs named after Manchester City players? It really says something that right now, this seems an entirely rational explanation for what is happening to her. 'I was calling you by a cutesy nickname you didn't ask for, just as you do with me. My name's Olivia, not Liv.' She has put on her most patronizing tone, the kind she would usually reserve for Jack or Saskia when they were being really gobby (or her father

Peter, for that matter). 'I was trying to make a point, but obviously it's been lost on you.'

Stephen laughs in a hollow way that suggests he does not find this in the least bit funny. 'Liv, are you writing a feature where you try out some new Hollywood craze that involves only saying what you think?'

'Yes!' exclaims Olivia, grateful for the excuse. 'There's this new, erm, self-help book out in the States that Oprah has been touting. It's about standing in your power and, um, owning your boundaries, and rejecting people pleasing. Apparently, women are going wild for it, Ste. WILD.' She makes a roar and turns her hands into claws. 'It's called . . .' She clears her throat as she tries to think on her feet, which are following Stephen towards the glass-box meeting room, the one where conference takes place. '*People Displeaser!*'

She realizes that she says this in a schlocky American accent, very loudly, so that half the office turns round to look at her – the half that hasn't already turned and stared in horror when she attempted to be a lion a moment ago. She closes her eyes in mortification, her mouth moving around like a fish in the hope that this might stop the cascade of words that seem to be coming out unbidden. Instead, it just makes her look like she's having some sort of episode, very possibly a stroke. Which, to be fair, is another potential explanation for her sudden verbosity. Perhaps it will turn out that she's quite unwell, that this is all the result of a major neurological event and she will end up being signed off for a couple of months, protected by the law, which now she comes to think about it is the dream of most working people over the age of thirty-five.

'Bonza,' she says, as she imagines being sedated for a prolonged period of time.

'Are you OK?' asks Stephen. They are by the very water

cooler where, just a few days ago, he completely changed her job description without once thinking to enquire about her thoughts on the matter, which, it occurs to her now, is almost certainly illegal and worth taking up with HR.

'Am I OK?' she parrots back. 'Nice of you to finally ask after, what?' She starts counting her fingers. 'Twenty-odd years of working together?'

'Sorry?' Stephen is now pretending that he hasn't heard her, a tactic she sort of respects, having long used it herself as a way to avoid difficult conversations with people.

'Nothing, I'm fine.' If she just focuses on keeping her answers short and simple, she will be able to limit the number of offensive comments she makes.

'You're speaking your truth, I like it,' nods Stephen. 'We need more women like you saying what they really think.'

'Speaking of women who say what they really think,' smiles Olivia, folding her arms over the slogan on her T-shirt, 'I wondered if you could point me in the direction of this new executive assistant, Rose.'

'Who?' Stephen looks annoyed.

'Rose, the new executive assistant in the pink suit, from the pub on Friday?'

'Don't know her. I just wanted to talk to you about the party if you've got a spare five minutes, which I know you do have because I'm your boss.' He motions towards his office, and nods for her to go first.

'And I just want to talk to you about Rose.' Olivia is now annoyed. She walks into his office and sits down on his sofa without asking. He stands over her, his brow furrowed in confusion. 'Rose, Rose, Rose. Maybe Rosemary. Possibly Rosie. Ros? About five foot six, pink suit, smokes roll-ups. Though of course she probably didn't do that in her interview for the job here. Quite precocious, which is good. I mean, I need that kind of energy in my life right now.' She sees that his face is as blank as her memory of Friday night. 'Not ringing any bells?' She has stretched out on the leather sofa, her Nike-clad feet hanging over one end of it. 'The woman I was smoking with outside when you walked in with Nina?'

'I've never seen you smoke, Olivia. I think I saw you for about ten seconds on Friday night, leaving alone.'

Olivia sits up straight. She feels her tummy lurch.

'So you haven't recently hired an assistant called Rose?'

He shakes his head.

'There's no Rose?' whispers Olivia.

'There's no Rose,' nods Stephen, like he's talking to an idiot non-savant. 'Do you need me to refer you to one of the mental health first-aiders?'

'Ahahaha!' Olivia stands up and makes her way to the door. 'That's a good one. Mental health first-aiders indeed. Most of us in here need time on a psychiatric ward.'

As if to prove her point, she blows a raspberry with her tongue. It's not a nervous tic she's ever gone for before, but in this moment, when absolutely everything she thought she knew seems to have been turned upside down, it makes a strange kind of sense.

If Stephen has never heard of Rose and she doesn't exist anywhere on the system, then who the hell is she?

10

Olivia stands in the corridor and, like a Co-Op Columbo, tries to assess the situation as it appears to her this Monday morning: that on Friday night, a Gen Z-er in a bright pink suit kidnapped and drugged her, while pretending to work at *The Morning*. Was this an elaborate way to get free drinks, or something more sinister? It all made about as much sense as a Christopher Nolan movie, without any of the redeeming qualities of Cillian Murphy, or a stirring Hollywood film score.

Olivia heads back to the safety of her desk. As Olivia approaches, she immediately spots Nina in her new office. It's really more of a small glass box, but the point is that it has a door. Sat at her pristine desk, the only belongings on it a bottle of Tom Ford perfume, a pale green Stanley cup, and a Chanel lipstick, Nina is ranting animatedly at her screen, slamming her mouse up and down on its mat, as Joe stands over her, rubbing her back in a consoling manner.

But with Joe, as with everyone in this place, he could just as easily be knifing her in the back.

Olivia sits down at her desk, littered with sachets of sugar, wooden hot-drink stirrers, Post-it notes and pictures of her children. She switches on her computer and wonders if there is something in the air. Maybe the moon is full, mercury is in retrograde, and all the stars and planets have realigned to wreak havoc on Earth? Why is it that she can suddenly see all the myriad ways in which she has allowed herself to be slowly boiled alive in this place, like a frog trussed up in a Zara frock and Charlotte Tilbury lipstick? What is happening to her brain?

'I can't BELIEVE they wouldn't delete these,' shrills Nina from her office, with the self-important air of someone who has just been made a national newspaper columnist. Olivia has to admire the speed at which Nina has settled into the role. Her first week on the job and already criticizing the overworked online moderators.

'I know,' slithers Joe. 'But see it as a compliment that all these morons wasted their weekends below the line on your column. And think of the engagement, darling!'

'I suppose it will have made the numbers look good,' nods Nina, temporarily mollified. 'But Jesus, where do these people get off? *Nina Hunt clearly only got this job because she's sleeping with someone at the top.* Liked two thousand eight hundred and ninety-two times, Joe. TWO THOUSAND EIGHT HUNDRED AND NINETY-TWO TIMES.'

Olivia writes the word 'BASTARDS' on a Post-it note, and realizes that she would have hated this aspect of the job, that no amount of praise from on high would be able to cancel out the endless negativity from arseholes on the internet.

'Think of the numbers, babe,' Joe reassures. 'Think of the numbers.'

'*Are you paid to write this drivel?*' Nina's head is craned directly at the screen as she reads out more of the vicious missives posted below her first column.

'Well, to be fair, you are,' nods Joe. 'And handsomely. Meanwhile, are they paid to write these comments? Now who's the loser?'

Olivia nods along at her desk, thinking that for all his many barbed asides, Joe does at least put in a good shift as a hype man.

'I'm tempted to log in and write that as a response,' snorts Nina.

'Look at this dude,' Joe says, leaning into the screen. 'HaalandIsLife? He's left about seven hundred comments. He's completely hot for you, look.' Joe points at the monitor.

'He absolutely wants to have sex with me,' nods Nina, in a way that suggests she isn't entirely upset about this.

'*Nina Hunt would be better off writing for the Beano than a once-great newspaper*,' reads Joe.

'*Nina Hunt?*' he continues, reading out another comment. '*More like Nina *unt.*'

Nina looks aghast at the C-bomb. 'Joe! What the fuck does HaalandIsLife even mean?'

'He's probably referring to the Man City player, Erling Haaland,' interjects Olivia with a sigh that ripples through her like a shudder. That name is following her around like a bad smell after an afternoon on the pickled onion Monster Munch. She dismisses the paranoia with a roll of her shoulders and a shake of her head, then notes the blank expressions on her colleagues' faces. 'Famous Norwegian striker, quite popular with ten-year-old boys.'

'Well, you know quite a lot about this HaalandIsLife troll, don't you, Olivia?' Joe narrows his eyes at Nina. 'Have you been trolling Nina under a pseudonym? Even I didn't think you'd be *that* provincial, Olivia.'

Everyone within a ten-metre radius has stopped what they are doing, Spidey senses alert to a spectacle about to unfold in front of them.

'Oh my god. Don't even try that playing-us-off-against-each-other bollocks, Joe. Not today.'

'You're not usually so defensive, Olivia.' Joe's face lights up at the shit he has managed to stir. 'Anybody would think you had something to hide.'

'Ironically, Joe, you've caught me on a day when I'm just about done with hiding.' She feels a fury building inside her, that after all this time working her behind off on the Women Rising programme for absolutely no thanks – or remuneration – this man would try to make out that *she's* the bad guy.

'Going to admit that you've been trolling poor Nina, then?' Joe is playing to the crowd now, warming to his theme. Olivia's seen him do this before with other colleagues – she's watched him toy with people for his own amusement, lapping up all the laughs he gets. She's always tended to cower behind him, and now his vitriol is aimed at her she feels ashamed of every time she's seen it happen and not called him out on it. His sense of humour has always been cruel, always been about taking someone down, usually a rival who threatens his place in the pack. She's never been that person, never posed a threat to him, and she marvels at how quickly his nose has been put out of joint by her simply saying a few feisty words to him on the escalator. The fact that he's nothing but an insecure, immature bully smacks her in the face.

'With all due respect to Nina, I have better things to do with my time than troll her.'

'Bit suss, though, that you know so much about this Haaland chap,' he says, with a flourish. 'Who else could it be, Olivia, if not you?'

'One of the thousands and thousands of anonymous men that this organization actively encourages to post misogynistic shit on its website every day?' Olivia shakes her head as if she's just had to explain Catholicism to the Pope.

'That's pretty convenient, isn't it, Liv?'

Olivia closes her eyes for a moment, tries to calm her breathing. She needs to respond, not react; she can't allow Joe to get her flustered, or she'll lose the argument entirely. And for once, she not only wants to have an argument – she wants to win it.

'You know, Joe,' says Olivia, spinning her chair slowly round to face him. 'I'm going to take responsibility for something today, but it's not what you think it is. I'm going to take responsibility for allowing you to suck my energy. To drain it, with your fake friendship and your back-stabbing and your manipulation. You're a vampire in designer clothing and the whole time we've known each other, I've let you suck on my blood. Whenever you've felt like shit, you've just dumped all of it on us without any consideration for what might be going on in our lives. And I've tolerated it, because I've been a pathetic, emotionally naive empath, who thinks the worst of myself and the best of everyone else in the hope that it might make you like me more.'

Out of the corner of her eye, Olivia notices people nodding along with her. She used to cringe when actors and creatives gave interviews talking about the importance of living-in-their-truth, but all these validating glances are giving her an inkling of how very intoxicating it is. 'Olivia, that is—'

'No, I haven't finished. You've always refused to own your bad behaviour. You've always put it on other people's backs, instead of taking responsibility for it yourself. You've just accused me of trolling the woman I've been mentoring, for Christ's sake. But I'm handing it all back, Joe. I don't need you to like me. I don't even want you to like me, when I really think about it. You're just someone I work with.'

Joe's lip quivers in shock. Nina sips on her Stanley cup, enraptured.

'Do you remember when you told me that someone over in Baghdad had been slagging me off? You pulled me aside and told me that he'd been having a go at my, what was it?' Olivia steeples her hands as she searches for the words that had pierced her in the heart back when she had first heard them. 'Beige copy and middle-aged ideas? And when you told me, Joe, you said it was because you wanted me to know you had my back. That you were looking out for me. Ha! I was really upset, and yet you expected me to be grateful for this *beautiful act of friendship*. You were just passing off nastiness as some sort of enlightening honesty.' The adrenalin is pumping through Olivia's veins now, courage finding its way from her heart to her mouth. 'But if you think I'm beige, then you should see my insides. You should see them. They're red-raw and raging with all the things I have wanted to say but swallowed down. Well, that stops now. I can promise you that from this moment on, I will tell you what I feel clearly and openly, and you won't ever find me hiding behind some pseudonym on the internet to do it.'

From behind her, she hears a slow hand-clapping. She turns to see Stephen, grinning like a man who has just watched his football team demolish the opposition in the Champions League final. 'Very impressive,' he says. 'Very impressive. I was just coming over to suggest that my new columnist and my new Anniversary Architect join us in conference, but after that performance, I don't know if I dare!' He laughs with all the soul of a clown in a collapsed circus.

For the first time in her career, Olivia doesn't feel the need to laugh along with him.

11

Olivia had always suspected that 'conference' was too grand a term to describe the daily editorial meeting that takes place in newspapers across the country, or what remains of them, and now that she is finally in it, all her suspicions are confirmed. If the word 'conference' typically means a gathering of large numbers of people in one place to discuss a shared interest, then the morning meeting fails on most counts, containing, as it does, a dwindling number of section heads all fighting with each other over terrible ideas they are paid pitifully to pretend to give a toss about.

'I'd like everyone to know that Nina and Li— I mean Olivia – are going to be joining us from now on,' says Stephen, sitting at the head of a large oak table, the type that probably costs more than her annual wage. The room contains eight men and now, thanks to Olivia and Nina, the grand total of three women, though Mary, the assistant editor, doesn't really count, owing to the fact she's basically risen to the top by refusing to have a personal life and adopting the same insidiously misogynistic views as all the other men in the room. 'Nina, as we all know from her blockbuster first column on Saturday, is the new voice of women on this paper. And Li—' Stephen corrects himself, 'I mean Olivia – is going to be the Anniversary Architect, in charge of all our birthday celebrations. Although you should also know that she's writing one last feature which involves "speaking her truth"' – he does quote fingers in the air – 'so there's no need to take anything she says today too seriously.'

Andrew, a sixty-something who rarely shows up before 11 a.m. and frequently takes two-hour lunch breaks, lets out a sarcastic little snigger. Olivia knows she could pretend not to hear it, just as she's pretended not to hear so many other comments over the years – the tired old ones about skirt length and necklines and the apparent vapidity of everything that appears in the features section of *The Morning*. The sexism had become less overt the longer she had been there, but it was still there, in every moment of being interrupted, spoken over, or simply not engaged with at all. Olivia knows that the comments about women's bodies have gone away not because any of the men have been enlightened, but out of self-interest, a desperate need to stay in their relative positions of power. And today, Olivia finds she cannot pretend she hasn't heard the snigger. She needs to say something, if only to make up for all the times she's said nothing at all.

'That snark is a bit rich coming from a man who's held the title of "letters editor" for fifteen years,' says Olivia, smiling sweetly. Andrew's face begins to turn beetroot red, or more beetroot red (his nose has always had the unhealthy glow of an all-day drinker about it), as he struggles to compute this combination of feminine charm and hostility. 'Doesn't your job just involve reading post and printing out the less mad and angry ones on the letters page? If a woman did that job they'd be called a secretary.'

Nina sniggers and attempts to pass it off as a cough.

'No need to get your knickers in a twist,' says Andrew. 'Although I'm probably not allowed to refer to your knickers without finding myself cancelled.'

'The frisson of cancellation is what counts for excitement

nowadays, old boy,' says Hugo, the thirty-something comment editor whose proudest achievement to date seems to be his admittance into a members' club that doesn't allow women.

Olivia rolls her eyes and decides not to waste any more of her energy on this conversation. Plus, she needs to be a bit careful. She is the main breadwinner in the house, and a job is extremely useful when it comes to paying a mortgage. Even if it is a job you don't want, haven't asked for, and that might actually have broken several employment laws, given the way it was handed to you.

She decides instead to stay quiet, a powerful, self-imposed silence. She sits and thinks about the version of her who existed before she met Rose, the one who felt genuine pain in her stomach at the thought of being on someone's bad side. It was visceral, the sensation she'd always had when there was a possibility someone might be cross with her – it pushed out all other feelings and thoughts and plans for the day, threatening to swallow her whole, like heartburn. Her only means of survival had been to defuse the situation and make sure that everyone was happy with her, by desperately fawning, and throwing compliments around like confetti. She *loved* everyone's ideas (even though she didn't), she *adored* that dress (even though she hadn't even noticed it), she *really enjoyed* that joke (she hadn't). Seeing the glow on someone's face as they received her compliments gave her a thrill that more than made up for the fact she didn't mean them. That others liked her was way more important to Olivia than whether or not she was behaving in a manner that meant she actually liked herself.

She picks up a biro from the table and starts chewing it in the hope that it will distract her mouth from getting her in serious trouble. She tries to avoid accidentally drawing on her own face and listens to the men in the room wang on about immigration and the tyranny of wokeness and the upcoming Euros, the recent injuries of several French players apparently the kind of important news that really matters. Olivia, for the sake of her cortisol levels and her blood pressure, slips into a sort of catatonic state, almost meditative – similar, she imagines, to the vows of silence that monks are forced to take for weeks on end as they enter the Buddhist faith. It's only when she hears Andrew discussing a famous singer in her sixties who has been stalked and followed by paparazzi on her holiday, hunted down until they could get a picture of her in a bikini, that she snaps out of it.

'She's deluded,' she hears Mary say, as she looks in disgust at the cover of a downmarket tabloid, which has pictures of the singer holidaying on a yacht splashed across it. 'As a woman of a similar age to her, I don't think this is a good look, and I think there's loads of us out there who would agree. We don't want to see it.' Mary screws up her face in distaste. 'I reckon a piece by another woman saying this would go down a storm online.'

Stephen nods. He has been given permission to be misogynistic by this token woman, and so he is happy. 'Nina, maybe you should write a column on why you're sick of seeing famous older women parading around showing off on holiday? But make it kind of sexy, and non-judgemental.'

'Right,' gulps Nina. 'I was actually thinking more along the lines of a piece about how great it is that once you get older, you no longer care what anyone thinks of you?'

Stephen shakes his head, still grimacing at the pictures. 'No, that's not the one for big numbers, Nina. If Mary is thinking this as a fifty-something middle-class woman, then there will be loads of other people out there thinking it too. Surely we need to listen to all women, and not just the ones who hold beliefs of neoliberal feminism? Isn't that what a proper truth-telling news organization should be doing, instead of simply kowtowing to popular opinion?'

'Well, I think—' Olivia starts to speak, but is cut off by Hugo.

'I have a good piece actually on how neoliberal feminism is hurting the women who need help the most,' he says, stroking the bumfluff on his chin seriously, 'and how rich, privileged Western women have forgotten their counterparts in places such as Afghanistan and Yemen.'

Olivia gapes. What would Rose say if she were here? She'd probably summon all her strength to upend the big oak table, covering the likes of Andrew, Hugo, Mary and Stephen in their coffees. She would point out how incredible it was that their utterly irrelevant thoughts about a woman's body had managed to morph into a discussion about how modern women were responsible for systemic oppression and abuse. Rose would take each and every one of these turgid tossbags to task for their toxicity, for their entitlement, for the absolute fucking arrogance of believing that anybody would actually give a shit about their view on this woman's swimwear choices. She'd probably say something pithy like: 'Is there an age where women should stop wearing bikinis? And if so, would you mind clarifying what that age is, so I can inform all the world's women and they can make a note in their diary accordingly? *Twenty-fifth birthday: do not wear bikini any more in case it offends Andrew Grey, the greasy-bearded letters editor of* The Morning *newspaper who is so overweight his belly is currently poking out from under his shirt?*'

Olivia smiles to herself, and then is suddenly hit by a flashback of Rose, taking her to task for a piece she once wrote about how boring Kate Middleton's fashion choices were, and how much she preferred Harry's then girlfriend, Chelsy Davy. Olivia had been shocked that Rose would even know about the piece – it had been written way back in the mid-noughties – and then she was shocked by the irony of writing such a mean-spirited little article just to appease her boss, without any thought for the wellbeing of the women she was writing it about (as if they read *The Morning*, she told herself). Olivia wonders where Rose is now. *Who* Rose is, more to the point.

'OK, Liv, you're not holding back today.' Stephen's nasal voice penetrates her brain and shocks her back into the moment. 'So what do you think Nina should do the column on?'

Holy shit, she said that last bit out loud. Andrew is ferreting around trying to tuck his shirt in across the table from her.

There's a part of her that knows she should stay quiet. That she should rise above it all and carry her feelings to a book club meet-up or a spin class, or any of the other sanctioned places where women go, in groups, to vent the rage they fearfully store up in their everyday lives. But there's also a part of her, a part that suddenly feels important, that knows that if she doesn't correct him now it will always, always be like this. She will spend the rest of her life simmering with fury while smiling sweetly, and nothing will ever, ever change.

'I think Nina should write a piece about the madness of a world where a sixty-year-old woman wearing a bikini is deemed shocking enough to make the front page. She should write the piece about how nuts it is that you've just spent somewhere close to twenty minutes pointing out the grossness of this woman's body, given that you're grown men – and women,' Olivia turns to Mary, 'who should know better. But mostly, I think Nina should do the column on whatever she damn well wants to, because you're paying her to write *her* opinions, not yours, or Andrew's, or Mary's. Furthermore, you're paying me to be the Anniversary

Architect, not to tell you what other people should write. And by the way, it's Olivia,' says Olivia, reaching across the table for Nina's notepad. 'Sorry, Nina,' she says, tearing out a piece of paper and writing her name in block capitals on it, before holding it up and showing it to the room. 'O-L-I-V-I-A,' she spells out. 'Not Liv. Not L-I-V. O-L-I-V-I-A.' She shakes her head. 'Honestly, I've told you this quite clearly already this morning, not that long ago, in terms that, had anyone used them to me, I would have listened to. And not only would I have listened, I would also have burned the information into my brain because there's nothing less terrifying than the possibility that I might do something to even vaguely upset someone. Pathetic, isn't it? Because meanwhile, you've already forgotten what I said, despite being the Oxbridge-educated editor of one of the biggest newspapers in the country, a man who is on speaking terms with the prime minister.'

Olivia pauses for a moment, enjoying with a mixture of horror and relish the speechless faces of her colleagues.

'Or maybe you just don't deem it important enough to take into consideration,' she says, standing up and heading in the direction of the door. 'Either way, it's a pretty damning indictment of the culture at this esteemed organization as it enters its centenary year.' She bows and curtsies as she says this, goes to exit, feels a blast of air from outside come flooding into the glass box as she turns the handle and pulls the door towards her.

'Leaving so soon?' sneers Hugo.

'I've been working here twenty fucking years, Hugo,' she says, sticking her middle finger up and turning on her trainer-clad heel. 'I'd hardly call this soon.'

12

A week ago, Olivia Greenwood would no more have dreamed of bunking off work than she would have entertained the idea of standing up to Stephen, Hugo, Andrew and their woman-bro Mary. Now she has done all of these things before 11.30 on a Monday morning, and she is both exhilarated and terrified in equal measure.

Which is in itself kind of confusing. She feels like some sort of contemporary midlife Jekyll and Hyde, fighting with two extreme versions of herself.

On her way to the train station, she stops at a Gail's Bakery. It's a place Olivia usually avoids – she prefers coffee that doesn't require her to remortgage the house. Also, she's normally the kind of person who limits herself to one cup a day, never after 11 a.m., which is officially the point at which she switches to something less likely to leave her a paranoid wreck: lemon and ginger tea, for example, peppermint, or – if she's feeling particularly daring – a mug of green. Today, she knows that having more coffee won't lessen any anxiety about her not-so-little outbursts at work this morning. But she also knows that she really, really wants a dirty-great-big cappuccino absolutely covered in chocolate, and since the anxiety hasn't arrived yet she's ordering an extra-large one.

She orders the second coffee and a cinnamon bun on the side, reasoning that the sugar and carbohydrate content of the latter might at least create a pleasant bed for the caffeine to nestle in.

She catches the 11.47 train back to her suburban station in Sussex, amazed at the emptiness of the service. She sits in what she has always considered to be the train's premier seat, equivalent to 1A first class on a plane (not that she's ever flown anything but cattle): next to the window, perched at a table, facing the direction of travel. Olivia cannot believe her luck. She hasn't sat in this privileged position since her early thirties, when she was heavily pregnant with Jack, sporting ankles that had swollen like rubber rings. Back then, people would take pity on her, though not before shooting her a glance that told her how resentful they were for it, how annoying it was that she would deign to leave the house and take up space with her massive, pregnant belly that was an inconvenience to everyone on this train, all of whom just wanted to sit down on their journey to work, and none of whom had asked her to get up the duff. Well, that's how it played out in her head, anyway.

Olivia slips off her shoes and puts her feet on the seat in front of her – another highly improper action she wouldn't have dared to carry out a few days ago, especially not with feet as blistered as hers – before biting into the cinnamon bun, allowing its sugary flakes to drop everywhere: all over her top, down her jeans, and on to the seat around her.

She has only ever pulled a sickie once, way back in her twenties, when she was in the early stages of her relationship with Nick. They had spent the Sunday on a pub crawl, even though it was a school night and she wasn't going to be able to ascend to the dizzy heights of journalism if she was permanently hungover. That may have worked in the old days, when most newspapers were written in a fog of cigarette smoke after a long lunch at a Fleet Street boozer, but this was the early noughties and editors wanted their trainees bright-eyed and bushy-tailed in order to see off this pesky thing everyone was calling the internet and the sudden availability of 24-hour news. Together, these innovations were threatening to steal the thunder of print, which liked to knock off by about 9 p.m. so it could go and get pissed at the pub, thank you very much.

'We need to ensure that people never tire of the feeling of printer's ink on their fingers,' bellowed Henry Wellington, the then editor of *The Morning*, in what was meant to be a rousing speech to the new trainees on their first day. 'We need your talent and your know-how and your . . .' He had waved his arms in the air. He was quite clearly pissed, and it wasn't even 4 p.m. As he searched his booze-addled brain for whatever word it was he was looking for, Olivia, Joe and all the other trainees marvelled at his impressive belly, barely contained under braces, and at the awards and framed front pages that lined his vast office, which they sat in like terrified four-year-olds on their first day of school. 'Your youthful ebullience!' Olivia got the sense that he wanted to jump for joy, but the man had long ago lost the ability to do much in the way of physical activity.

'Yes, your youthful ebullience is what we need to get us through this next challenge that journalism faces,' he continued, hitting his stride after his momentary lapse. Olivia had felt so proud that she had earned a place in this room, being addressed by a national newspaper editor, a job she was told so many others wanted but only a precious few ever managed to secure. Proving to herself she could get the job had been as important as the job itself.

She pictures it now and cringes. All that endless harping on from management about how many people were waiting behind her to step into her role – the pressure of it had kept her in the job long after most sane people would have walked out (during that first, drunken, rambling rant from Henry Wellington, perhaps).

'But if we can keep the printers rolling while the Nazis were bombing the shit out of us during the Second World War, then I damn well think we can keep them rolling as things like web pages and emails and search engines try to steal a march on us! Honestly. What a load of crap!' He shook his head sadly and wandered over to the corner of the room that contained a cabinet full of whisky decanters and cut-glass tumblers. The trainees watched mutely as he poured himself a drink and then raised it, like a drunk uncle performing an impromptu toast at a wedding.

'To manning the helm, and to the future!' he slurred.

The trainees picked up their mugs of tea and bottles of water and made feeble attempts at returning the gesture.

The message was loud and clear: the elder statesmen of the paper (there were no stateswomen, other than Selina, who had last come into the office in 1998) were allowed to live it up. They had earned the right to, after all! But the young whippersnappers were to be at their desks at all times, coming up with ways to stave off the threat of the internet, just in case it did happen to take off and become a permanent thing.

Had Olivia known then what she knew now, would she have stayed?

Probably. After all, it wasn't as if she had possessed the balls to do anything daring until about forty-eight hours ago.

Olivia was one of the few trainees to have taken the editor's little speech seriously. She had her routine, which involved *Coronation Street* and ready meals and staying up only as late as *Newsnight*, at which point she went to bed and hoped the programme's major talking points would percolate in her head overnight, becoming fully formed ideas that she could sprinkle into any conversations she had the next morning with her superiors – and everyone was her superior, including the bloke behind the till in the office canteen.

Olivia drifts back to the soft memory of those early days of her relationship with Nick. That Sunday he had been able to convince her to go on the pub crawl, saying that he was in PR and they had met through work, so technically hanging out with him was all part of the job (even if that involved nothing more laborious than drinking vats of red wine, eating Yorkshire puddings, and later, snogging each other's face off in a cocktail bar on Clapham High Street). It was mid-Happy Hour that Nick announced he wasn't actually working the next day, and that Olivia should bunk off and spend her Monday in bed with him instead. She had whipped out her BlackBerry and emailed her boss saying that she had come down with food poisoning and wouldn't be in.

Olivia winces now, at this willingness to drop all her boundaries the moment a nice man asked her to. But as she sat there on that barstool, with Nick's hands on her thighs, his feet touching hers, their noses grazing each other as they giggled and kissed and giggled and kissed, this email felt like the best idea she'd ever had. It felt liberating. It felt, now Olivia came to think about it, similar to the sensation she got when she stormed out of Stephen's office earlier.

But when she woke up the next morning in Nick's fusty-smelling sheets, the eighties-style radio-alarm clock on his bedside table telling her it was 9.57 a.m., she thought she was going to expire from shock. She was going to be late for work! No, she wasn't, because she had sent an email to her boss telling him she wouldn't be coming in! Which was worse, almost, because it meant she had lied to her boss! Surely that was a sackable offence? Olivia needed to check the email! To make sure that it didn't contain spelling mistakes or grammatical errors that would give away the fact she had been drunk and making shit up! But where was her BlackBerry? And how was she going to find it without waking Nick, who was sleeping soundly, and who she didn't want to annoy because annoying him would also be unthinkable, worse almost than the fact her mouth felt like an animal had curled up and died in it and her breath probably smelt similar and ohmygoodness what if she'd farted or snored in the night? She couldn't know until he woke up and looked at her adoringly, but she didn't want to wake him up in case it pissed him off. She rummaged on the floor until she felt the BlackBerry's keyboard, picked it up, and then, with dawning horror, saw its battery had run out and she was nowhere near a charger (Nick had a Motorola flip phone, RIP). So she crept out of the bed, got dressed in the manner of Marcel Marceau, then exited Nick's flat and fled for her own, where she spent the day in fevered terror that someone might have seen her on either the fifty-minute Tube journey, or the twenty-minute bus journey from the Tube to her shitty little shared flat in the most far-flung corner of north London. Was she going to be sacked? Dumped? Both? She had collapsed into bed that night in utter panicked exhaustion. She'd have been better off dragging herself into work where she would have at least been paid to have a hangover, and she vowed to never bunk off ever, ever again.

How would she react if she were sacked now? As she begins licking her fingers so she can dab up the remaining flakes of the cinnamon bun from the table, she fantasizes about an imaginary universe where she doesn't have to work or pay bills or parent both her children and her husband and her own dad and rely on her stoned little sister for childcare. A world where she could do whatever she wanted, where people bent themselves into pretzel shapes to meet her needs. A world where she, like Nick, had the guts to quit her stupid, mainstream semi-corporate job and live by her principles.

But what are those principles? And what does she really want? If someone was bending over backwards to meet her needs, what would she even be asking of them? The questions opened up gaping big spaces, and she didn't know how to fill them.

She wishes she could say that she would set about changing the world, engaging in activism and making things better for the next generation – the kind of things that would make her look like a good person, an unselfish one. She briefly wonders why she isn't a better person, and then stops herself. Would a man ever beat himself up for not having an earnest-enough fantasy? Or for staying in a shit job to support his partner as they pursued their own dream?

Olivia is dabbing another flake into her mouth when she is rudely interrupted by a bloke plonking himself down in the seat next to her.

She is completely flummoxed by his presence. The train is almost empty and there are about seven hundred other places he could sit. She shifts in her seat, closer to the window, and he shifts in turn, spreading his legs and moving into this blessed bit of personal space she has managed to carve out for herself. She doesn't want to look at him, because that might signal something she isn't supposed to signal, but from the corner of her eye she can see that he is smartly dressed in corduroy trousers and a dark green wool jumper. She angles her entire body so that she is facing the window, her back turned to him.

'Enjoying that bun, are we?' He speaks in what Olivia can only describe as a guffaw, in the kind of accent that she has got used to, having worked most of her adult life at a newspaper staffed almost entirely by men who left Eton, went straight to Oxford, and then into *The Morning* newsroom, on some sort of Fuckwit FastTrack. 'Or what remains of it, har har har!'

Olivia takes a deep inhale, rolls her shoulders, and continues to stare out of the window.

'You sure do have an appetite,' he continues saucily, nudging her in the ribs.

The comments are an echo of many others like it, that she's heard before. Instantly it stirs the dreadful memories of times when she truly believed that if she could just restrict what she put in her body, then everything would be better. Of a seventeen-year-old who couldn't make sense of why she loathed herself, but was sure that her physical body was the most likely place she would find the answer – in a more pronounced clavicle, a more jutting hip bone, a less rounded bum, a more concave stomach. She did not want to be the kind of person that men looked at and accused of having anything as unseemly and unladylike as an *appetite*. She didn't want to be the kind of woman that blokes described as 'liking her food', or that a grandparent might refer to as having 'child-bearing hips'.

'I beg your pardon?'

'I said that your bun eating is awfully impressive!' He is relentlessly cheerful, it clearly not occurring to him that there might be a world in which a woman sitting alone on an empty train might not want to be provided with a running commentary on her snack choices. 'I've been watching you savour it from the other end of the carriage, and I thought to myself, "She looks like the kind of jolly girl who is in need of some company," so I took a gamble on coming over and saying hello.'

His right hand slips on to her left thigh.

Olivia knows, in this moment, what she would do if this

had happened four days ago. She would have turned and smiled politely, keen not to make a scene, or offend this man she doesn't know and hasn't asked to know and whose hand she certainly doesn't want to feel creeping up her thigh. Then she would have made up some sort of excuse about needing the toilet, bundling up her stuff and scurrying off to another carriage where she would spend the rest of the journey desperately hoping that he hadn't followed her, questioning what she had done to invite his attention – was her bun eating unnecessarily suggestive? Did the way she licked her fingers signal some sort of proposition? – before coming to the conclusion that she was almost certainly the problem for reading too much into his innocent gesture. The man was probably just trying to be nice, he was only a product of his time and circumstances and, honestly, it wasn't as if he had done anything *too* invasive, and why did she have to go and make it awkward by getting up and moving seats?

But this has happened today, and Olivia Greenwood will not do any of these things. She will not let this thoughtless man impinge on her personal space in the name of being polite and remaining cordial. Where has being polite and remaining cordial ever got her, anyway?

She will not be made to feel uncomfortable for simply existing. She will not punish herself for having the audacity to relax as a solitary woman on an almost empty train in the middle of the day. She will not be a welcoming thigh for an entitled old man. She thinks of Rose, the feminist angel who now sits on her shoulder, and decides to use the powers the mysterious young woman has bestowed on her for the greater good. Just as Superman found that the destruction of his home planet and subsequent death of his parents had given him the power to help people on Earth, so Olivia Greenwood will accept the extinction of every people-pleasing bone in her body and turn that fiery energy against all the perverts who blight the UK's local train services.

She clears his hand from her leg roughly and looks at him straight in his slightly bloodshot eyes, notices the poppy on his Barbour jacket, even though it's April.

'There's no need to be quite so hostile!' he says, putting his hands up in a manner that suggests she has pointed a gun at him.

'I think you'll find there is, actually,' says Olivia.

'I was just trying to be friendly,' squirms the man.

'Do I look like I need a friend? Do I look like I'm sitting here crying out for friends?'

'Well, we all know that a woman losing herself in sweet treats usually needs a little TLC.'

'Oh, do we now? Do they teach that at dickhead school?'

'I beg your pardon!'

'No, it was me who was begging the pardon a moment ago, when you so rudely sat down and put your hand on my thigh, as I innocently sat here eating a bun because I'm hungry. And do you know why I'm hungry? I'm hungry because for my entire life, I've been told that women are only allowed sweet treats when they're having a bad time. When they're suffering. When a man dumps them, boo hoo hoo.' Olivia mimes crying with her fists. 'Why else would a lady dare ruin her figure, unless she was in a significant amount of distress? Because, as we all know, women must eat dainty little rabbit food or risk looking unattractive to the opposite sex.'

The man rolls his eyes, huffs at her. 'I was only trying to be civil.'

'Civil!' She removes her feet from the seat in front of her, goes to gather her bag from under the table. 'Is that what you call it?

If you truly wanted to be civil, you'd have stayed in your seat and stopped staring at me as I was eating my cinnamon bun. You'd have left me well alone instead of coming over here and feeling me up, you dirty old pervert. Do you spend your day riding up and down the Southern train line so you can target women on their own? Shame on you!'

'How dare you!' Now he stands up, as the train slows down in its approach to a station. 'I am not a pervert, I'm just a retired man going about his day trying to make polite conversation. I wasn't feeling you up and nor would I want to.' He spits this out, as if his rejection might somehow provide the final, wounding blow. 'Honestly, what has become of this world, when you can't even say hello to a lady and accidentally brush her leg without being accused of impropriety!'

'Oh my god, are you for real?' Olivia stands up too now. 'Do you have daughters? Granddaughters? Have you ever thought to ask them how often they are bothered by men just going about their days, trying to make "polite conversation"?' She does quote marks in the air as he stands in the aisle, looking terrified. 'You know, when I was about twenty-nine, I was walking down the street looking absolutely miserable because guess what? I'd just had a miscarriage. The second in a year. I was feeling absolutely wretched, as I'm sure you can imagine, but obviously I couldn't take time off because, you know, women's trouble.' She does jazz hands. 'I mean, I'd basically given birth to a blood clot in the toilet two days before, and I was telling myself that it was OK because at least I didn't have to have a D&C this time. Do you know what a D&C is, sir? Has anyone ever explained to you what it involves?' Olivia moves across the seats and into the aisle, because she needs him to hear this, she needs him to hear this on behalf of all the people who haven't heard it. 'A D&C stands for dilation and curettage. Sounds good, doesn't it? It basically involves a nurse scraping out your uterus.'

He winces and moves back as the train pulls into the station. 'I don't need to know, thank you very much.'

'Oh, you do, you absolutely do. Because if you know this, then maybe you'll think twice about invading a woman's space to say a jolly hello. Anyway, there I was, walking down the street near the office, and I'm crossing the street at some traffic lights, and a man in a fluorescent yellow tabard is coming towards me, in the opposite direction, and do you know what he says to me?'

The man in the corduroy trousers and woolly jumper continues backing up the aisle towards the door, Olivia following in his wake, despite the fact that she is easily a head shorter than him. He backs into the glass doors to the vestibule, and now Olivia is standing right in front of him, her cappuccino in one hand and the empty Gail's wrapper in the other.

'He says, "Cheer up, love, it might never happen."'

Olivia stands in silence, unexpected tears now pricking her eyes.

'You're mad,' says the man.

Olivia lets out a deranged cackle. 'Wouldn't you be?'

'I was only trying to be nice,' he says, pressing the door button. 'Can someone HELP?' He is shouting down the train. 'Please, I'm being harassed!'

Olivia continues her demented laughing. 'You're being harassed!' She tries not to spill her coffee as she clutches her stomach in mirth. 'I'll give you harassed!'

Then she throws the remainder of her cappuccino over the man, just as the British Transport Police appear on the platform.

13

In the car home from the police station, Olivia recounts to Nick the details of her day with the same breezy nonchalance that she might describe a trip to get her nails done, or the shopping.

'They arrested me for antisocial behaviour,' she explains, as she clicks in the seat belt of the passenger seat, 'when in actual fact I was performing an act of public service, given that the man was a dirty old pervert who couldn't keep his hands to himself. It might not have helped when I told the officer that as a member of the British Transport Police, he had all the authority of a policeman in Toytown, but if these guys actually did their jobs and arrested all the weirdos who use the country's railways like Youporn, then maybe I wouldn't have had to empty the contents of my coffee in his general direction. It's not as if I *wanted* to waste the rest of my really quite expensive Gail's cappuccino on that twat's woolly jumper.'

'Can you slow down a bit? I'm trying to take this all in.'

'Shan't,' snaps Olivia. 'It's not my fault you can't fucking multitask.'

'Hey,' says Nick, pulling out into traffic. 'I'm not the prick who just felt you up on the train.'

'Turns out that prick is "an upstanding Tory councillor from Worthing who also volunteers with the Scouts".' She puts on her poshest, most pompous accent for this. 'I mean come on, he's an obvious wrong 'un! Both of those things are clear red flags.

Also, he said that the coffee I threw was scalding hot, when it was lukewarm at best.'

'I don't understand how this has led to you being possibly taken to court with the threat of a Community Protection Notice. You wouldn't normally say boo to a goose. What's got into you?'

She suddenly feels like it's 1985 and she's being told off for throwing a tantrum over Lily breaking her Barbie doll. Olivia spent so much of her childhood being chastised for displaying distress about things that really 'weren't that bad' in the grand scheme of things – forgetting her homework at school, the button falling off her cardigan, her mum leaving early to go to work and not waking her up to say goodbye. Nobody was beaten. Nobody was molested. Nobody died tragically. So what has she ever had to complain about?

'Are you saying I shouldn't have reacted to it?'

He slaps the steering wheel in frustration. 'No, Olivia, of course not. I just want to know what's going on. I want to know how I can help. You've been distant as fuck for the last few months and now you're being lairy as fuck. Are you having an affair or something?'

Olivia rubs her eyes with the heels of her hands. 'Where the hell would I find the time to have an affair, Nick?'

'That sounds like exactly the kind of thing someone who is having an affair would say!'

'I'm not the one spending all my free time at CrossFit.' She stares at the rain that has started to splatter the windscreen.

'Has it ever occurred to you that I might be trying to improve myself for you? For us? I feel like we've completely drifted away from each other since your dad moved in. I know it must be weird that they've split up, but you can talk to me, you know. You don't have to close shut.'

'Maybe it's got nothing to do with my parents splitting up. Maybe I'm feeling closed off from you now that you've got your new career, new friends, new hobby. Now that you're out there doing something that matters, while I'm being paid to draw up guest lists for a fucking birthday party. You had the guts to get out of the wanky world of media, and I'm stuck in it, too cowardly to get out. We've got nothing in common any more.'

'That's bollocks, we've got loads in common, like . . .' Nick prods at the radio to turn off a traffic bulletin.

'Like we both seem to spend a lot of our time wanking, instead of having sex with each other,' huffs Olivia, cutting her husband off. 'Don't think I didn't notice you beneath the duvet when I came back from my shower the other day. You used to be all over me first thing in the morning, but now you treat me like you've woken up next to a pile of crinkly dead leaves.'

'You've hardly been giving off sex vibes recently.' He switches gear.

'Perhaps I don't give off sex vibes because I don't sense they'd be much appreciated. It's pretty hard to compete with a rowing machine.'

'It's perfectly normal to have a hobby, Olivia, something that interests you outside of work. Maybe if you got one you might be a bit happier.'

She searches for something pithy and cutting to say, finds nothing. She must have used up her allotted sass quota today, what with all the events at work and on the train. They pull on to their driveway and Nick parks up in front of their 1970s semi, where through the living-room window they can see a cosy display of domesticity Olivia has rarely witnessed in her life: her dad sitting on the sofa with a cup of tea as Saskia and Jack stand in front of him laughing uproariously, making hand gestures that suggest they are playing charades.

She hears the satisfying thud of Nick's car door closing, unbuckles her seat belt and follows his lead into the house, the beep-beep of the vehicle locking heralding their arrival.

'Mum!' squeals Jack, rushing into the hallway and flinging himself at her as she starts to remove her jacket.

'My sweet Jack-in-the-box!'

'Hello, chaps!' trills her dad, as he stands up and moves to the frame of the living-room door, clutching his cup of tea. 'We were just playing some games while we waited for you to come home.' He is bright, breezy, a complete stranger to his daughter.

'That's nice,' Olivia grins, finding she genuinely means it. 'And you managed to make yourself a cup of tea.'

'Oh no, Saskia did!'

Saskia shrugs, then slumps back on to the sofa.

'She made it with some of her funny pea milk,' continues Peter. 'And while at first I wasn't too sure, I have to say I've developed somewhat of a taste for it.'

'Oat milk, Grandad.' Saskia smiles.

'Whatever it is, it's a long way from the milk we had when I was a child,' Peter says.

'I'm going to start making dinner,' interrupts Nick, picking up the post from the doormat. 'I'll throw some sort of stir-fry together, shall I?'

Olivia spins a hundred and eighty degrees so she is facing Nick. 'Absolutely not,' she announces. 'After the day I've had, I want something comfortingly unhealthy.'

'Pizza!' shouts Jack.

'Not just any pizza,' nods Olivia. 'Takeaway pizza, with the really gooey plastic cheese, and garlic bread, and also those chicken wings that only the unhealthiest takeaway places always sell. Plus lots of garlic dip. And vats of ice cream to finish.'

Saskia makes a face. 'Mum, that sounds disgusting.'

'It does sound rather out of character for a Monday,' nods Nick, who is sitting on the stairs taking off his shoes.

'Yeah, it's definitely got more of the feel of the first Friday of a school holiday,' says Saskia, who plonks herself down next to her dad.

'Well, usually kids don't complain when their mum comes home and announces she wants to splurge on takeaway.'

'It's not that I'm complaining,' says Saskia, shrugging off her father as he attempts to put an arm around her. 'It's more that it's Meat Free Monday and I think it's important that we stick to this routine for the sake of our health but also the environment. Consistency is really important, Mum, you always say that.'

'I don't mean with your diet,' says Olivia, appalled that her words have been misconstrued. 'I mean with schoolwork and bedtime and other boring things like that. You're allowed to have pizza on a Monday occasionally, babes.'

'I know I'm allowed to,' sighs Saskia, 'but maybe I don't want to. Not all of us crave nutritionally bankrupt food.'

'No food is nutritionally bankrupt,' says Olivia, feeling a sudden panic. 'It's just food that we are allowed to enjoy!'

'Well, I like the sound of Meat Free Monday,' chimes in Peter, being uncharacteristically diplomatic in his old age.

'You can have meat-free pizza,' points out Olivia. 'Anyway, fuck Meat Free Monday!' She drops her bag on the floor.

'Olivia!' Nick stands up in horror.

'Permission to say fuck!' Jack jumps up and down.

'Jack, that is enough.' Nick is doing his best serious voice.

'Jack, that is enough,' Jack parrots back.

'Well, I'm going to get a takeaway for me and Jack while you guys have a dreary old stir-fry. We can have a pizza party, can't we, darling?' Jack dances around in excitement. Olivia skips to the kitchen, grabs a flyer that has been attached to the front of the fridge by a magnet shaped like a flip-flop that was bought many years ago in Alicante airport, and watches dispassionately as a flurry of school certificates and old save-the-dates fall to the floor. 'Oops!' she says, sitting down at the kitchen table and punching the number of the takeaway into her iPhone. 'Hello! I want two extra-large pepperonis. With EXTRA pepperoni. You have a buy-one-get-one-free deal on medium Meat Feasts? I'll take one of those too. Well, two of them, I suppose.'

'Olivia,' mouths Nick, who is now standing in front of her, his face crumpled in submission.

'And I'll have one of every side,' continues Olivia. 'Yep, every single side you have on the menu. Yep. I'll pay by card now over the phone, thanks ever so much.'

When the pizzas arrive, Olivia and Jack vacate the kitchen to make way for the stir-fry crew. 'We're going to eat on the sofa,' explains Olivia, to the delight of her son.

'Mind you don't drop sauce on the cushions!' stresses Nick, tearing at a roll of kitchen towel which he insists they take with them.

'Sure sure,' says Olivia, whisking it away. She walks across to the living room, which is actually just the other half of the kitchen until they can afford to get an extension like everyone else on the road, and plonks herself on the floor, the boxes of pizza placed on the coffee table to appease her husband.

'So, my darling,' she says, getting on to her knees and pushing open the lid of the box, 'tell me about school today.'

'It was . . .' Jack bites down forlornly on a mozzarella stick. 'It wash shine,' he finally replies, with his mouth full.

'You're not being very convincing, Jack. Or is that just the gob full of takeaway?'

He points at his mouth and chews until he can swallow. 'I dunno,' he shrugs. 'I'm having some problems with the football boys.'

'Urghh, not the football boys,' says Olivia, conspiratorially.

'They don't include me in anything. I keep trying to swap Match Attax cards with them, but they just take all my good ones and then tell me to go away.'

Olivia feels her stomach twist at the awfulness of this. She wants to immediately march into the houses of each and every one of the football boys and tell them exactly what she thinks of them. Instead, she takes a deep breath. Sometimes, even she has to concede that there are more important things than giving entitled boys a piece of her mind.

'I bet you nobody swapped Match Attax cards with Erling Haaland when he was at school,' she says, taking one of the mozzarella sticks.

'What do you mean?'

'I mean, Erling Haaland was probably a bit of an outsider when he was younger, because he had so many special things about him, like you. Like you, he was really good at football. Like you, he was probably clever and funny and maybe he even knew how to do a Rubik's Cube in thirty seconds, although I doubt it because I think only you are special enough to be able to do that. Anyway, like you, he could probably make people laugh with cracking roasts of his family members. Comedian as well as a footballer.' She doesn't say anything about Haaland looking like a character from a J. R. R. Tolkien book. 'And when you have loads of special things about you, like you or Erling, then people who don't feel special, or who don't understand what it feels like to be special, they tend to leave you out. I mean, you can't blame them, right? Like, it's not really their fault that they haven't been taught what it's like to feel on the outside of things. And special people do feel on the outside of things.' Olivia picks up another piece of pizza, chews for a bit. 'When I was your age, I felt like such an outsider, like I reacted in the wrong way to everything. I couldn't understand why everything felt so hard, while everyone else seemed to find things easy. Auntie Lily, for example. She was always smiling, but I felt sad the whole time. And instead of being able to talk about the sadness and explain it, I just sort of hid it and covered it up, because back then it wasn't the done thing to talk about sadness or any feeling, really, other than happiness. I thought there was something wrong with me. But there wasn't anything wrong with me. I was just a bit different, like you're a bit different, and Erling Haaland was a bit different. And as Erling Haaland proves, being a bit different isn't a bad thing, not if you're allowed to embrace it. He shows that there's just reams of people, and some of them like to be unapologetically themselves, while others feel they have to go along with the crowd and try to fit in. We all end up taking the first route, eventually, I promise you. You can only ignore yourself for so long before you come bursting out. So forget about the football boys ignoring you. The most important thing is you don't ignore yourself, believe me.'

She shoves a slice of pizza in her mouth.

'Can I tell you something, Mum?'

'Of course you can, honey,' she smiles.

'You've got tomato sauce all over your chin.'

'Oh, I am glad,' she says, picking up another slice, and smearing it over the rest of her face. Jack begins to cackle. In the kitchen, Nick and Saskia turn to see what is going on, and the laughter proves contagious. Olivia happily munches on the remainders of the slice that aren't now in her eyebrows, lashes and hair. She may not be sure if she still wants to be a journalist, but she knows this moment is exactly what she needs. There is nowhere she'd rather be than here.

14

In need of a proper clean, Olivia runs the most decadent bath of her life, the type you can only have when you don't give a damn about using up all the hot water. She pours in half the contents of a lime-green bottle of Badedas that she finds in the cupboard under the basin – it might well have been there since before they moved in – and lights a dusty old Yankee candle that Nick bought her for a birthday several years ago, a putrid shade of custard that allegedly smells of vanilla cupcakes. The thought makes her gag, but she's committed to her Luxury Lifestyle Bath now, and she's not going to let something like the lack of a Diptyque candle divert her off course.

Plus, there is a soft glow of condensation on the shower screen, the flame flickering on the walls, which is all very handy when it comes to disguising the pubes on the floor, the hair in the plughole, and all the other disgusting bits of the Greenwoods' bodies that get sloughed off and never properly cleaned up because, despite there being a chore rota, she's the only one who ever seems to adhere to it.

Olivia drops her clothes on the bathroom floor, instead of putting them in the laundry basket (nobody else does, so why should she?), then climbs into her boiling-hot candlelit Luxury Lifestyle Bath and considers shaving her legs. Her armpits. Maybe her bikini line? She tries to think of a time she's had a bath to do anything other than make herself less hairy and more appealing. They've lived in this house for almost ten years, but has she ever once sat in this bath for the purpose of relaxation? She has sat in it with little children, to wash their hair or pull lice out of it like some sort of mama gorilla. She has sat in it with god knows how many tonnes of exfoliating salt, scrubbing her skin until it's softer and smoother. She has sat in it to remove excess hair, by which she means all hair that isn't on her head or framing her eyes. She's even sat in it fully clothed, with a towel thrown over herself in an attempt at disguise during a game of hide and seek . . . But until now, she's never sat in it just because she can. She's never allowed the hot water to keep running over her feet, never cleared the rubber ducky or the tiny green soldiers Jack long ago stopped bathing with, never asked for fifteen minutes to herself to just unwind, as all the Boots adverts suggest she might like to. She's usually distracted by the mouldy grouting, wondering if a combination of bleach and baking soda might clean it, or counting all the toilet-roll tubes on top of the cistern that she's allowed to accumulate as a sort of pathetic protest against slovenliness and mess. She looks at the mouldy grouting now only to find it is gleaming white; searches for the cardboard tubes only to realize they are no longer there. And no, it's not a trick of the candlelight. Someone has *cleaned*.

Why should she use this precious free time to shave her legs? She might throw out her razor altogether. And does she really need to pay to have her most intimate areas agonizingly waxed once every six weeks, all her pubic hair removed because good god, what if she actually had the temerity to look like a grown woman down there? No. She will no longer submit herself to all the painful procedures that she's been told make her more of a woman, but actually make her feel like less of one.

'Love me, love my bush!' she hollers to nobody in particular, kicking her legs up and splashing a whole load of water on to the floor in the process.

She picks up her phone from the edge of the bath to check she hasn't accidentally got it too wet, sees a notification of an email from Stephen. Well, here it is. The termination of her contract. The suspension of her job pending an investigation. You can't behave the way she did today and just get away with it. The idea of being sacked sends an excited shudder through her. That's probably not a good sign, is it, that at the thought of losing her job she feels more relief than anxiety, especially not when they have a mortgage visible from space. She opens the message and feels a stab of disappointment at its contents.

> *Loving the energy you brought to conference. You really set the cat amongst the pigeons, stuffed it to those pompous pricks in the room, who actually put in a full day of work as a result. Keep it up – wonderful to see you keeping them all on their toes!*

Olivia feels the thrill of validation rush through her, notices how cheap it is, and how quickly it replaces the disappointment. Then she flings her phone on to her pile of clothing before sinking herself under the water, which is pleasantly, almost painfully hot. She sees how long she can hold her breath, comes up just as she begins seeing stars behind her eyes, and is hit by a crystal-clear image of herself dancing in a dingy bar surrounded by Rose and a group of cheering young Gen Z-ers, remembers feeling the same starry sensation as she threw her body around with abandon.

She's snapped out of her reverie by a hard knock on the bathroom door.

Olivia bares her teeth in the general direction of the source of disturbance. 'Not now!' she growls.

'Just checking you haven't fallen into a carb coma in the bath,' tuts Nick, entering the room.

'Your concern is sweet,' sighs Olivia, realizing her relaxing Luxury Lifestyle Bath has officially come to an end. 'But not needed. I am alive and well and thriving after imbibing more mozzarella in the last hour than I have in the last twenty years. Also, at seeing how Dad cleaned the bathroom today.'

'Sweet Jesus,' exclaims Nick, admiring the pristine nature of the non-suite. 'He even threw away all the empty toilet rolls.'

'Right! It is incredible, really, given he's about as keen on cleaning and tidying as Lily.' Olivia hears a slosh as she removes the plug and lifts herself out of the bath. 'You know, she has all this beef with Dad about him not being present, but she's got way more in common with him than she cares to admit.'

'Speaking of Lily, I was wondering if that's what the last few days have been about?' Nick throws one of the towels from the door at his wife. 'Maybe you're upset because your mum's throwing Lily a fortieth birthday party? I know you always feel like she gives you a much harder time of it.'

'I'm not jealous of Lily, if that's what you're saying,' says Olivia, wrapping herself in the towel, blowing out the Yankee candle and plunging them into darkness. 'Though I don't know why everyone treats her like a helpless child.'

'Little bit of sibling rivalry causing you to act out over the last few days, maybe?' Nick opens the door for his wife, moving out the way to let her through.

'Honestly, Nick, I really object to you dismissing my legitimate discomfort about the codependent dynamics in my birth family as sibling rivalry.' She storms down the landing towards their bedroom. 'It's a bit rich coming from an only child who grew up in a thatched cottage, doted on by his loving, perfectly sane parents.'

He trails his wife into the bedroom, where she is stunned to see the bed has not just been made but made as if it belongs in a five-star hotel, the linen changed and the duvet flattened into the sides, the pillows puffed expertly as if waiting for a princess.

'Did you even use fabric conditioner?' Olivia picks up one of the pillows and sniffs it suspiciously, before flopping down on to the duvet and staring up at the ceiling.

Nick perches on the bed, raises both his hands as if in surrender. 'Wasn't me. And I have to say, I thought it was sweet that your dad was really making an effort with the kids today. It was a nice thing to come home to. He is trying.'

'Totally adorable.' Olivia rolls her eyes and props herself up on to her elbows. 'Have I ever told you about the time I caught him drunkenly snogging the magician's assistant in the cupboard under the stairs at my sixth birthday party?' She puffs out her cheeks. 'He told me he was helping her get well again after she'd been sawn in half.'

'I hadn't heard that one, actually.' Nick shifts up the bed next to his wife. 'I feel for your mum, she basically married her own dad.'

'Oh please, she had agency. Nobody made her do anything.'

'OK, but it must be hard to square the sad old man downstairs with the lady-killing Casanova you describe from your childhood.'

Olivia turns and looks directly at her husband, feels a softening in her body for the first time in months. He's right that her parents' break-up has had an effect on her – it's terrified the life out of her, in fact. She had always thought that they would somehow muddle along, despite all their obvious problems. But seeing her mother snap so suddenly and throw her dad out, long after everyone thought Tina had simply accepted her lot, has shaken the admittedly flimsy foundations of family that exist in her brain.

'I've spent my whole life trying to make my parents' marriage work, I think.' Olivia reaches across and takes Nick's hand, is relieved when she feels his stubby, hairy fingers close around hers. 'Isn't that tragic? Everything I've done, from going to work at *The Morning* to having a family of my own, has been about being the perfect daughter. If I could be the perfect daughter, then maybe they'd be happy? I know it sounds absolutely fucking ridiculous, given that I am a grown adult, but hear me out, right?'

Nick nods.

'So a few years ago, I had to interview this psychiatrist for a feature about the child mental health crisis. It was all about making your kids happy. And she said that, really, the best way to make a child happy is to work on your own happiness. We think as parents that working on ourselves, doing therapy or whatever, is selfish, that it takes away from time we should be spending with our kids, but actually, it's the most selfless thing you can do because all our issues are basically inherited from our parents, who inherited them from their parents, and so on and so forth until the dawn of fucking time. She said that any issue we don't deal with in ourselves, our kids will have to deal with instead. We just hand it all down for the next generation. Most troubled kids are just barometers for issues going on in their own homes. They're weathervanes, essentially.'

Nick looks as if he is working hard to follow what she is saying, bless him.

'So anyway, when I was young and I had all my, all my . . .' Olivia still finds it hard to say the word.

'Your anorexia?' Nick clasps her hand tighter.

'I was going to say my issues, but I suppose anorexia will do, yeah.' She shakes away the memories of those long months away from school, the frustration that came off her mother in waves, who had once again had her career interrupted by the need to care for her daughter – her daughter who was, this time, suffering from an illness that only existed in her own head, rather than the appendicitis, which Olivia couldn't actually be blamed for, no matter how inconvenient it had been at the time.

'All those difficult times I had when I was a kid, where I felt like I just overreacted to everything, every tiny bit of criticism from a teacher or every apparent snub from a friend, I think I was just a normal kid who happened to feel things strongly, and who had picked up on the fucked-up nature of my mum and dad's relationship, in lieu of anyone else allowing themselves to. I took on all the family issues as my own. But I couldn't ever have made my parents' marriage work because it was always fucked, as this divorce in their seventies shows.'

'Oh, Olivia.' Nick puts his arm around his wife. 'Sometimes I look at you and I find it impossible to see all the pain that I absolutely know is in there. You're so smiley, so upbeat, so *capable*.'

'It's the compliment I've always dreamed of,' smiles Olivia, nuzzling into her husband's armpit.

'You know what I mean. You just get shit done. You want to make people happy. It gives you genuine joy. It's one of your most glorious qualities but you're really fucking good at hiding the fact that it often exists at the expense of your *own* happiness.'

'Until recently, I'd hidden it so well that even *I* didn't know how miserable I was. I just thought it was normal to always be striving for the next thing to validate myself with, be it a house extension or a promotion at work.'

'There must be some things that make you happy.' Nick kisses the top of her head, talks into it.

'There are *some*,' says Olivia, shaking him off as she sits up straight in bed and stretches herself out.

'Oh yes?' he says, trying not to show he is disappointed that she's moved out from underneath him.

'Yeah, I can think of one or two things that make me feel content,' she purrs, her voice lowering a little. 'But I wouldn't want to be accused of giving off *sex vibes* . . .'

'You don't need to worry about *that*, my love.' Nick turns and begins to move towards her on the bed. 'This new bolshie version of you really is infuriatingly . . .'

'Infuriatingly what?' she says, releasing her towel so that it falls to reveal her bare breasts.

'Infuriatingly sexy,' he growls, clambering on top of his wife.

15

The next morning, Olivia wakes not to the usual screams of her children, fighting over the toaster or the last keto protein bagel, but to her husband, delivering her a cup of tea.

'What did I do to deserve this?' she says, propping herself up against the headboard and sipping from the WORLD'S BEST MUM mug that Saskia and Jack gave her on Mother's Day three years ago – a mug that had then ended up unused, hidden at the back of the cupboard by other, sturdier mugs, and the plague of plastic water bottles that seemed to amass in various kitchen crevices like locusts. Olivia looks at it, remembers the mug she and Lily gave their dad, and briefly wonders how Tina managed to stick it out for so long.

'I don't want to go into the finer details of what you did to deserve this,' Nick says, planting a kiss firmly on his wife's lips, 'because it might get me excited and we'll all be late for work. But let's just say I very much appreciate this new, vocal version of you that seems to have emerged in the bedroom.' He raises his eyebrows, and then trots off to the non-suite where he begins to sing 'Shape of You' by Ed Sheeran.

'That's really not giving me sex vibes!' Olivia cries, as she sips her tea.

Downstairs, her father is sitting with the children, buttering toast for Jack. 'Morning, Mum,' smiles Saskia, sweetly. 'Grandad's just been telling us about the time you and Auntie Lily played a pink and a blue toothbrush in your ballet recital.'

'Well, he would remember that,' mutters Olivia under her breath, 'it being the only performance he ever attended during our childhoods.'

'Is it OK if I wear my new Primark dress to Auntie Lily's birthday?' continues Saskia, oblivious. 'It says black tie on the invitation so I thought a black dress would cut it.'

'Does it now?' Olivia wanders over to the kitchen counter where the invitation sits under one of the discarded pizza boxes, the top left corner now steeped in oil. She picks it up and reads it. 'Does Lily know it's black tie? The last time I saw her wear a smart dress might well have been the pink one she had to wear in that ballet recital. Anyway, you can ask her tonight, Sask, it's her evening again.'

'I'm not wearing a tie,' mopes Jack.

'I don't think I even have a tie any more,' sighs Peter.

'I'm sure Nick will be able to sort you both out in time.' Olivia smiles inwardly as she sees Saskia washing up her plate, goes to kiss both her children on the top of their heads. 'Now, shall we get going so I can get you to school in time to avoid a detention or me missing the train?'

'Actually, Grandad is going to walk us,' says Jack.

'He is?' Olivia looks at her father in something approaching astonishment.

'I am! It's a lovely day for a walk, after all.'

Olivia looks out the window at the grey sky, the low-hanging clouds and the drizzle that has just started to speckle the paving stones in the garden. She shakes her head and expels her disbelief in a big sigh. 'OK, well if you're sure.'

'Never been surer of anything in my life.' Her father does a little salute, nods his head.

Olivia briefly wonders if they have all gone through a wormhole to another dimension, then says a cheery goodbye.

On the train, Olivia takes her usual place on the luggage rack, where she reasons that she can at least sit alone, without risk of being felt up by any old Tory perverts. She puts in her AirPods before hitting play on 'My Heart Will Go On'. With an uncharacteristic clarity and confidence, she decides that there is nothing she can do for now about the possibility of a criminal conviction, and furthermore, there doesn't seem to be all that much she can do about finding Rose. That maybe, given the uptick in everyone's behaviour at home this morning, she doesn't *want* to find Rose. If Olivia has always been the type of person who worries when she has nothing to worry about, now she has become one of those mystifying humans who genuinely believe that there's no point obsessing over things you can't control. Rose had appeared out of nowhere and told her some hard truths, and maybe that's exactly what Olivia needed. Maybe she had to think of it like a one-night stand, except she'd come away from it with some self-enlightenment instead of an STD.

As Celine Dion blares out, full blast, Olivia smiles and allows herself to think about last night. Here she was, forty-four years old and married for almost twenty of them, and for the first time in a good few years, Nick had made her come.

It wasn't that sex with her husband had previously been unpleasurable. He had, for a long time, gone out of his way to please her. But as their relationship wore on and other things took priority, Olivia had never quite felt able to get in the zone. She was tired, her body had changed to accommodate the two babies it had carried and birthed, she was on her period, or she just wanted to be alone. So Olivia had begun to fake an orgasm to get it all over and done with. As a woman who grew up in the eighties and nineties, one who had been weaned on a diet of magazines that promised to provide you with the perfect tricks to please your man, she had learned to derive a lot of her pleasure from the pleasure she could give, from the look on his face as he came, the satisfied grin and the flushed glow. That was often her reward for sex – not an orgasm, but the validating knowledge that she had been able to deliver someone else one.

Today, in the year 2024, it seemed incredible to her that she had only ever encountered one man other than her husband who had actually made an effort to make her come. She had met Josh when they were both freshers. He was squat and solid and attractive in a very plain way that meant he'd had to learn other tricks to snare members of the opposite sex. But Olivia had come to see his focus on her pleasure as some sort of perversion, a perversion that had in part led to her subtly ghosting him for a while in the hope that he would dump her (she was far too terrified of upsetting people to ever dump anyone herself). Why would a man actively want to bury his head in her vagina? (Her vagina that she's only recently discovered was actually labia, thanks to an interview she had been forced to do with a 'Sex Positive' blogger who had started a campaign to educate women on their own bodies.) Vagina, vulva, labia, fruit, mineral, vegetable, the point still stood: she was appalled and embarrassed by everything down there, spent a small fortune each month on keeping it tidy so as not to upset the Gods of Bikini Lines.

But last night . . . well, last night! Something had come over her, and it wasn't her husband, or at least not until she'd given him permission to. She had spent hours ordering him around, expertly directing and instructing him until his tongue brought her to the brink. She didn't know what was more enjoyable – the experience of actually allowing Nick to give her an orgasm, or the fevered concentration on his face as he set about delivering it. 'Fuck, that's sexy,' he growled, as she lay there, bucking and whimpering under him.

As the train hurtles towards London, Olivia lets herself acknowledge an astonishing fact: that her husband has always wanted to devour her. He's always wanted to bury his head between her legs and make her come. The only thing that's changed is that she's started wanting him to again.

Olivia Greenwood is beginning to believe that she damn well deserves it.

16

Olivia stares at the steaming-hot bowl of pale green and beige food in front of her and knows that she has finally cracked the code. She's spent sixteen years obsessing over the ultimate family meal, the right ratio of vegetable, fibre, protein and carbohydrate that will enable her children to grow up strong, healthy, and with zero food issues, unlike her. If she could just be the perfect percentage of Nigella Lawson (while also maintaining the appropriate levels of Jessica Ennis-Hill and channelling the right amount of Helen Mirren), then she could break the cycle of dysfunction for Saskia and Jack. It wasn't much to ask, was it?

But an orgasm and a decent night's sleep have shown her what umpteen lifestyle pieces about being the perfect parent couldn't: that when it comes to recipes for happiness, a simple bowl of cheesy pesto pasta knocked up in ten minutes is best.

'What exactly are we eating here?' Saskia stirs the contents of her bowl suspiciously.

'It's pasta, babes,' says Lily, helpfully.

'I can see that.' Saskia raises her eyebrows in frustration. 'But what *kind* of pasta is it?'

'I'm calling it Pasta à la Gooey Cheese,' Olivia interjects. 'With a touch of pesto.'

'There's not a single vegetable in it,' Saskia complains.

'Actually, that's not true. There's basil in the pesto, and I've boiled up some peas if you want to add them.' Olivia points at a colander sitting unloved on the kitchen worktop. 'Now, shall we talk about our days? I'll start. I'm being allowed to write one last feature, on being a People Displeaser. It means I get to say whatever I want without worrying about the consequences!'

'Woah, cool!' beams Jack.

'That sounds utterly horrific,' shivers Saskia.

'Actually, it sounds a lot to me like being an old white man,' sighs Lily. 'Doesn't it, Dad?'

'What's that, darling?' Peter seems to be at a safe level of inebriation, the type that thankfully only enters the conversation when asked to.

'I said that doing whatever you want without consequences must be quite relatable for you.' Lily stabs her fork into her penne.

'Actually, Lil, I'd say it was more applicable to Mum right now, given that she's off living her best life while we all clean up her mess.'

'Well, isn't this lovely?' Nick lifts a cheese-sodden spoon to his mouth.

'Glad you agree that Dad's a mess, finally,' smiles Lily.

'That's not what I was saying, Lil.' Olivia pulls an entire lump of melted cheese out of her bowl with her fingers, shoves it between her lips.

'Is this really the time and the place for us to be having conversations about your childhood?' Nick shakes his head, clearly the only proper grown-up at the table this evening.

'Dad's right, Mum.' Saskia rolls her eyes almost out of her forehead. 'It is pretty unhealthy and narcissistic to be discussing your own issues in such an unboundaried way in front of your kids.'

'Boundaries! Narcissism!' Lily claps her hands together in

delight. 'Can you imagine how different our childhoods would have been if we'd known about these things!'

'Everyone's mother suffers from narcissistic personality disorder nowadays, Lily, didn't you know?' Olivia is aware she sounds sulky, but if there's anyone in this world she can be sulky with and know she'll be forgiven, it's her sister. 'I know our mum does.'

'Not this again,' sighs Lily. 'You're forty-four, Olivia! Are you really saying that our mother has a serious psychological illness simply because she finally decided she'd had enough of his . . .' Lily looks at her father, and then her niece and nephew '. . . carousing?'

Peter chews vacantly on his pasta.

'I'm just saying that she has a special way of putting herself first, that's all.'

'As an only child,' Nick interrupts, 'I have to say I'm quite amazed that two people with the same childhoods could have such a varying view of them.'

'It's not that surprising, Dad,' sniggers Saskia.

'I think it's because your mother doted so much on you, Lily,' Peter nods towards his youngest child, 'and was so hard on Olivia, that perhaps I was softer on her to make up for it. To make up for my many, many shortfalls as a father.'

Everyone turns and stares open-mouthed at him.

'What?' He shoos them away with his fork. 'Don't be so surprised that I am listening, even if you all think I'm a doddery old drunk.'

'Think,' seethes Lily. 'Anyway, sis, putting yourself first isn't always a bad thing, you know. Mum's really coming into her own now she's able to focus more on herself, and not worry all the time about what he's up to.'

'Lily's right.' Peter suddenly perks up. 'Your mother is entitled to want a bit of space. Though I must say she's missing out on wonderful family times, not being here.'

'That's so funny,' says Lily. 'She said exactly the same thing about you, Dad, for the two decades of wonderful family times you were usually absent from when we were young.'

'I didn't always get things right,' concedes Peter, 'but I'm trying to make up for it now.'

'Only because Mum stopped putting up with you, and you realized you needed someone else to sponge off,' Lily tuts. 'I'm pretty sure you'd be in the pub right now otherwise.'

'I'm really loving the texture of the pesto pasta,' announces Nick.

'Is "pesto pasta" a euphemism for whatever it is between Dad and Lily?' Olivia gets up to help herself to some more stodgy carbohydrates.

'I could definitely get used to this,' beams Jack. 'Cheesy pasta every day and Auntie Lily and Grandad replacing the endless bickering between Mum and Saskia.'

'We are not having cheesy pasta every day,' interjects Nick.

'And we don't endlessly bicker,' snaps Olivia.

Saskia silently spoons some peas into her mouth.

'Anyway,' says Olivia, shifting her tone to alert all to the fact she is about to Change the Subject. 'We're digressing. How was school today?'

'Oh, it was great.' Jack doesn't look up from his food. 'I'm taking a leaf out of your book, Mum, and telling everyone what I really think. And do you know what?' Jack leans back in his chair, looking terribly pleased with himself. 'It's making me really popular. Even Jonathan asked me if I wanted to come round one day soon and play Roblox with him.'

'Jonathan?' Olivia is surprised – Jonathan is well known as

the leader of the football boys, who have never exactly welcomed her son.

'Yep, Jonathan,' nods Jack. 'He says he's going to get his people to speak to my people about arranging a sleepover.'

'That's great, darling.' Olivia feels touched that their conversation yesterday could have had an effect so quickly, but her moment of contentment is broken by a manic vibrating on her wrist. 'Ah, there's my watch, letting me know that there's something else to do, another *thing*, just in case one of the many other *thing*s has distracted my oversaturated brain, causing it to shut down and forget.' Olivia pulls her phone from her pocket. 'Let me look. Oh, wow, it's a humdinger, guys! One from Mum in the Fabulous Fryer Ladies group!' She flashes the screen around the table, where everyone tries not to look too keen to read it.

'I didn't know you had a WhatsApp group without me,' mopes Peter.

'You're not missing much, Dad. Let me read out what's just come in from Mum. *Where is your RSVP card, Liv????*' Olivia pulls a goofy face. It wouldn't be fair to say that this is the last straw. The last straw was encountered at some point on Friday, somewhere between her 'promotion' and taking drugs with Rose. But it is a straw nonetheless, one of those elaborate, bright pink ones with a twist in the neck that you used to have in cheap cocktails.

'I don't want you to think that I'm not looking forward to your fortieth birthday, Lily,' Olivia says, while spooning even more cheese into her bowl from a packet of pre-grated Cheddar. 'So please don't take what I'm about to do in any way personally. Anyway, we know that this is really all a ruse for her to unveil her new boyfriend.' She begins to read out loud as she types.

Dear Mum, I'm afraid you're going to be waiting for that RSVP card for about as long as I've been waiting for you to realize you have NARCISSISTIC PERSONALITY DISORDER (look it up). You can take this as my reply – the Greenwoods will be there, along with your ex-husband, the one you kicked out when you decided you couldn't be arsed with all that in-sickness-and-in-health bollocks they make you say on your wedding day.

PS. You more than anyone know how much I hate being called Liv, so please don't do it.

She hits 'send', smiles at her shocked family members, then flings her phone on to the table before emptying the packet of grated cheese into her gob.

'Way to show Mum all the wonderful fun family times she's missing out on,' Lily says.

'Awfully kind to RSVP on my behalf, darling,' Peter nods.

Olivia's wrist vibrates again, this time a pointless news alert about the weather. She unbuckles the watch and drops it into the pint glass of water that sits in front of her. Then she takes her phone, stands up, and makes to leave the table.

'I think I've had enough,' she says, walking towards the stairs.

'I think we all have,' grimaces Lily, beginning to clear up.

In the cocoon of her room, Olivia collapses on to the bed and surveys the ridiculous plastic rectangle that rules her life. She opens WhatsApp, sees that the message to her mother has been delivered, and that her mother is already typing a response.

Olivia does what anyone would do.

She leaves the group.

Olivia smiles to herself as she imagines her mother's indignation at first reading the message, and then the words *Liv has left the group*. Olivia has never left a WhatsApp group before. But if previously Olivia had been horrified whenever she'd seen those words flash up, wondering why a person couldn't just archive a group, or mute it, to avoid hurting anyone's feelings . . . today she gets it. She completely gets it. She wants her mother to know that she is done with playing the good girl, the nice girl, the compliant girl, the kind girl. She wants her mother to know that she isn't, actually, a girl any more, but a woman, and she's sometimes a bad one at that.

Emboldened by this act of derring-do, Olivia scrolls through her WhatsApp feed, painstakingly leaving any group that has ever annoyed her – which is most of them. Goodbye Class 9T, au revoir Yoga Girlies, adieu Monday Eve Coding Class Pick-Up Rota. With each *Exit Group* she feels lighter, brighter, bouncier, less weighed down by the expectations of others. She goes to her settings and switches off the function that allows people to see she's online, or that she has read their message. (In a world where Donald Trump has access to the nuclear codes, she doesn't need the stress of wondering if Jane from yoga is quietly offended because she hasn't yet replied to her message about meeting up for a coffee to discuss Jane's new organic, sustainable yoga-block business.)

She feels a brief stab of shame about all the other, unanswered, unread WhatsApp messages that are contained within her phone, the ones from school parents and PTA representatives and book clubs she optimistically joined but never quite got round to attending. Then she promptly dismisses said shame, and deletes them too.

17

Olivia doesn't rush out of bed the next morning. Nick's here, Lily's here, even her dad's here, passed out, no doubt, in the garden shed. One of them can keep the good ship *Greenwood* afloat while she spends a few more minutes sinking below the bed sheets, avoiding the start of the day. 'You do breakfast,' she mumbles into the pillow, when the alarm goes off on her phone. Nick gets up silently, and she returns safely to slumber.

She exists in that dozing state somewhere between dreamland and the dawning of a new day, until she hears a thumping on the door and opens her eyes to see Lily, standing in her kimono.

'Oh hi,' Olivia says, propping herself up while scrambling for her glasses on the bedside table. 'How did you sleep?'

'You know me,' Lily shrugs, sitting on the end of the bed. 'Never happier than when on a sofa bed, a floor or someone's couch. It's the bonus of living a nomadic life.'

'Is that what we're calling it now?'

'Ah, there she is,' Lily shakes her head. 'Olivia Version 2.0. I thought I'd come in and check on you, but I won't stay if you're going to be an arsehole.'

'Sorry I've not yet managed to hang the bunting out or blow up the balloons.'

'Are you OK, sis?' Lily rubs her eyes.

Olivia gets up and walks towards the chest of drawers and her contact lenses. 'I don't think I am, no. The Gen Z colleague who gave me the gummy also tore a strip off me, and it's caused some kind of epiphany. It's like I've lost the bit in my brain that prevented me from seeing what a doormat I'd become and everything that was holding me together has just come undone. Whenever I feel a pressure to do something just to please someone else, I get so angry. It's like I'm suddenly overwhelmed by decades of pent-up rage.'

'Well, you've been swallowing it down your whole life, so no wonder you need to unleash it,' says Lily, tightening her kimono. 'Unleash away. But don't get so lost in fury that you poison the rest of your life with it. Mum dropped the ball when we were kids, I'm not denying that, but at least she was trying to handle the ball. Whereas Dad, he had no bloody interest in it. He couldn't drop the ball because he never picked it up in the first place.'

'Yeah, but he never belittled me, did he?' Olivia stabs a contact lens in her right eye.

'He never did anything at all for you, or any of us. Where was he when you were off school for months? I know Mum handled that badly, but have you ever thought maybe it was just because she was doing it all alone?'

'Don't do that,' snaps Olivia.

'Do what?'

'Make me feel like I was a burden that had to be shouldered. I didn't choose to have anorexia any more than I chose to have appendicitis.'

'I know that, Olivia. You really don't need to get all defensive with me. I'm just saying that she was doing her best with the limited information and resources that existed in 1997 when it came to supporting a severely ill child with an eating disorder at the same time as a husband lost in alcoholism.'

'He was hardly an alcoholic back then.'

'But how do you know that, Olivia? We weren't married to him. There's all sorts of shit we weren't privy to. He didn't just become a raging piss artist in the last couple of years. That's not how the illness works, you know that. I'm not excusing Mum for how she sometimes handled it. I'm just saying that she was trying, in her own, weird, Mum way.'

Olivia thinks back to the day, when she was seventeen, that Tina was called into school for a Very Important Meeting. Olivia was, if nothing else, a conscientious student with excellent grades, and as a result, Tina couldn't work out what could be so serious as to require her coming into school in the middle of the day, when she needed to be at work delivering yet another dreary pitch about the ketchup account. She had delayed the meeting three times, until the headmistress had been forced to step in and call her personally, demanding that she come in about an 'urgent pastoral matter'. When Tina walked into the head's office, Olivia felt a strange mixture of terror and relief – terror at the prospect of what was about to happen, but relief that perhaps it might finally all be over, and someone could make her better.

She couldn't say when she had stopped eating. It had happened gradually, over the course of a year, the level of food she ingested slowly getting lower and the subterfuge around it getting higher until finally she felt caught in a vice-like grip between these two things, all her energy channelled into controlling what she put in her body and what people thought she had put in her body. But one teacher had noticed her stuffing the cake in her blazer pocket, and then depositing it in the bin, and then there had been the morning she half-fainted in assembly. Bulking herself out with extra layers had gone a long way towards masking the fact her body was shrinking, but she had recently developed a light dusting of fur on her face, a clear giveaway that all was not well.

Tina was appalled. She had immediately got Olivia an appointment with an eating disorder expert who had suggested that Olivia be admitted to hospital, 'as a precautionary measure'. But Tina thought that was a bit much. After all, Olivia hadn't fainted again, and she'd watched her eat on two separate occasions in the preceding week. Wasn't there something else they could do, something less drastic? The doctor had said that Olivia needed to have some time off, come for twice-weekly therapy sessions, and be watched like a hawk in between. Her mother had taken some of her precious annual leave to hover over her daughter in what felt like an almost constant state of resentment.

Olivia sits back down on the bed next to her sister. 'I know it sounds ridiculous that I still can't let it go. But I can't forget the time she told me off for not being able to diet like a normal teenager. "You always have to take it too far!" She said that to me, Lily. And I don't understand how she could have been so ignorant as to think my studying for my exams was a sign I was better. The only thing it was a sign of was me transferring my mad perfectionism from food to schoolwork.'

'Speaking of perfectionism,' sighs Lily. 'I could be making something out of absolutely nothing, and I'm sorry if this seems like I'm overstepping the mark. But is Saskia OK? She was quiet as a mouse and barely ate anything last night.'

Olivia turns to her sister and looks directly into her eyes. She senses Lily's concern that she has just made everything worse, that she is about to be banished from the house quicker than you could say 'Olivia Greenwood has left the group'. But there is also a softening around her sister's eyes as they start to glisten, and Olivia feels her shift closer.

'Promise me, Lily, that you will never, ever, ever worry about overstepping the mark when it comes to the kids?' She cradles her sister's chin in her hands. 'Anything you even vaguely suspect, the slightest thing you think is wrong, you promise to tell me? I always need you to be direct. I don't want the Fryer family's pathological fear of confrontation to come before Saskia and Jack. However hard the thing is to say, I *always* want you to say it to me. Nothing matters more.'

Lily nods her head vigorously. Olivia stands up, lets go of her sister's chin and kisses her forehead. 'Good,' she says. 'You're right, I have been an arsehole, totally caught up in my own anger. I don't want to make the same mistakes Mum did. Thank you, Lily. Thank you.'

Tears, a hug with Lily and a strong coffee later, Olivia finds her daughter bent over an open workbook in the kitchen, the crumbs of a keto bagel on a plate next to her. 'Morning, darling,' she says, bending down to envelop her child in her arms. Saskia sits up, her back ramrod straight, and begins to squirm in her chair.

'Mum, what are you doing?'

'I'm just giving you a hug. Aren't I allowed to give you a hug?'

'You're so weird,' she says, trying to get rid of her mother with a shrug of her shoulders.

'It's OK to be weird,' says Olivia, sitting down next to her. 'Weird is good. Weird is cool. You do you and all that. I just . . .' Olivia looks at the empty plate. 'I just wanted to check you were OK, that you'd had breakfast.'

'I'm OK,' nods Saskia robotically, 'and I've had breakfast.'

Olivia reaches her arm across the table and puts it over her daughter's right hand. 'I also, I just wanted to . . .' She stumbles for the words, notes the look of quiet, bored disdain on Saskia's face. 'I wanted to say that however busy or distracted I seem, however mad it might feel with Grandad and Auntie Lily here, however annoying it might be that me and Dad keep arguing about his CrossFit, none of it is more important than you.' She shakes her head, puts her arms around her daughter for another hug, whispers into her ear. 'None of it.'

It takes a moment, but then Saskia leans back into her. No words are said, but in this one moment of closeness, none are needed.

18

Olivia comes to the next morning and all is quiet. Her husband is still asleep, the children are not arguing, but most of all – she suddenly realizes – her brain is not a seething cauldron of resentment and rage.

What the fuck?

She looks at her phone: 5.53 a.m. Double what the fuck. When was the last time she naturally woke up this early, without any resistance whatsoever? She creeps out of bed so as not to wake Nick and heads downstairs where – extra extra what the fuck with whipped cream on top – she makes herself a coffee, sits quietly at the kitchen table, and enjoys some time to herself.

Alone. In peace. Her head a serene stream as opposed to the constantly whirring washing machine it has been for . . . ooh, forty-odd years?

She reads back her message to her mum and instead of fury feels a strange sense of pity for her. She realizes that ever since she became an adult, she has been a willing participant in the drama dynamic that exists between them, and that she can just as willingly change it – just as Tina decided to do with Peter. And speaking of her dad, if even he can have the self-reflection he did the other night, then surely Olivia can too? The last few days, she has been getting all the pent-up rage out of her system, and now she knows it is time to really put FRANK, FEARLESS Olivia Greenwood into action. No more whingeing and messing around.

At work, she shuts herself off from the bullying and bitchiness of Joe and Stephen by taking herself to her safe space, a dreamland of beauty and lust where anything feels possible. Her Net-a-Porter wish list.

This wish list has always been a place where she has quietly squirrelled away all the things she has most coveted, but has never had the confidence or money to buy. Today she zeroes in on a skin-tight leopard-print minidress that costs the grand sum of £585. This is a sum she does not have in her personal current account. Her joint account with Nick, however? Well, that's another story altogether, it being the place where they put their monthly bill and mortgage payments, but also, crucially, their monthly savings, so that over the years they have accumulated a small but not insignificant amount that they like to have as a cushion should anything go wrong.

As she watches Joe tapping away at his keyboard, Olivia decides that, technically, something has gone wrong. Not the potential criminal conviction, nor the derailing of her career. No. The thing that has gone wrong, Olivia realizes, is that she has spent so much of her life making herself smaller, smoother, less Olivia, essentially, in case she were to offend or upset a load of people who have never had her best interests at heart. Or any of her interests at heart, for that matter. It is that she has spent so much time actively displeasing herself, in the hope of pleasing others. It is that she has gone out of her way to turn herself into a sort of human chaise longue for strangers and acquaintances and, urgggh, Stephen to get comfortable on, without once considering the fact that her back hurts, and her feet are starting to get really fucking sore. Her need to be likeable, to always be good-natured and amenable, this is the great thing that has gone wrong in Olivia's life.

So she checks that the skin-tight leopard-print minidress is still in stock, allows herself to feel sad about the fact she has never worn leopard print, or a minidress, not even in her twenties, let alone now she is staring down the barrel of the menopause, presses 'add to cart', rummages around in her tote bag for her wallet, finds the joint account card, types it into the website, adds the magic three-digit code that unlocks all the money, presses 'place order', feels a delicious thrill as the webpage reloads and doesn't ask her to answer any extra security questions from her bank, then, joyously, announces that her order has been processed and is on the way.

She feels good. She feels like . . . the kind of woman who wears skin-tight leopard-print minidresses. What other kind of woman is she?

Olivia checks that nobody is looking at her screen. She searches for the vibrator she'd once read about, the one that actually sucks on your clitoris as well as pulsating on it. She has thought about this invention at least five times a day since she first heard about it, wondering at the type of woman who would have the chutzpah to order it, let alone use it. Well, she is that type of woman. She is! She may not have been a week ago, but now she is, and she doesn't intend to waste a moment more of her life denying herself the orgasms that are so rightfully hers. She clicks on a website (thankfully no alarm is set off by her searching 'clitoral stimulator' on her office computer) and sees there is a special discount for new customers. She hits 'add to cart' on the 'sonic sucker', which looks much less frightening than it sounds. Out comes the joint account card again – Olivia knows Nick won't object to this purchase – and in go the digits, though this time their bank does want to carry out an extra security step before allowing the purchase to go through.

Of course it would be tricksy on this, thinks Olivia, who now has to go into an app on her phone and approve an alert. *IS THE PURCHASE FROM ORGASMS INC. YOURS?* screams a notification on her screen. She clicks 'yes', imagines herself as Meg Ryan during that scene in *When Harry Met Sally*, chuckles to herself, then becomes aware that Nina is standing next to her, staring at her monitor.

'Working hard, I see?'

'I can share the link with you if you want?' smiles Olivia mischievously.

'That would be great,' sighs Nina, flopping down in the chair at her now-empty, former desk. 'I'm going to need to let my work rage out in some way when the day ends and I finally get home.'

'Want to talk about it?'

'Not really, but I suppose that as my mentor and the head of the Women Rising programme, I should probably put it on record to you that our editor is a complete and utter cockwomble.'

'Oh yes?' Olivia looks at Nina.

'He asked me to write a "quick, pithy on-the-day piece",' Nina does quote marks in the air, 'about the pop star in the bikini. And after the scene in conference the other day, I wrote what I thought he would like as opposed to what I actually believe, which will teach me to be a disingenuous prick because he totally bawled me out for it. Said it was way too bitchy, which is a bit rich coming from a man who's spent much of his life putting ticks and crosses next to pictures of famous women in frocks.' Nina lowers her voice. 'He told me that I needed to write for the female reader, and not the trolls who comment, and that if I couldn't hack the deranged witterings of people below the line, then maybe I wasn't cut out to be a columnist. Then he stood over my shoulder as I rewrote it to his liking, which was my original liking. I fucking hate him.'

'I hope you told him you fucking hate him. He'd probably get off on it.' Olivia finds herself oddly relieved that she is only having to deal with the bullshit of being Anniversary Architect.

'I was sad you weren't there to say it to him for me. I would have loved to see how you would have brought your People Displeaser energy to proceedings. How's that going for you?'

'Well, Nina, I'm finding it oddly liberating.' Olivia spins in her chair. 'I feel like if you'd thrown the level of drama I'm experiencing in my life right now into my life a week ago, I would have gone into an obsessive spiral. I was only OK if everyone else was OK. But now I couldn't give a fuck.'

'So I can see.'

'It was like when Joe accused me of trolling you the other day. That would have mortified me before. I couldn't cope with anything other than accusations that I was spreading joy. Like, there was this time at secondary school when the headmistress stood up in assembly and announced that someone's Game Boy had been stolen from their locker. I hadn't taken it, but that didn't stop me from obsessing over the possibility that the head might *think* I had. I went out of my way to appear dutiful and good, volunteering to help whenever a teacher asked. I spent an evening consulting my timetable and making a list of all the places I had been, just in case I was asked for an alibi. It turned out the Game Boy had been lost, and later found down the back of a sofa by an embarrassed parent, but I still spent the rest of the academic year worrying about all the ways I could accidentally find myself in trouble.'

'Christ, that sounds exhausting.'

'It was,' nods Olivia. 'It is. But this feature, it's freed me from that. I'm not going to bankrupt myself emotionally in order to make Joe or Stephen happy, and neither should you. We can't spend our lives moulding ourselves into the kind of people who endlessly help others but always abandon themselves.'

'I'm glad I came for this chat,' nods Nina.

'I'm glad you did too.' She notices Joe walking over to his desk, raises her voice. 'Us women need to stick together, especially in this nest of vipers.'

'Amen, sister.' Nina notices Joe, high-fives Olivia, and then returns to her office as he slithers uncomfortably into his seat.

Olivia ignores him, returns to her Net-a-Porter wish list. She had long marvelled at people who had the ability to have an argument with someone and then move on without first resolving it – they had always seemed to Olivia like exotic creatures – but now she realizes she is one of those people. She decides to do what most humans do when a massive fucking elephant walks into the room – she ignores it, instead of cosseting it and pampering it and attending to its every need.

Olivia is shocked at all the energy she has wasted, trying to make everyone happy. She is horrified by it. Of course she was never going to rise to the top at work, when so much of her time has been taken up trying to be everything to everyone. Like so many other women of her generation, she has been told time and time again that she can have it all, as if it was somehow a good thing. It was a gift that her mother and grandmother had never been allowed, so she better bloody take advantage of it to avoid seeming ungrateful, or spoilt. But she realizes now that even this notion of 'having it all' is a poisoned chalice, an image of perfection that no man had to ever bother even trying to aim for. And it had removed any chance of a level playing field. Every morning of her teens, Olivia and all her friends had woken up knowing they needed to be a wife, a mother, a captain of fucking industry, whereas all the boys had to do was finger someone and vaguely think about their GCSE coursework. It was exhausting. It was endless. It was incredible that any of them had got to their forties without committing mass murder. And as Olivia sits at her computer, thinking about how hot she's going to look in that leopard-print dress, it dawns on her that she doesn't want to be a superwoman any more.

Astonishing as it may sound, she just wants to be herself.

19

A couple of hours later, as Olivia is about to dig into a luxury prawn sandwich from M&S, a message appears in her inbox. It's from Nina.

> *Lunch in my office so we can really put the world to rights?*

Olivia picks up her sandwich and coffee, sticks a finger up at Joe, and heads over to the glass box.

'Apparently, my girl-power bikini piece is the most-read article on *The Morning* website today.' Nina sits at her desk with a lunch that consists of a single boiled egg and a handful of spinach. 'Incredibly, Stephen has just emailed with a breakdown of the figures and a self-congratulatory message which reads *Good thing we went with my idea, eh?*'

'What a fucking prick.' Olivia leans back in the other chair. 'I really hope that his wife cheats on him and gives him an STI that makes his cock fall off.'

'Poetic,' nods Nina, holding her boiled egg between her fingers. 'Just you wait until you hear the rest of it. He genuinely believes that the big numbers are because everyone hates what I'm saying so much that they're all clicking on it to tell me. And he's over the moon that they're trolling me. If anything, he wants them to troll me even more.' Nina hands Olivia her phone, so that she can read his email for herself.

'*Brilliant numbers, you're really keeping them on the site* is his response to a load of people frothing in the comments about a sixty-year-old woman's cellulite? What a time to be alive.'

'Exactly why we became journalists, right?' Nina looks conspiratorially at Olivia, who is increasingly unsure as to why she became a journalist at all. 'Anyway, I appreciate you sticking up for me in conference. If only they actually listened to the women they so generously invite into the room, as opposed to just having us there as window dressing.'

'It was a great piece, Nina. The most important thing is you managed to get it into *The Morning*, which is a miracle in itself. You heard the way their brains work. If you hadn't had the guts to suggest that body-positive idea, you know they would have just commissioned someone to write the same old tripe.' Olivia affects the haughty accent she uses for her mum. '*Why DO female celebrities of a certain age still insist on flashing the flesh?* or some such crap. Forget about the trolls. Just be thrilled you've exposed them to some critical thinking on the subject of women's bodies, no doubt for the first time in their lives.'

'You know, I reckon it's all a bit of a game to Stephen,' Nina says, when she's finished chewing her egg. 'He got me to write his stupid, bitchy piece even though he knew I didn't want to, as a way of showing that he has all the power. Then he reverted to the first idea I came up with, and passed it off as his own. I don't know why I thought being given this column would somehow make him treat me with respect. If anything, it's just exposed me to even more of his twattery.'

'Well, now you know why Selina Martin never came into the office.' Olivia takes a breath, watches as her phone vibrates across the desk. She picks it up, and there it is, the thing she's been expecting ever since she fired off that message to her mother during dinner the night before last – a WhatsApp from her mum so long she has to press 'more' to get to the end of it.

Olivia – just how hard would it be for you to think about others for once? It's your sister's special birthday. And as for leaving the group, which is our one remaining bastion of togetherness . . . well, that's just spiteful, I would say.

I have tried to be a good mother to you. I had hoped that having children of your own might make you realize the emotional burden that comes from being a parent. But perhaps you have got lucky with Jack and Saskia and can't see how very painful it is when you have a child who seems to hate you. I got many things wrong but I don't think I deserve this treatment now that I am entering my dotage, and trying to carve out an independent life for myself after so many years of running around after your father. I have apologized for my endless faults and think that by now we should all be grown up enough to move on from them. I have gone out of my way to make sure Lily has a special day for her fortieth. You know she doesn't have the family or security that you have, that she gets very lonely. You had lots of people to make a fuss over you when you turned forty, Lily just has you and me. Please don't make me feel like I am being difficult for simply requesting you fill in a RSVP card – one I have already been kind enough to pay the postage for (I know these things make you young people laugh, but this means a lot to me and you could at least humour me this once).

All that being said, I do love you, and hope that this finds you and the family well.

Olivia lets out a demented laugh that could also be a cry. 'I hope this finds you well!' she says in her haughty accent, doing a little curtsy in her seat.

'Everything OK?' Nina says, chewing on her spinach.

'You know what, Nina?' Olivia turns to her young colleague. 'No, everything is not OK. It's not OK that you've been made to feel like you're reliant on casual misogyny to make a living, and it's not OK how Stephen's behaved in the last forty-eight hours. Or ever.' Olivia feels the tamped-down rage preparing to unleash, as Lily might say, dislodged once more by the message from her mother. 'Do you know, I used to go out of my way to mollycoddle him? I was so scared of him that I'd tiptoe round him like some traumatized dog.'

'Err, I do know actually,' Nina nods. 'I mean, I'm here for this new version of you, Olivia, with your big-girl pants on, but I'm not going to lie and say it isn't a surprise, given that your career advice has always been a *teeny-tiny* bit on the passive side up until now.'

'Fair enough.' Olivia stands up, pats down her thighs. 'But now the big-girl pants are on, I'm in no hurry to take them off.' She grabs her coffee, and heads in the direction of Stephen's office.

Over the years, Olivia's done this walk in her head what feels like a thousand times. She's done it in her demented, deluded fantasies in which Stephen made her his star columnist. But she's also done it in her demented, deluded fantasies where she exposes him for his behaviour all those years ago, and he is dragged out, sacked, made an example of, *The Morning* becoming a meritocracy rather than a company based entirely on chauvinistic nepotism. But she never at any point imagined this: her storming into his office in the middle of the day, to tell him off for being inappropriate and unprofessional.

Olivia imagines the remnants of the Erling Haaland gummy still working away, its tiny blue crystals taking root inside her. She gulps her third cappuccino of the day down, shakes her body in some ludicrous attempt to release all the liquid anxiety she's just drunk, and then marches with her head held high to Stephen's glass box. No time like the present and all that.

'Ah, Olivia,' says Joanna, who is guarding Stephen's office like a Rottweiler in an LK Bennett frock. 'He's just chatting to the letters editor, but he'll be free in a moment if you want to take a seat.'

'Thanks, Joanna,' she says, raising her empty cup to Stephen's ever-dutiful PA. 'But I'm sure whatever he's talking to Andrew about can wait.'

Joanna rises as if to stop Olivia but is not quick enough for the Anniversary Architect, who storms in and gets the editor's attention by throwing her Gail's cup towards the bin next to his giant oak desk. For a moment it looks as if it is going to hit him in the head, but it sails past his astonished face, landing with a satisfying thwack in the centre of the waste-paper basket.

'Hi, Stephen,' she says, plonking her bum down and making herself comfortable on one of his many sofas. 'Just need a moment with you to talk through a few things.'

'Right.' Stephen nods his head seriously, then ushers an incandescent Andrew out of the door, shutting it firmly behind him. He perches on the end of his desk and looks at Olivia with a pinched smile on his face. 'Go ahead,' he says, a note of irritation in his voice.

She swallows and tells herself she is more than capable of going toe to toe with this absolute moron.

'Well, there's a few things, Stephen,' she begins. 'And while I'm writing this People Displeaser feature, it seems the perfect time to raise them. For a start, I need you to know that I object to what happened in conference on Monday.'

'You object?' He begins laughing pompously. 'Your Honour! Was there a particular moment you'd like to raise in court?'

'There was,' she says, her voice firm, her face stony, her mission undeterred. 'Long before you made me an Anniversary Architect, you put me in charge of the Women Rising project, which suggests that this company has some sort of interest in gender equality. That it takes a stand against sexual discrimination of any sort.' She lets that hang for a bit, assesses him for any nervous tics, but he has the cool, calm demeanour of a snake. 'Subsequently, I think it's important that I raise the way that everyone was talking about that pop star's body in conference. We shouldn't be discussing the pictures at all, frankly, given that they were a clear infringement of her privacy.' She sits up straight, steeples her fingers in a manner she believes to be businesslike. 'Nor should you have spoken to Nina in the way I'm told you did later, especially as she was only following your orders.' She sees a redness begin to creep across his face, senses that she might be gaining ground. 'I thought you would appreciate this feedback and understand that I wouldn't be doing my job properly if I didn't bring it up. I thought it best if I just mentioned it to you, casually in conversation, instead of making it formal with HR.'

Stephen nods along, looking at the floor. 'Thanks for that, O-liv-i-a,' he says, clearly enunciating each syllable. 'I really appreciate your candid evaluation of everything. I'll endeavour to do better next time.' He smiles with all the sincerity of a politician on polling day. 'And I'm glad you're here. I was going to come and find you later today as it happens. It seems we have a problem.' He pauses dramatically in an attempt to place the ball firmly back in his court, where he likes it. Olivia smiles sweetly, tucks a stray hair behind her ear. She refuses to be cowed.

'Specifically, we have a problem with this group called Stop the Press.' He gets off his desk, goes to his big leather chair, sits in it and puts his feet on the table. A real willy-waving move, if ever Olivia saw one. She maintains a straight face – she's not going to give him an inch to add to that tiny, flaccid cock of his. 'They're some pathetic group of university dropouts who fancy bringing down the nation's newspapers in protest at . . . well, fuck knows what? Being part of a generation of woke wet wipes?'

'Sorry, what?' Olivia is trying to readjust her expectations of this conversation, which have changed rather swiftly.

'Stop the Press, Olivia. Come on, pay attention. They're targeting us, looking for ways to mess things up, and I'm not going to let them. I need your help. They've been sending communiqués, Olivia,' he says, seriously.

'Communiqués?' repeats Olivia, wondering if Stephen thinks he's in a 1950s spy novel.

'Well, messages. They've sent emails announcing their intention to scupper our celebrations and "expose our secrets".' Stephen does quote marks with his fingers, then looks away and clears his throat. 'Obviously, they're using empty threats and we almost certainly have nothing to worry about, but I just want you to be alert, OK? If you get even a sniff of these fuckers trying to blow things up, I want you to tell me.' He slams his hand down on his desk, removes his feet and sits up straight. 'Because there is no way I'm letting a bunch of self-righteous twats fuck up *The Morning*'s big moment.'

Olivia nods mutely.

'Listen, I know I can trust you, Olivia. I've always been able to and now I've seen your true mettle with this People Displeaser feature, I feel like I can depend on you even more. You have hidden depths I didn't know about. There I was thinking you were all sweetness and light and baking cupcakes with your kids in Bromley...'

'Haywards Heath, actually, Stephen.' Olivia gives an unhappy little sarcastic smile. 'I've never even been to Bromley. And I've never baked a cupcake, for the record, although I don't think that baking is necessarily a sign that someone is a weak-willed pushover for doing it with their children. Baking requires skill and precision, unlike editing a national newspaper. I wouldn't fancy your chances in a fight with Mary Berry.'

'You see! There it is again, that streak of sass!'

Olivia thinks that all men who use the word 'sass' should be sent to some sort of prison for crimes against cringe, the keys thrown away for evermore.

Stephen leans back in his chair, a look of smug self-interest plastered across his features like face cream. Olivia can see his bright red socks, his hairy calves, and suddenly feels unwell. She coughs and stares out the glass-box window at Joanna, who is browsing a holiday website while her boss isn't looking.

'You're a wily fucker and I love it. You keep confidences, do you know what I mean?' Olivia shifts uncomfortably on the sofa, not liking where this is going. 'You know what you have to do to get on, and I respect that. You've come in here to pull me up on my admittedly shoddy behaviour and show Nina the sisterhood is alive and well, which is big of you because we all know how devastated you are, Olivia, that she got the job you wanted.' He sucks air through his teeth, and then expels it in a big, long sigh, as he allows what he has said to fill the atmosphere around them. 'But I know you're the right person for this Anniversary Architect gig. I couldn't have given the job to anyone else. And if you make this party a night to remember, then I will reward you for your hard work.'

'A night to remember?' Olivia is just repeating things now, while she tries to work out how to gain lost ground.

'Yep. A night that goes down in history – not just *The Morning* history, but media history. I want all the naysayers on social media who wang on about us being "legacy media" to know what a legacy truly is. I want them to see what we're all about, the power we have. I want celebrities. Big celebrities. From stage and screen and sport. I want a lavish location, no expense spared. I want red carpets, epic entertainment—'

'Dwarves serving platters of cocaine?'

'I can no longer tell if you're being serious or not.'

'I can no longer tell if *you're* being serious or not.'

Stephen spins in his chair, like a toddler enjoying Bring Your Child to Work Day. This is his sign that the conversation has deviated too far from its intended path. Despite being the editor of a national newspaper, he isn't emotionally advanced enough to deal with any exchanges where he isn't fully in control.

'Listen, I've had a word with the chief exec and the finance officer who agree with me that this is an investment opportunity, a chance to bring in a new audience, a new generation of *The Morning* readers.'

'They agree with you,' nods Olivia, raising her eyebrows. 'So what does this all mean, Stephen?'

She knows full well that after her opening salvo, he is trying to both butter her up and give her a warning, but she wants to lull him into the belief that she's still a bit clueless to his Machiavellian ways. She can, after all, use people pleasing to her advantage.

'It means that you have a massive fucking budget for the party and I want to do it sooner rather than later, to neutralize the threat of Stop the Press once and for all. I was thinking we should be ready to go in about a month, six weeks tops.'

'OK.' Olivia takes a deep breath. 'So not content with completely changing the remit of my work with no warning, you're now telling me I have to organize a party with six weeks' notice?'

'Six weeks tops,' says Stephen.

'Six weeks tops,' repeats Olivia. 'Well . . . I'm going to need some help, then.'

'This is a solo project.' Stephen wags his finger at Olivia, as if she is being naughty. He can't for a minute stand someone else trying to wrestle control from him. 'I know that you're more than capable of handling this assignment on your own. You hardly need help – you're Olivia fucking Greenwood.'

'I am Olivia fucking Greenwood,' smiles Olivia fucking Greenwood. 'And I want some people to help me with the boring administrative stuff that a project like this requires. I'm not wasting my time calling up venues and publicists, begging B-list celebrities to come and be part of our celebrations. That's way below my pay grade. Which isn't particularly high, but we can talk about that another time, perhaps as you're about to release your next gender pay report.' Olivia flashes him a rictus grin. 'But in the meantime, what I really want is some staff.' If she managed to track Rose down, she could hire her to be her assistant. That would be fun.

'I'm afraid that won't be possible, Liv.'

'Olivia. My name's Olivia.'

'Yes, well however you want me to refer to you, it doesn't change the fact that this is a one-woman project.'

'Is that right?' Olivia leans over to pick up a bottle of the executive spring water that sits in the middle of the conference table. 'A huge budget for the party, but no budget for staff to help me put together the kind of celebration that this organization doesn't just deserve, but needs, if it's going to last another century? The kind of event that will be talked about for months on end, generating buzz and influence and changing the way that *The Morning* is perceived by a new generation of subscribers, a younger generation. No budget for staff to create the kind of event that will make you look like a once-in-a-generation newspaper editor, a Harold Evans for the twenty-first century?' She pauses for a moment, allowing this to permeate Stephen's not inconsiderable ego. 'But budget for your sparkling water?' Olivia waves the bottle in the air, then puts it back on the table. 'Not to mention all that champagne you bought in the pub on Friday to celebrate Nina becoming *The Morning*'s new star columnist.'

'OK, Olivia, now isn't the time to air your grievances—'

'This isn't a polite request,' Olivia says, rising and making her way to the door. 'It's a demand.'

20

Deepti Batra is far more thrilled to be made temporary assistant to the Anniversary Architect than Olivia was to be given the role.

'Gosh, it's a real privilege to be working with you . . .' Deepti attempts to look furtively at the notebook that sits hidden on her lap under the canteen table '. . . Olivia. Yes, thank you, Olivia.' She nods her head vigorously. 'I'm really very grateful for this opportunity.'

'Oh my god, Deepti, your politeness is adorable but you don't have to pretend to me.'

'Pretend?' Deepti begins to look panicked. 'I'm not pretending. I'm genuinely thankful for every opportunity afforded to me on this internsh—'

'It's OK, Deepti. I don't need your gratitude, I just need your help.' Olivia peels the wrapper off a KitKat. 'Now why don't you tell me a bit about yourself?'

'Well, I, um, I went to Rushey Mead Academy in Leicester,' says Deepti, looking coyly at her hands. 'Then on to read History at Manchester University.'

Olivia remembers the time when her entire personality was her A-level grades and university choice. She realizes that, give or take two kids, a husband and a semi-detached house, it still is. 'Sounds pretty impressive to me,' says Olivia, clearing her throat.

'I thought so too, until I pitched up for the internship here and clocked that I was the token hire to tick a few diversity and inclusion boxes. I've spent most of my time being a general dogsbody, making cups of tea, while the other people on the internship, people with names like Lucas and Edward and Little Lord Fauntleroy, get to gallivant around the country doing actual reporting. Sorry, I don't mean to sound rude. It's just . . .' Her face flushes.

'No need to apologize,' smiles Olivia, taking a big bite out of her KitKat. 'It all sounds very familiar to me. Listen, this isn't news, and it isn't going to make Little Lord Fauntleroy jealous. But that's a good thing, believe me, because you don't want to be on the same wavelength as Little Lord Fauntleroy. I've had two decades of journalistic experience and I promise to impart some of it to you while you work on this project with me. And the good news is that this project is an editor's special. If we can pull off the party and impress him, it will help your connections no end. It may not result in a byline, but believe me, those can come later. You've got all the time in the world for bylines. Now you can focus on showing how keen and competent you are. Keen and competent, keen and competent!' Olivia waves her KitKat in the air then takes another bite out of it. 'This is way more important than being on the news desk.'

'Really?' Deepti perks up.

'Yes, really. So you've heard of Stop the Press, right?'

'Of course!' Deepti lets out a gasp. 'STP. The people who keep throwing bright pink paint over journalists and editors?'

'The very ones,' says Olivia, mouth full of chocolate.

'I did think about joining them,' sighs Deepti, 'but, you know, need to pay off student debt and all that.'

'Right,' nods Olivia. 'Sure. Anyway, STP. Well, the thing is, Stephen has heard that they're planning to threaten this centenary celebration we're putting on, and we need to make sure that doesn't happen.'

'How can we do that?'

'By using our investigative journalism skills to find out about them, of course, so that we can STP-proof the party.'

'Oh, right.' Deepti pulls out her phone. 'I mean, we could start by looking at their Instagram?'

'Surely that's too obvious?'

Deepti shrugs and hands her phone to Olivia, who begins scrolling through a selection of black and white pictures of STP members at protests. Shots where the only colour in the frame is the pink paint poured over some shame-faced journalist standing outside their office. Candid shots of group members, huddled round kitchen tables as they work late into the night, plotting the downfall of the 'corrupt MSM'. And multiple shots of a young woman, on a march, her hands holding crudely created cardboard banners, bearing the wisdom STOP THE PRESS. A woman with short, white-blonde hair and furious grey eyes.

Rose.

Olivia sits in Gail's, alone, having slipped out of the office for a moment to herself. The barista has started giving her the cappuccinos for free, a sure-fire sign that she is spending far too much time here, not to mention money.

But it's the only place that she can get her thoughts together, without Deepti or Stephen bothering her, or the grunts that echo from Nina's glass box every time HaalandIsLife drops another comment under her column. And Olivia needs the quiet right now to work out what she is going to do about the fact that she went on a wild night out and revealed her soul to one of the founding members of a group whose sole aim is to destroy the industry that pays her salary, and in doing so, most of her monthly mortgage.

The Post-it note containing the contact email for Rose sits on the granite table in front of her, fluttering in the gentle breeze of the air conditioning which the manager could really do with switching off, given the weather is that especially cruel late-April brand of icy cold. Rose's email had been easy enough to find, hardly requiring the skills of a trained investigative reporter – there on the website, under the 'About Us' section, lay the pictures and contact details for every member of the 'Executive Activism Team', which sounded to Olivia about as nonsensical as the title of Anniversary Architect.

Olivia may not want the antidote to the gummy any more, she might even be glad about everything that's happened since. But she needs to know what, exactly, she told Rose and what, exactly, Rose is planning to do with that information.

But she needs to do it in a nice way. A way that doesn't provoke any ire from this woman she so recently shared many intimate details of her life with.

She begins composing emails.

Dear Rose, I hope this finds you well. I just wanted to see if we could arrange a time to meet again and perhaps discuss our night out in a grown-up and sober way. Yours, Olivia.

Too formal.

Hi Rose! I hope you are well, and don't mind me reaching out to you – I tracked down your details and I thought I would just check in as I had so much fun the other night. Fancy doing it all again?! xx

Too perky. Too fake.

Rose – I wanted to get in touch as it has come to my attention that you are not who you say you are. Don't worry, I'm not cross, I just wanted to figure out what it is you want from me, and if there is a more honest way that we could communicate. I'm pretty sure I told you things that night that I've never even told my own husband, and given that level of candour on my part, I feel it would be such a shame to ruin it by us not at least trying to have a conversation on a more equal footing, one based on trust and integrity.

Way too understanding. Not to mention worthy.

With a start, she realizes that she doesn't need to be nice to Rose. She doesn't owe her anything, because Rose is the one in the wrong – the one who lied and tricked her into revealing things that were better off left in the past. Why is this her natural setting? Rushing to apologize even when she hasn't done anything? It's Rose who should be sitting somewhere composing messages to *her* – it's Rose who should be feeling cornered and on the spot. By trying to be polite and nice, she is thinking like the old Olivia. The Olivia who Rose had so effectively deconstructed that night in the pub. If she sends a pleadingly pathetic message to her, Rose will know that she holds all the cards, that the ball is firmly in Stop the Press's court. Olivia's not going to behave in the very way that got her into this mess in the first place.

She writes quickly, and without bothering to reread.

Rose (at least I think that's your name). If you know what's good for you, you'll call me, ASAP. OR ELSE. My number is at the bottom. PS. This is Olivia. No more Mrs Nice Girl.

She hits 'send', gulps down her free coffee, and strides back to the office with a sense of majestic purpose.

21

The leopard-print minidress doesn't quite fit, but in a way that Nick finds slutty and sexy and which means it ends up taking Olivia an hour and a half to get ready for Lily's party, as opposed to the usual rushed twenty minutes. She's waited aeons for her husband to give her an orgasm, and now she is averaging one a day – two, if Peter is particularly insistent about doing the washing-up, thus giving her and Nick more time alone – she isn't going to let anything get in the way of her coming.

'I think we should have a break, just the two of us.' Olivia is still sitting on top of Nick, straddling him after a two-orgasm extravaganza. 'I've been looking at places for a cheeky weekend, maybe after I've got this bloody centenary celebration out of the way.'

'I'm very impressed with how you've handled this career curveball, I have to say.'

Olivia feels a momentary sinking in her stomach, as she checks her phone and sees that Rose still hasn't replied to her email. She throws it back on to the bedside table and looks at Nick, who is gazing adoringly at her with puppy-dog brown eyes in a way she'd almost entirely forgotten about. She rolls off her husband and falls flat on her back next to him in the bed, noticing that all that takeaway food and all those cinnamon buns are definitely making her boobs bigger.

'In fact,' says Nick, also admiring his wife, 'everything about you right now is impressing me. You're like Olivia Greenwood, but on steroids.'

'Maybe that's what happens when we get older.' Olivia shrugs. She gets up and starts re-dressing, completely unbothered by the fact she stinks of sex. 'We spend the first forty years of our life trying to be someone else, and the next forty trying to be ourselves. And if we're lucky the people we've married still fancy us rotten.'

'Well, you can count me in for that weekend away, that's for sure.' Nick jumps out of bed, pads to the non-suite and even closes the door.

Olivia stares in the mirror, trying to ignore Saskia's panicked calls from downstairs that they are going to be late.

'It's OK, darling, we'll be there with plenty of time to spare,' she shouts out the door, before returning to her reflection. The invitation said 7.30 p.m. drinks for 8.30 p.m. dinner, which everyone knows means 'turn up somewhere around 8', and as it's only a half-hour drive away, they're still on track to be ever-so-slightly early. Anyway, Olivia is no longer marching to the beat of her mother's annoyingly insistent drum. Everything feels a bit quieter in Olivia's head at the moment. It's like someone has turned the volume dial down on the chorus of demands she was constantly alert to – demands she made of herself too. How many steps she needed to do, how many calories she needed to stick to, how much protein she could eat in a day.

She stands in front of the mirror. Though the anorexia is now in the past, Olivia's still spent her whole life gripped by its echo, so attuned to the less extreme but nevertheless disordered eating habits that society has somehow passed off as normal. She's deprived herself of cream and cheese and carbohydrates and all of the other very best things on the planet, 'treating' herself instead to tasteless alternatives with half the calories and not even a quarter of the fun. It's like a metaphor for her own character transformation over the last couple of weeks: having spent most of her life carefully extracting all the most delicious bits of herself so she could be a low-calorie version of Olivia Greenwood, she is now existing in all her scrumptious full-fat glory.

The extra pounds she has gained recently have hardly hindered her sex life, more like they've done wonders for it. She feels like some sensual Rubenesque portrait, whereas previously she was simply existing like Edvard Munch's *The Scream*. Then there's the effect it has had on her complexion. She leans in closer to the mirror. She's stopped slavishly lathering extra-strength retinol all over her face each night, and yet she appears ten years younger. The added weight is plumping out not just her bosoms but the emerging wrinkles on her face that are beginning to sneak in now that her next botox top-up is due. She glows with the joy of mozzarella sticks, the potential of prawn crackers. And this feels like one of the greatest revelations of all – realizing that she can take pleasure in food, and herself, all at the same time. That the two are inseparable, even, one absolutely impossible without the other.

'Why does nobody tell you that it's OK to take up space?' she whispers to her reflection, smoothing down the leopard-print minidress as she speaks. 'Why do we willingly go out of our way to make ourselves smaller?'

Nick returns from the non-suite, pats her on the bum, and dresses quickly in an old suit from his PR days, which is slightly too roomy from all the CrossFit. She watches him as he loops his tie, puts on cufflinks, thinks how proud she is that he had the guts to leave that world and do something meaningful, something worthwhile. She wonders what she would have done with her life, if she hadn't been chasing a career she thought would impress everyone else. Sure, she had enjoyed those days of university journalism, but real-world journalism had quickly proved to be completely different, and yet she'd still stuck it out this long, waiting for someone to let her know she was really good at it. She wonders, now, why she'd allowed other people's validation to mean so much more than her own. How much further she might have gone if she'd actually allowed herself to believe that she was really good at journalism, and refused to take all the bollocks that had been handed to her by tossers like Stephen. Maybe, by now, *she'd* be one of those tossers like Stephen.

Her mind wanders to all the alternative worlds out there, where she didn't study herself into sickness so she could get to a top university and then on to the graduate scheme of a newspaper where she now works as a glorified party planner. Might she have run away and joined the circus? Travelled the world like a bum, finding herself, in the style of Lily? She's never had the time to stop and think about this, never really considered the possibility that she could also make a change and spend her life doing something she wanted to do. What a danger women would be, if they were all given the time and the space to learn about themselves. If they were left to do as they pleased, and allowed to make mistakes with the same wild abandon as their male counterparts. Some of them would undoubtedly take over the world, though there would be plenty of others who might simply decide to lie down and wank all day, just as men did. Olivia is beginning to suspect she might fall into the latter category, although that could just be the years and years of sexual suppression rising up and spilling out into the world. Maybe it would eventually calm down, and then she could go on to run the United Nations. Or maybe she'd realize she wasn't built of super-ambition, resilience and steel, and be OK with that, choosing instead to do something that mattered to her. Whatever the case, it would be nice to find out, wouldn't it?

She snaps out of her reverie, runs her fingers through her hair in lieu of properly brushing it, and then makes her way downstairs, where Nick greets her with a whistle. Everyone is assembled in the hall in their smartest clothing – everyone except Jack, who is in a Man City kit, teamed not-so-neatly with his Crocs.

'Won't you be cold in that?' asks Nick, staring at his son's sandals.

'Oh for god's sake,' Olivia laughs, chucking on some eyeliner in the hallway mirror, admiring the post-sex glow that is infusing her cheeks in lieu of blusher. 'If you're worried about anyone being cold it should be me, in this incredibly slutty dress.'

'You shouldn't use the word "slutty", Mum, it's not exactly empowering, even if you are being sarcastic.' Saskia is in head-to-toe black, doing a good impression of Wednesday Addams.

'I'm not in my sarcastic era any more, Saskia. I'm in my "say the first thing that comes into my head" era. Anyway, do you like it?' She does a twirl. 'The leopard-print minidress, that is? You know, I've realized that it's not older women in miniskirts that anybody needs to worry about. It's us standing here, owning our own majesty!'

'Oh my god, Mum, are you having a hot flush or something?' Saskia cringes into her sleeve.

'I'm just doing my job and embarrassing you, sweetheart. Promise I'll try and snap out of it when we finally meet Lady Muck's new boyfriend.'

Jack scrunches his nose up. 'Who?'

'Clive, your grandmother's new fancy man, who we are all going to bitch about afterwards to make Grandad feel better.'

Peter doffs an imaginary cap at his daughter, a far-off look in his eyes. They pile out of the door and into the car, where Olivia tries to ignore the smell of booze emanating from her father in the back.

He's his own person. She isn't responsible for him. And as she prepares to see her mother for the first time in months, she wishes that she, too, had downed some vodka. To extinguish the nerves that sit somewhere deep beneath her leopard-print mini-dress. To get rid of the ominous feeling that weighs so heavily on her. To dilute the worry chewing away at her. To feel certain that she won't return to her old, people-pleasing ways.

22

Tina stands at the entrance to the private room at the back of the restaurant, guarding the guests inside. Her hair has been expertly ironed into a sleek, black bob, not a hint of grey to be seen, while her face has been set in make-up, the foundation caking in every crease and crevice. When it comes to cosmetics, Tina has never been a less-is-more kind of person. A real pearl of wisdom from Olivia's teenage years was nothing to do with knowing her own worth, or standing her ground, but 'if in doubt, darling, put some more mascara on'. This evening Tina is dressed in a black trouser suit with pointy kitten heels, a Vision Express version of Victoria Beckham. Her energy is clear: nobody enters the sanctum without crossing her first.

'Darlings,' she greets them, her smile a sort of sticking plaster on a snarl, or so it seems to Olivia. 'How wonderful it is to see you all, I've missed you so!' She launches herself at her grandchildren, begins pecking them on the cheek. 'Saskia, black suits you! You look amazing, darling!' Olivia feels something violent and primal in her stomach, a sort of urge to gather her daughter into her arms and take her immediately away from her mother, and her tired old obsession with the way people look.

'Saskia doesn't just look amazing, Mum.' Olivia reaches in for an air kiss. 'She IS amazing. She's doing so well at school.'

Olivia turns to her daughter and realizes with a start that Saskia looks exhausted – hollow-cheeked and washed-out, like she might be coming down with something. Perhaps it's an excuse to exit early, before she says anything she might live to regret.

'Well, it's just absolutely delightful that you're here. Now, if you could make your way into the private dining room, we can be getting on with the evening.' Tina eyes Olivia like she is a barely tolerated plus-one, rather than a human she carried in her womb and squeezed out of her vagina almost forty-five years ago. 'I was going to say you can leave your gift for Lily on the table at the back, but I see you haven't actually brought one.'

'I ordered it,' says Olivia, thinking on her feet, 'but it still hasn't arrived. You know what those delivery companies are like.' She tuts and rolls her eyes dramatically, unwilling to concede victory to her mother this early on in proceedings.

Olivia enters the private dining room, which is actually a conservatory in which the restaurant owners have cobbled together a selection of unevenly shaped tables and chairs in the hope of creating the atmosphere of a state banquet. She wonders if Tina let Lily choose who could come, or if she vetted the guest list first. As Olivia's mind ambles over her mother's incredible control freakery, she feels her phone vibrating in her bag. She reaches in to look at it and sees a text from a number she hasn't saved. She opens it and gasps.

It's Rose, call me.

Olivia steadies herself. 'You are a grown woman, you are a grown woman, you are a grown woman,' she says silently to herself, again and again and again. She needs to have this conversation in her own time, on her own terms, rather than here as she tries to navigate her way round all the traps her mother has inevitably set for her, possibly even without realizing.

I will text you later with details on meeting up TOMORROW, Olivia taps out, channelling her mother.

She walks up to Lily, who looks genuinely thrilled to see her. 'Wasn't sure you'd actually make it, sis,' she laughs, nervously. 'Was a moment back there when I thought you might go rogue.'

Olivia puts her arms on her sister's shoulders, feels a rush of affection for her that seems somehow embarrassing, here in the presence of their mother, who has always liked to point out their numerous differences, as if they should be warring states and not amenable siblings.

'Happy birthday, Lily,' she smiles. 'You've not aged a day since you were twelve.'

'You can talk.' Lily ruffles Olivia's arm. 'You appear to be reverse-ageing. Who is this sexy motherfucker I see before me, showing off her legs in leopard print?'

'If you can't wear leopard print to your sister's fortieth, then where can you?'

'A sex party?' Tina's voice cuts through the air, followed by a high, tinkling laugh. Lily smiles awkwardly, Olivia rolls her eyes. 'Only joking, darling,' Tina lies, brushing Olivia's shoulders. 'Now, will you come and meet Clive?'

Olivia turns around, ready to say something pithy . . . but there, to her surprise, stands the cord-wearing groper from the train. She gulps. A flash of contempt crosses Clive's face, one that Olivia sees despite his best attempts at disguising it with a crooked, entitled smile. Maybe it shouldn't come as a shock that her mum is in a relationship with the oily creep from the 11.47 to Brighton. She thinks about throwing a glass of champagne over him, just in case he needs reminding who she is – but stops herself. This is Lily's night, and however shocked Olivia is to see this man here, her mother isn't to blame for his actions on the train the other day.

Olivia puts on her most Tina-esque grin. 'Gosh, Mum, you won't believe this but me and Clive have actually met before.'

Clive's ruddy face has drained of colour. Olivia gets a perverse kick from imagining his terror at what she's about to say.

'Clive and I, darling, Clive and I.' Tina sighs, takes Clive's hand in hers. 'Now tell me, how on earth have you two met?'

Clive clears his throat to speak, but Olivia isn't allowing him to get the upper hand, not this time. 'We commute on the same train, Mum,' she says. 'It's quite the gang we've got going up and down the line from Sussex to London, isn't it, Clive?'

'I didn't know you commuted, Clive,' Tina says, before turning back to Lily and Olivia. 'Clive doesn't commute, on the train of all things, he's far too busy running the council here!'

'Well, Tina,' Clive begins, before stopping to clear his throat. 'I sometimes do have reason to go up to Westminster and meet with some of the party bigwigs, and it's far more cost-effective to go by train. It also stops anyone attacking me over my eco credentials.' He smirks, his voice as haughty and horrible as before. 'So yes, your daughter and I have had the pleasure of meeting previously.'

Olivia says nothing. For now. Her father's here now, anyway, barging in, breaking the tension with all the subtlety of a neutron bomb. 'Ish thish your new fanchy man, Tina?' he slurs, offering the hand that isn't gripping a glass of wine.

'Yes, Peter, this is my partner, Clive,' Tina tuts. 'Please be civil. Now, it's time for everyone to sit down for the meal,' she continues. 'Please take your places and no messing with the seating plan, I've rather meticulously arranged it all myself!'

Olivia finds her name card at a sort of ante-table at the far end of the room, where she has been seated alongside her children, her father, and two of Lily's godchildren. That's right, she's on the kids' table, and incredibly, this fact delights her. Right now she can't think of anything worse than being put next to that pervert Clive.

While the main table receive their prawn cocktail starters, a waitress plonks in front of Olivia a dish filled with bubbling macaroni cheese. 'Well, aren't we lucky that we get to eat something half-decent, rather than that rather eighties-looking party menu over there.' Olivia begins to crudely dish out great big dollops of mac and cheese on to everyone's plates, her father ignoring his in favour of the bottle of wine he seems to have extracted from a waiter.

Saskia looks morosely at the meal.

'Beige and congealed like all the best party food!' Olivia beams, genuinely delighted with the dish. 'Are you OK, Sass?' She watches her daughter poke at her food with a fork. 'You're looking a bit peaky?'

'I'm not feeling great, that's all.' She shifts stiffly in her chair. 'There's something going round at school and I think I'm a bit off my food.'

'Well, if you need to go home just say the word.' Olivia is wondering if willing her teenage daughter to be ill so that they can leave a family event early makes her a terrible parent, or merely a passably piss-poor one.

'I'll have yours,' says Jack, who has already wolfed down his portion and is now helping himself to his sister's.

'Let Sass try a bit, Ja—' Olivia begins, but she is cut off by the sound of the spoon on the side of a champagne glass once more.

'My lords, ladies and gentlemen!' Clive stands up and addresses the room around him, with all the confidence of a man who thinks nothing of groping strangers in public. Why does it surprise Olivia that he would feel entitled to make himself the master of ceremonies? 'Would you please give a round of applause to the mother of the birthday girl, Mizz Tina Fryer!'

Tina laughs in a high, tinkly way, then stands up as everyone around her begins to clap. She rearranges her features in a faux-bashful way, one that actually gives her the look of someone experiencing a minor neurological event. 'Oh please, there's no need!' she demurs, in a manner that suggests the opposite is true. 'You're too kind, too kind!'

Tina lets the applause die down, though there's a glint in her eye that implies she wouldn't be put out if it went on a little longer. 'Clive, thank you for getting everyone's attention, and for being here with me tonight on this beautiful evening where we get to celebrate my gorgeous Lily.' She looks down adoringly at Clive, who takes her hand in his and kisses it. The room coos as one, with the exception of Peter, who makes a retching noise that everyone pretends not to have heard. Tina does her tinkly laugh again, though there's little sense of real humour in it. 'I don't want to distract you from this most delicious dinner,' she says, commanding the room again, 'but I just wanted to say a few words to mark this special occasion, the fortieth birthday of my darling daughter' – she looks lovingly at Lily who tries not to grimace too hard back – 'and to also thank you all for coming.'

Tina pauses, makes sure she has everyone's attention. 'So all of you know Lily, but not all of you know just how much she has powered through over the years. She's always been such a bright, happy child, thinking endlessly of others, and she's often given the impression of having not a care in the world. But she's been a rock to many of us during our darkest hours. Both myself and her sister can attest to the incredible support she provides to those of us who are lucky enough to have her in our lives.' Tina sniffs, as if the emotion is too much and she will surely be overcome.

'As a child, Lily was quiet, but forever thoughtful. When she was a little girl, she would donate her pocket money to the donkey sanctuary in Devon, so it shouldn't surprise us that she has grown up always putting others first. She never stops, also devoting much of her time to spiritual practice, as so many of you know, not to mention looking after her niece and nephew.' Tina pauses. Lily takes a deep breath. Olivia grits her teeth. Peter stares in disbelief at the empty wine bottle he is trying to pour into his drained glass. 'I can't tell you how proud I am to have such a caring, considerate daughter, one who always goes out of her way to look after me and doesn't let a day go by without ringing and checking in. That we are all here tonight, together, to celebrate this most remarkable human, is a tribute to how loved and adored she is. I am so proud of her. Would you please all raise your glasses to my darling Lily Fryer.'

The room does as it's told. Peter stands up, his empty glass aloft. 'I'd like to make a shpeech!'

The room falls quiet and stares at Peter as he sways from side to side, like a Weeble that has just been gently wobbled. Lily holds a hand in front of her face, clearly wanting to disappear. 'Waiter!' cries Peter. 'Waiter! I want shome more sho I can make a toasht!'

Olivia stands up, her own glass held in the air. She knows what she has to do. 'What Dad means is that he'd like *me* to make a speech.' Olivia grins broadly, pulls her skirt down, motions for her father to get back in his seat. 'Yes, hi everyone, if you wouldn't mind just diverting your attention for a moment to the kids' table.' By now everyone in the room is exchanging awkward glances, wondering if they are about to witness some sort of surprise flash mob, organized especially for Lily's fortieth. No such luck. 'So yes, I would love to say a few words about my little sister, Lily, if that's OK.'

Lily gives Olivia permission with a genuine smile.

'The thing about Lily is that she is kind and considerate, as our mum just said. She is caring.' Olivia hoicks her skirt down once more. 'She is the most compassionate, empathetic soul I have ever met, and I don't know about you all, but I'm bloody glad to have Lily here to sort out all our chakras.'

Gentle laughter fills the room. Even their mother seems to relax.

'So, to give you an example of how amazing Lily is as a sister. Mum is right when she says she's the person we go to when we are experiencing our darkest moments. Um, when I was seventeen, and Lily was about thirteen, I was really ill for a bit.' She notices Tina shift uncomfortably in her seat, Clive taking her hand in his for support. Peter is still trying to extract wine from the empty bottle. Olivia removes it from his grip, shushes him with a piercing glare and then turns back to her audience.

'Where was I? Ah, yes, when I was ill. I mean, Lily was thirteen, and she was massively into Boyzone at this point.' Her sister shrieks in embarrassment, as everyone begins to laugh. 'Sorry, Lil. But it's true. Her room was covered in posters of Ronan Keating. She was OBsessed. She'd spend hours going all dreamy-eyed about him with her friends. Anyway, what I mean to say is that Lily had her own, rich teenage life going on, right? She didn't need her annoying older sister, moping around sick. But that's the thing about Lily. She never treated me like an annoying, older, moping, sick sister. Every night, she'd come and sit with me in my room and tell me about the things we were going to do when we were glamorous young women in the not-too-distant future, when I was better and she was married to Ronan Keating. I was going to get into Cambridge, and Lily promised me she was going to visit with Ronan, who would introduce me to his bandmate Shane, who would obviously fall head over heels in love with me.' Olivia looks saucily at Nick, who grins back. 'Every night after dark, Lily would creep into my room, get into bed with me, and hug me. She would tell me she loved me and she needed me and that we were partners in crime.' Olivia wipes an eye, finds it wet. 'The truth is, I couldn't exist without Lily. I *wouldn't* exist without Lily.' She looks towards her sister, whose eyes also seem to be leaking. 'I want you to know that me, and Nick, and Saskia and Jack, we are so goddamn lucky to have you. You give us life, and hold us together, and I'm sorry if I don't always let you know just how much we appreciate you. So yes, if you could all raise your glasses to Lily, my little sister, but mostly a total fucking legend.' Olivia brightens, grabs her glass and raises it in the air. 'Lily, everyone!'

'Lily!' cheers the room.

'Thank you, Olivia darling,' says her mother, standing up again. 'Now that the speeches are over, I hope you all enjoy your evening!'

The guests return to their food, while Tina pulls out her chair, and heads towards the kids' table.

'Peter!' she says, growling at her former husband. 'Could you not make a scene for once?'

'Mum,' says Olivia, putting her hand on Tina's arm. 'Shall we go outside and, um, cool off?'

Tina takes a deep breath, steadies herself, nods. Olivia grabs her arm, and they head into the main restaurant, buzzing with Saturday-night diners. Together they silently criss-cross the room until they reach the ladies' loos, where they stand face to face with one another in front of the old, battered tampon machine offering Lil-Lets for two 20ps.

'I can't believe he'd turn up in such a state to his own daughter's fortieth.' Tina looks as if she's about to blow a gasket. 'He's an absolute disgrace, an embarrassment.'

'He's an unwell man, Mum,' Olivia murmurs. 'Maybe if you'd got him help rather than chucking him out, he wouldn't be making such a fool of himself now.'

'Why won't you accept that our marriage is over, and it has been for years? If I told you some of the things . . .' Tina stops herself, folds her arms across her chest. 'For the first time in my life, I'm having an honest, transparent relationship with someone who looks after *me*, Olivia. Someone who I don't have to clean up after and turn into the recovery position at night so he doesn't choke to death on his own vomit.'

Olivia winces. She can't bear it – the thought of her dad being so out of control, the knowledge that her mum has unwittingly shacked up with a new bloke who is every bit as much of a liability, just in a different, more sinister way.

'It was awful, Olivia. You don't even know the half of it. Why am I to blame for everything?'

'Would it be better if I was smiling sweetly and laughing cheerfully instead?'

The fight seems to go out of Tina. 'You could at least pretend to be happy for me.'

'I've spent my whole life pretending to be happy, Mum. Pretending to be happy has been my entire fucking personality since I was a small child. It's never enough. Or rather, I'm always too much. Too emotional, too sensitive, too . . . Too much like *me*. I've been tamping it all down for bloody decades now, not entirely successfully, I'll admit, but just so you know, I am constantly, continually, trying to pretend to be happy – for you and for everyone else.'

'Well, I could say the same, you know,' huffs Tina. 'All I've ever done is try to keep the wheels on the track, to make sure our family was happy, that you girls had what you needed. But I'm always the one at fault. When I threw your dad out, I thought maybe if you could all see what he's really like, you might understand. I've spent years trying to help him but he won't be helped, and eventually I had to accept that it wasn't my responsibility to get him well. He's not a child, Olivia.'

'Yeah, well, it's not as if you excel at helping those, either, is it?' The words taste bitter and nasty and instantly flood Olivia with regret.

'I can't believe you'd say that.' She turns away from her daughter, slams her manicured hand against the tampon machine. 'You're forty-four, Olivia! You can't still honestly hold that childish belief that I wasn't there for you? It's like you've completely rewritten history. That little tribute to your sister, you made it sound as if you were orphans left to fend for yourselves.'

Olivia turns away in a sulk. The seventeen-year-old version of herself is running the show, and right now she feels like she has to let her. 'I feel like you never want to be near me, Mum. You seated me on the kids' table with your much-detested ex-husband!'

'I put you there because you're the only person I could think of who would be grown up enough to watch over things!' Tina stamps a kitten heel on the floor. 'Not everything I do is out of some deranged vendetta against you, Olivia. Believe it or not, I love you. I've always loved you.'

Olivia desperately wants her mum to reach out and hug her. She wills Tina to do it.

'I'm too old to still be having these arguments. It's not for me any more. I'm trying to move forward, instead of looking backwards, as I have every right to do now I'm in my twilight years. I'm sorry I didn't get it right with you, Olivia. I did my best, I really did. You can't keep being angry with me about it for the rest of my life when you have your own to live.'

'Mum, I . . .' Olivia pauses as she feels her wrist vibrate. There's an alert from Nick on her watch, something about her dad, and being needed back at the table.

'For fuck's sake,' she whispers at her arm. 'I need to go and parent my father.'

Olivia turns on her heel, tears stinging her eyes, and heads to the private room. She's greeted by Nick, who is holding a glass and a general air of mortified surrender as her dad wrestles with one of the waiters over a wine bottle. His valiant attempts are thwarted by the server, who swiftly raises the wine bottle up and out of the way. The sudden change in direction sends Peter off balance, arms flailing as he staggers and falls backwards on to the table, arse-first into the dish of macaroni cheese.

23

It wouldn't be correct to say that the car journey back is silent, on account of the endless belches that erupt from Peter's throat, and the horrified 'eww's that come from Saskia. But otherwise, everyone in the car is subdued, grateful to no longer be trapped in the private dining room from hell.

'We really are one messed-up family,' says Jack, brightly.

'I didn't know you were ill when you were young,' says Saskia, quietly. 'What was wrong with you?'

'Oh, it was just a bad bout of, um . . .' Olivia feels her fingers start nervously drumming against her thumbs, wills them to stop. 'Tonsilitis. Terrible tonsils, I had.'

She looks at Saskia, who still seems drawn and tired. Maybe she should have said something bland and boring during her speech back there, something that hadn't drawn attention to a time everyone would rather forget. Maybe she should have bitten her tongue, behaved like the adult, the *mother*, that she really needs to be right now, for Saskia and Jack's sake. Maybe not everything needs to be said, and certainly not by her.

If earlier in the week her truth-telling had seemed like the empowering words of a newly awakened and independent woman, she feels like this evening's reality is revealing just how far she's falling short as a mum. How much she's turning into her *own mum*. The conversation with Tina was awful but it cleared some air – air that had been left to fester for too long. Does she really want to be having arguments with Saskia in twenty-five years' time about how badly she let her down? She needs to be emotionally mature now, not when her kids have grown up and moved out and the damage will already have been done.

'Your mum's new boyfriend seemed . . .' Nick turns briefly from the steering wheel to check on Peter, who is passed out, his head resting on a window, drool dripping from his mouth. 'Well, he seemed very right and proper.'

Olivia continues to bite her tongue. Now is not the time to tell him that Clive is the handsy man from the train.

'Poor Gran. Poor Lily.' Saskia puts on her headphones, presses 'play' on her phone, considers the matter closed.

Olivia knows that her daughter has a point. She takes out her phone and begins to text her sister.

> *I'm sorry for ruining this evening. I'm sorry for abandoning you with Mum after humiliating her so publicly*

Immediately, Olivia sees her sister begin to type.

> *You didn't ruin it because it was already ruined from the get-go! I should have told you but I already celebrated with a party a few weekends ago, an amazing couple of days away that my mates organized in Margate. I'm still trying to recover from it. This one was just to humour Mum . . . and we sure did that, eh?*

PEOPLE PLEASER

> *I don't think I humoured Mum at all, certainly not during the row we had in the loos. I was a bit of a dick. I should have risen above it, been the grown-up*

> *Olivia, in this relationship, you're not the grown-up. She is. You're her child. Maybe just try not to see her as the enemy all the time?*

Olivia stares at this message, feels herself begin to cry.

> *When did you get so wise, little sister?*
> *Thank you. Love you xxx*

By taking that Erling Haaland gummy, she has unleashed a cascade of truth, a veritable domino effect of honesty. She's had a sharp epiphany: Olivia has to face up to the fact that she isn't a child any more. She is a grown-up.

Arriving home, Saskia storms upstairs and slams the door, while Nick goes and plays FIFA with Jack in the living room. Olivia props up her stumbling father, guides him to the shed, opens the slightly stuck door and has a good look at this room he calls home. There's a small pile of neatly folded clothes on a chair, a selection of books about Roy Orbison, the little electric heater she got to make sure he doesn't freeze to death out here. It's all a bit tragic. Why does she find it so much easier to accept her dad's failings, but when it comes to her mum she boils with anger and hurt?

As he crashes around, trying to find his way to the bed, Olivia notices a picture on the tiny table, next to the Buddy Holly books. It is of the Fryer family on a holiday to Majorca back in the early nineties, one of the few trips they ever went on together. Olivia and Lily were usually packed off to camps the day after school broke up, spending weeks at a time practising tennis, and swimming, and arts and crafts, with an ever-rotating cast of minders who were probably only just out of school themselves. She looks at the picture, the two sisters dressed in matching pink dresses with bows, her mother and father standing behind with their arms around their children, smiling. They look like a normal family, a happy one, but Olivia has only one memory of the holiday itself.

The girls had been left in the apartment with a babysitter, though who that person was Olivia can't recall now. Similarly, Olivia has no memory of the finer details of that evening, other than her waking up at some point to the shrill shouts of her mother. Olivia turned in her little single bed and looked towards Lily, who had also been woken up. She put her index finger to her mouth, signalling for them both to stay quiet, then pulled the sheet up over her head in a way that she could hear Lily copying. Tina was shouting words that neither Olivia nor Lily could understand – they were as foreign as the Spanish the babysitter spoke – and their father was shouting similarly strange words back. They were, Olivia realized later, swear words, the kinds of words that parents weren't supposed to say and children most definitely weren't supposed to hear. There was the sound of something smashing, and then of their mother crying. But in the morning she was bright and breezy, as if nothing had happened, and Olivia had decided she'd made the whole thing up, a dramatic fever dream that, if she were to mention it to her mother, would seem like it had been invented to ruin an otherwise perfect holiday.

Now, looking at the picture, and her drunken father stumbling out of his trousers, she suddenly knows that it had been all too real. Her father must have spent most of his marriage drunk out of his mind. Olivia feels first a wave of relief, that she wasn't making it all up, next a stab of guilt that Tina had worked so hard to hide it, and then sadness that her mum had got it so wrong in the process. Is she feeling sorry for Tina, after everything? She tries to imagine what it would be like if Nick was almost entirely absent, a feckless alcoholic, and is hit by the confusing realization that it's possible to feel sorry for someone you were pretty sure you hated this morning.

'Time for bed, Dad,' she says. 'Time for bed.'

Her father collapses into the Ikea day bed he sleeps in, and Olivia pulls the duvet around him, switches the electric heater on so that he won't be cold. She turns him on his side so that he is in the recovery position, remembering her mum's words from earlier.

'I'm sorry I let you girls down,' he whispers, putting his arms around his eldest daughter. 'All of you.'

Despite Olivia's desperate, deep-seated need for validation, she is not particularly good at receiving it. The hug from her father leaves her feeling curiously disconnected. She knows it to be a normal, paternal activity, one that millions of dads across the country carry out umpteen times a day. She's seen Nick do it with their kids, witnesses it all the time. And yet she has no memories of her own father taking her or Lily into his arms, ruffling their hair or trying to smother them in kisses, as they desperately scrambled to escape (which is what happens now if either she or Nick dare to try and embrace Jack and Saskia). Did it happen and she's just forgotten, choosing to remember his absence instead?

One by one, she knocks on her children's bedroom doors and goes in to give each of them a goodnight hug. 'Love you, Mummy,' whimpers Jack, her baby boy already in a half-sleep.

'Your dress tonight kind of slapped,' Saskia tells her, the unenthusiastic compliment feeling like a lottery win to Olivia. Then she goes to her own room, and lies on her bed, staring up at the ceiling. Surely her dad must have hugged them. That awkward embrace in the shed cannot have been the first time that the two of them have ever cuddled.

'I've got no memory of either of my parents hugging me,' Olivia says as Nick walks into the room. 'Isn't that odd?'

'I mean, odd feels pretty normal at this point in proceedings.'

'Have I told you about the time I answered the house phone to a weeping woman asking to speak to my mum? I went and got her, and then listened as she called the lady on the other end of the line, and I quote, a "home-wrecking whore".' Olivia puffs out her cheeks. 'That was a fun way to spend a Saturday morning.'

'I'm sorry, Olivia.' Nick shifts over and puts his arm around his wife, kissing her on the ear.

'My poor mum,' she whispers into her husband's shoulder.

Olivia hears his breath slow, unwraps herself carefully so as not to disturb him. She looks up at the ceiling, wide awake. She has spent most of her adult life in a state of extreme hypervigilance, constantly scanning the environment for danger, in the form of an upset relative, a disappointed mother, an annoyed friend or an angry boss. She's tired of it.

She grabs her phone from the bedside table, opens up WhatsApp, and taps out a new message to Rose.

I know you're planning to take The Morning down, have import-

ant information, but we have to meet in person. I will see you at Brighton train station, next to the piano, tomorrow at 1 p.m., she writes. She watches the ticks turn blue, sees Rose typing, then feels a lurch in her chest as the message appears on her screen.

Fine, have it your way, writes Rose. *But remember to bring plenty of fags.*

24

Olivia feels strangely confident as she waits for Rose to arrive at the station. If anything, she's excited for the twenty-something to hear the new strength in her voice, the about-turn in her character. She imagines Rose congratulating her for her sudden ballsiness, then feels a stab of disappointment that she is still so caught up in trying to impress her. She needs to pull herself together and become FRANK, FEARLESS OLIVIA GREENWOOD before Rose arrives. Today she means business, and she won't be messed around any more.

She gets to the station piano fifteen minutes early. Hardly an arch power move, but she wants to be calm and collected by the time she sees Rose. She can't bear to listen to the gaggle of small children stabbing tunelessly at the piano keys as their parents check through train tickets, so she scampers to the M&S and hides by the sandwiches where she can keep an eye on the station. The clock strikes 1 p.m., and Rose is not there. Five past one, and Rose is not there. Ten minutes past one, Rose is not there. Olivia keeps her eyes on the piano, and her phone, alternating between varying states of hypervigilance – observing the piano, the time and her WhatsApp inbox. Now this is a power move.

Finally, at 1.27 p.m., the woman who turned her world upside down just a couple of weeks ago saunters up to the piano, not a single fuck given, and – seeing Olivia is not there – sits down at the stool, where she begins to play a faultless rendition of Concerto No. 3 by Rachmaninov.

'Who *is* this woman?' Olivia says to herself, as she starts to make her way out of M&S, knocking over a display of Percy Pigs in the process.

'Fuck!' Olivia begins picking them up, and then, realizing that Rose is finishing her masterpiece and standing up as if to leave, drops them back on the floor.

A small crowd has gathered around Rose and now applauds her. She stands beside the stool, bowing in a manner that suggests she is used to such public displays of adoration. Olivia walks towards the young woman, who is wrapped in the sort of brightly coloured oversized scarf favoured by either the very old or the very young but nobody in between, and rearranges her expression as best she can so that she gives the impression of being both FRANK and FEARLESS. She has a lot of mascara on – Tina would be proud.

'Rose,' she nods, seriously, tightening her cardigan protectively around her in a way that she hopes seems hostile.

'Ah, Olivia.' Rose turns. 'I wondered when you might show up.'

'I've been he—' Olivia remembers that for the purposes of today, she is not the kind of person who arrives early. 'You're lucky I showed up at all, frankly.'

'Sure.' Rose laughs. 'Anywaaaaay, I hope you're going to reimburse me the train fare. This place is bloody miles away from London. But now I'm here, I might as well make the most of it. Let's at least get to the seaside, shall we?'

'You don't get to dictate the terms of today,' barks Olivia, annoyed because that's exactly what Rose is already doing – the younger woman now heading towards the station exit, confident that Olivia will follow. They begin the walk down the hill to the beach.

'Well, this is the most awkward second date I've ever been on,' says Rose, as they weave in and out of the tourists plodding cluelessly down the street. 'You could have at least bought me a bunch of flowers.'

'Are you trying to be funny?'

'No, I'm just making small talk while you decide to give me the information you've promised.'

'That's a bit rich coming from you, Rose.' For the first time, Olivia turns and looks her in the eye. 'You've hardly been forthcoming with your own information, have you? You said you were working for *The Morning* and now I've discovered that, actually, you're working against it. Plus, you, you, you *drugged* me!'

Rose hoots with laughter for several moments as they carry on past empty storefronts and a Wetherspoons already packed with drinkers. 'As I recall it, you went along quite willingly with the whole evening.'

'You lured me there under false pretences.' Olivia sees a free bench on the seafront, scurries towards it before some gormless tourist eating fish and chips can grab it. 'And had the gall to lecture me about being dishonest! You and STP are all about truth, and honest journalism, but it turns out you have all the morals of a hack from the *News of the World* circa 1996.'

'It's not the same,' spits Rose, sitting down next to her. 'We're doing it for the greater good.'

'How have you got any clue what the greater good is? You're a child. You don't have a clue about the world.'

'Oh and you do, as a 44-year-old woman who's somehow allowed herself to be fobbed off with a bullshit job title that puts you one step closer to redundancy?' Rose rolls her eyes. 'I'd hope by the time I'm your age I won't still be in a position whereby I'm continuously fucked over by a bunch of wankers with names like Jasper and Freddie.'

'I'll have you know that I've never worked with a single person called Jasper or Freddie.'

'OK, Hugo and Andrew then.'

'How do you know their names?' Olivia gasps.

'Are you for real?' Rose's nose scrunches up in incredulity. 'I know their names because you told me them the other night.'

'Wait – why are you talking about redundancy?' Olivia is struggling to keep up with everything.

'Babes, you know that as soon as you've put on that party, they're going to let you go. I just hope you have a good contract.'

'You haven't got a clue about the world I work in, Rose. If that's even your name. For all I know, you could have found out about Hugo and Andrew from your undercover snooping.'

'Oh wow, you really don't remember, do you?'

'I remember some parts, just not all of it,' snaps Olivia, as she watches a seagull swoop down and steal the flake off a little girl's ice cream.

'Well, here's what I remember about our night. I was there at the pub hoping to pick up the odd titbit of intel from a slightly inebriated journalist during a brief, unguarded moment at the bar, and instead, the universe delivered me you, Olivia Greenwood. The jackpot. And don't pretend you didn't get something out of it as well. I offered you the opportunity to offload about a bunch of arseholes you've put up with for far too long, but never actually done anything about, much to the detriment of other women trying to get into journalism, who have to put up with their shit too—'

'Oh PLEEEEEASE,' interrupts Olivia. 'I'm now responsible

for every woman in journalism? It's so easy for people your age to show up on social media with all your ideals and principles but no actual fucking clue as to the realities, and attack women like me for letting the side down.'

'That's not exactly the vibe you were giving off before, when you gratefully accepted the opportunity to rant about the tossbags you have to work with, without once questioning anything I said about them. You properly let rip about Hugo and Andrew, and how I should stay away from them because you'd heard bad things about their wandering hands. But have you ever reported them to HR? No. Do you remember telling me you reckoned Nina must be shagging Stephen because he likes them young?'

Olivia lets out a sort of strangulated moan that seems to originate deep in her soul. 'I said that?' She momentarily holds her head in her hands.

'Yep, that was a dick statement straight out of the misogyny playbook.'

Olivia shakes her head. Who was that person from a fortnight ago? She feels like that version of herself is a ghost, haunting her from afar. She does not want to be that woman ever again. She can't believe just how much she's woken up to in such a short space of time. Or, she can – but she feels equally ashamed and relieved about it.

'You know, Stop the Press exist to help people like you, Olivia, not to work against you.'

'I don't need your help, thank you very much, and even if I did I would prefer not to be tricked into receiving it.' Olivia stares at some children throwing pebbles into the slate-grey sea.

'The only person tricking you right now is yourself, Olivia. I get that you were looking out for me as a younger woman in the industry, warning me off all the twats and pointing out potential pitfalls. It was a wonder to meet a person who works at *The Morning* who seemed to have actual morals, even if only briefly. When you said you had info you needed to give me, I thought you were going to come over and be our mole on the inside. But you're just another self-serving hack out to protect yourself. How predictable.'

'Listen, you should know that there are laws against what you did.' Olivia glares at Rose, who does not return her gaze. 'If a journalist pretends to be someone they aren't in order to get a story *under false pretences*, they'd quite rightly be disciplined and written up by the Independent Press Standards Organisation. Which exists so that Stop the Press don't have to. It would be good if you subjected yourself to the same standards that journalists do.'

'What would you know about journalism?' Rose finally looks at Olivia.

'Don't be so impertinent!' blasts Olivia. Christ, she sounds exactly like her mother. 'What is it exactly you're trying to achieve? You're messing with people's careers.'

'Do you understand how terrible the people you work for are?' Rose straightens her back in a sort of fury. 'Do you know that your editor is the reason I don't have a mum any more?'

'What?'

'Stephen. He's the reason my mum's dead.'

Olivia turns her body around fully so she is facing Rose. Suddenly, the intensity of her expression doesn't look like rage. It looks like pain. 'I, I don't understand, Rose,' she says, softly. 'How can he—'

'Stephen basically stalked my mother for several months, back when I was a kid and he was a reporter who thought he could pass off his behaviour as journalism. It was during the financial crisis. Not that I knew what a financial crisis was, I was like seven or something. My mum worked at a big bank, as an executive assistant to the guy who basically ran the big bank, and then suddenly the big bank she worked for was in the news because it had to be bailed out by the government. I mean, none of this meant anything to me as a kid at primary school. I just knew that Mum's work was stressful.' Rose takes a deep breath. 'That there were changes at the top and she now worked for someone new, and she'd been really upset about it all. Then one Sunday, I woke up and Mum was telling me that there had been a change of plan that day and I was going to stay at my dad's as a special treat. When we left the house there were all these people with cameras sort of lurking by the front gate, shouting her name. It turned out that my mother was on the front page of a tabloid, exposed as the lover of her ex-boss. She'd been having an affair with the man who was held responsible by the government, and the press, for the bank's downfall and the loss of thousands of jobs in the process. Turned out that he'd been seducing my mother while Rome burned, and expensing it. And Stephen, who was a reporter at the paper, had got wind of it and spent months, and I mean months, having them followed. My mum had done absolutely nothing wrong other than be taken in by a lying prick, but that happens to most of us at some point, and she didn't deserve to have her life upended and her picture printed everywhere, under headlines such as BONKING CRISIS STRUMPET. The worst thing is that Stephen had been trying to blackmail my mum into doing a kiss-and-tell interview with him. There were hundreds of messages on her phone when they found it. The last one was sent the day before the piece came out, as if he didn't already have the six-page spread written and ready to go. His last text said something like *You still have the chance to do things on your terms, but come tonight you lose that opportunity*, as if he was doing her a fucking favour. The whole spread, all the coverage, Olivia, it was about my mum, and how if it hadn't been for her, maybe this man wouldn't have brought the bank down. It basically blamed her for all the job losses, as if she was some seductress and not a single mum from Forest Hill who read me a bedtime story every night and took me swimming every weekend.'

Rose wipes her eyes, and Olivia gently places a hand on her shoulder. 'That's just . . .' Olivia places the other hand on the centre of her own chest, as if to keep in all the feelings that have appeared there, pushing at the surface to get out. 'That's just fucking awful, Rose.'

'Yeah, well trust me, it gets much worse. My dad being the absolute twat he was, he wouldn't let me go back home with all the journalists around. He told me that Mum needed some time to herself, and that I could go back in a few weeks, and that was that. But I never did go back. Mum killed herself a month later – not that Stephen or any of the papers were interested, given that they'd already moved on to their next scandal. And that's why I work for Stop the Press, and not *The Morning*. That's why I do what I do. And it's why I'd hoped you'd brought me here to tell me more about that nasty hypocritical arsehole, and how he likes to take advantage of women like Nina. I thought there might be more to that story. Just the way you spoke about him, it felt like . . .' Rose shakes her head. 'Neverfuckingmind. I've told you my truth, so I guess we're even. Now do you understand why I "tricked" you?' she says, making sarcastic quote marks with her fingers.

'Fuck,' says Olivia. 'That's, I mean, that's . . .' She can't find the words, can't quite untangle all the thoughts that are flying around in her brain. Thoughts about the awfulness of what happened to Rose's mum, feeling desperate enough to kill herself and all because a newspaper wanted a quick scoop that would beat all the competition. Thoughts about her own mum, unwittingly loved up with a pervert. And her own well of hot shame, the secret she hasn't told anyone, ever.

'That is just appalling, Rose.' She tries to put her hand on the young woman's, but Rose snatches it away and stuffs it in a pocket. 'I'm so sorry.'

'An apology doesn't mean very much if you aren't going to help me,' Rose tsks. 'So if that's all, I'm going to leave now.'

'No, don't go.' Olivia closes her eyes, shakes her head. 'No, you can't leave. There is something I need to tell you about that nasty hypocritical prick, actually. There *was* something about the way I spoke, you're right. And if you can trust me with the story of your past, then I'm going to trust you with mine.'

25

Olivia tells Rose everything, and there isn't a football-shaped gummy or a pint of Kronenbourg in sight – just the sad juggling clown, and some seagulls picking at a bin full of discarded fast-food cartons.

She tells Rose about the time, way back at the beginning of her career, when she had made the mistake of going out for a drink with Stephen and a few other members of his team. About how humiliated she was by her apparent inability to handle her drink, and the nightclub she found herself in with him, somewhere round the back of a mainline train station.

About the way he pushed her into the disabled loo and up against the wall. How he had grabbed at her tights and the foul taste of his grotesque, jabbering tongue. How she had frozen. How the next day, they seemed to have silently agreed to laugh it off, as if he hadn't tried to force himself on her, as if he hadn't—

'He assaulted you,' says Rose, blinking in almost disbelief.

'I mean, I wouldn't go that—'

'Olivia, babes, he absolutely assaulted you.'

Having waited for so long to speak to Rose again, Olivia now can't bear to hear her voice any more. She can't bear to have someone else tell her what happened that night, because then she might have to say it, and if she says it, somebody might accuse her of being a drama queen, or self-involved, or difficult, or any of the other things she has spent a lifetime trying to avoid being called. 'Please, you don't need to say it,' she says, catching her breath. 'I know you mean well but I, I just can't, not yet.'

'I get it, but man I hate it.' Rose gives Olivia the smallest of smiles to let her know she's not having a go at her. 'Like, these men, they absolutely count on the fact that we'll feel somehow responsible.'

'I know all of this,' nods Olivia. 'Like, I know it in my head, but somehow it hasn't quite dropped to my heart. Like, women of my generation, women of your mum's generation, we all had to navigate the wandering hands and the inappropriate comments without anyone there to back us up. I'm not saying it's easier for women your age, I know you have your own battles and I know there are still absolute bellends out there . . . I threw coffee all over one on the train, but that's another story. There wasn't any social media when it happened. There weren't swathes of women talking about what happened to them, no Me Too. There weren't groups of people there to hold and support you if you made a complaint. There were just more fucking men, everywhere you looked.'

'And that's why we're here, Olivia. That's why we set up Stop the Press. We're here to help you call out this kind of shit.' Rose shuffles a bit closer and takes Olivia's hand. 'You don't have to stomach this kind of behaviour any more.'

'I'm really sorry about your mum.' Olivia uses her other hand to wipe away a tear. 'I'm really sorry that I must seem so lily-livered to you. Fuck, how is it that I still think that what happened all those years ago was my fault? I still sort of blame myself for being drunk, when I know that if you told me something like that had happened to you, or if my daughter did, I would be absolutely fucking apoplectic with rage on your behalf. I'd tell you that you could be drunk and dancing on a table in only your underwear, and it still doesn't give anyone the right to shove their tongue in your mouth and try and put their hand down your pants. And yet for the last twenty years or so, I've gaslit myself to believe the opposite. I've done Stephen's bidding for him.' She shakes her head, squeezes Rose's hand. 'But it's time, isn't it? It's time I started to do my own bidding. I just need to do it on my own terms. It can't be on yours, because that would be just as disingenuous as the version of me who blamed herself for what happened with Stephen.' She leans towards Rose, bumps their shoulders together. 'I mean, that version of me was having such an intense midlife crisis, I went on a night out with *you*.'

'Fair enough, boomer,' laughs Rose. 'Fair enough. So are you going to share your terms with me?'

26

The website for Stop the Press makes for particularly depressing reading. More depressing even than any of the increasingly deranged comments that get posted under Nina's articles on *The Morning*'s website.

She revisits Rose's not-so-little venture on the train back from Brighton, all the while chomping down on a bag of Percy Pigs – the lure had simply become too much as she passed through the station on her return journey.

> *Stop the Press is committed to creating a media landscape that is truly free. Currently, our national newspapers are a disgrace to journalism . . . and most importantly, to democracy.*
> *They are funded by the few, for the few – and the dwindling numbers reading them are a reflection of this. We want to provide a viable alternative to the mainstream media, one that exists without misinformation or bias and which truly serves the people, instead of lying to them.*

Olivia bites off an ear, reads on.

To do this, we have made it our mission to expose the harmful practices of many of the so-called journalists who work for national newspapers, and other sections of the legacy media. We achieve this through rigorous research and our own investigative journalism. It is our hope that through shining a light on the darker parts of the national press, we will both detoxify it and force it to cover subjects that truly matter: subjects such as the climate crisis, war, famine, and the oppression of displaced people.

Olivia imagines what the likes of Stephen, Hugo and Andrew make of Stop the Press's mission statement, their cynical, poisoned minds no doubt reading it as virtue-signalling wokery. But what, exactly, were they doing with journalism, other than using it as a way to feel powerful and important? Weren't they being every bit as virtue signalling and self-righteous, just in a way that only benefited themselves? Olivia reckons that the story about Rose's poor mum was probably the last time Stephen actually did any reporting, and what was the noble goal of that particular news item, exactly? Olivia googles the banker, finds the old reports on the websites of various tabloids, the tenor of each story being that without the 'pernicious influence' of Rose's mum, her married lover might not have played so fast and loose with British taxpayers' money. Words like 'harlot' and 'seductress' jump out at Olivia, and she wants to cry for the woman, for Rose, their lives irrevocably shattered for the sake of a cheap red-top thrill.

But she also wants to cry for herself, for the twenty-something version of her who had felt that the only way to survive was to deny all her feelings, to double down on her shame and be belittled by someone who had actively hurt her. Everything in her told her the world would side with Stephen; she couldn't even see a glimpse of a place that would believe and accept her version of events. Now, for the first time in her life, she has encountered the smallest of outposts where she has felt strong enough – safe enough – to reveal her truth. And in that space, all the hurt and anger she's had to tamp down over the years has begun to bubble up.

She puts an entire Percy in her mouth, chews. She is going to sink that motherfucker like the *Titanic*. She is the iceberg that is going to bring him down. She doesn't know how she's going to do it, but she knows she is going to enjoy watching him disappear beneath the waves, taking everything he stands for with him.

Olivia looks out at the tracks, as the train seems to have ground to a halt. She stares at the blocks of new-build flats that back on to the railway, the windows into other people's neat and ordered lives. She sees the back of a baby, bouncing in a Jumperoo, the infuriatingly jolly music of which Olivia can still recall now, a whole decade on from her last experience of new motherhood. As she watches a mother beaming down at her gurgling baby in its bouncer, she feels bile rise in her throat. She feels a sort of rage at herself, for not being able to understand that time as magic, for giving so much of her energy to her overlords in the office, the ones who had stay-at-home wives and nannies and cleaners and who didn't have to worry about getting their figures back, or their careers back, or anything back, actually – for it was all there waiting for them obediently, never daring to go anywhere, because it belonged to them and always had done.

Her phone buzzes with a notification. She ignores it, puts it away in her tote bag. The conversation with Rose has dislodged things that she'd never properly allowed herself to admit before . . . things she had kept hidden neatly inside her, so neatly that even Nick was not privy to them. What is she doing with her life? How has she got to this point, a woman-child who is terrified of speaking up for herself, or expressing even the most basic of needs and truths?

When Olivia thinks about this now, she can see with absolute clarity what it has been about. She has had no sense of self. She has never learned to trust her own thoughts and feelings. At home, any expression of emotion that didn't involve being good or happy was translated by her mother as attention-seeking and unwanted. Olivia wonders now what is so wrong about a child seeking attention – perhaps, if they are doing that, you ought to damn well give it to them. But she'd never been able to apply that empathy to herself. She had hung on to her childhood belief about being an attention-seeker with all the devoted fervour of a cult member. To let it go would be to cease to exist in any meaningful way whatsoever. And yet, like it or not, that encounter with Rose has shifted something inside her. Somehow a space has opened up, a place in which she can begin to build a structure that safely houses the courage of her convictions.

And now that space exists, she has to start putting things right. She has to begin living her life in a way that suits this new, adult version of herself, rather than the terrified little girl cowering inside her who has been running the show up until that fateful Friday she met Rose. She needs to run with her new-found control. She needs to get shit done. And she needs to start with Nick.

*

Olivia cooked the idea up as she lay in bed that night, wide awake, ruminating over all the memories of her early career that had started flooding her head. It was as if they had been unleashed by the younger woman's terrible story, set free by Rose's trademark tone, so familiar despite the fact the two of them had only actually met twice.

How could that be possible? How could one night out have managed to upend her whole life?

As Nick snored merrily beside Olivia, his sleep disturbed by nothing more pressing than the contents of the next morning's CrossFit workout, she was hit again and again by memories of incidents that involved rampant sexism, wild misogyny, barely concealed bigotry.

Was this perimenopause? Was some strange hormonal fluctuation responsible for the veil dropping away to reveal the truth about all the grubby, grotesque details she'd somehow managed to blank out for a good couple of decades? She'd read about women her age becoming fully fledged insomniacs, and she wondered if it was because deep in the dead of night, their bodies were finally giving up all the terrible misogynistic shit they'd hidden inside them in a simple effort to carry on.

But her brain had been waiting for the moment when she was finally ready to face the reality of herself. She hadn't been altered by the Erling Haaland . . . she had merely been given permission to be herself, without any filters. And she wasn't going to throw that away now. She could never unhear it, or unsee it.

She began to hatch her plan, finally falling asleep at some point after 4 a.m. It started to slot into place the next day, when Jack received an invitation to a sleepover the next weekend, from Jonathan, of all people, the head of the football boys. The WhatsApp had come through unexpectedly, given that Olivia had managed to exit every school group in existence, but Jonathan's mother was obviously a better woman than her, and had managed to track down her number.

Jack's excitement had been instant, replacing any of the remaining collective horror about what had taken place at Lily's fortieth, and it allowed her father a chance to start making up for his behaviour. Sheepishly, Peter had suggested that she and Nick go out for dinner that Saturday, with him watching over Saskia. 'You mean Saskia watching over you?' Olivia had shot back, nobody bothering to argue with her.

Olivia had decided that what she needed to tell Nick required more than a dinner. It required privacy, and time, and space. So she had expedited the night away, moving it from after the centenary party to the very next weekend. She had sold it to Nick as an opportunity for them to spend twenty-four hours in bed, with the vibrator that had just arrived, and he had agreed that this was a very good idea indeed. Saskia had initially moaned at the prospect of being left with her fuckwit of a grandfather, but had quickly relaxed her resistance when she realized it meant she could essentially be alone in the house, without her annoying brother or parents there to bother her, or eat any of her protein bagels.

Olivia had chosen a hotel not too far away, a place that had a last-minute offer on, including dinner and a half-bottle of champagne and box of chocolates in the room upon arrival. She thought it was going to take more than a half-bottle of champagne to let Nick know what she needed him to, but it was at least a start, and after her gleeful shopping spree she didn't feel she could afford anything better.

Once they were there, with their tiny chocolates and thimble of champagne, Olivia was going to tell Nick everything. About

Rose, about what happened all those years ago with Stephen, and about her other intention, the one she's not yet fully formed herself. She's going to get it out in the open so she can come up with some sort of solution, like the grown-up she is. Like the adult she has only very recently become.

27

The hotel looks very little like the picture on the website, which failed to feature the giant crane behind the main building, in situ for the major refurbishment that is taking place, wing by wing, of the country-house estate. Still, as Nick drags her suitcase along the gravelly entrance, Olivia thinks she is hardly in any position to complain about something not being what it said it is. Being catfished by a hotel is the least of her worries.

'It's going to be amazing once it's done,' says the receptionist, a girl who can't be much older than Saskia. 'There's going to be a spa pool and a sauna,' she says, tapping their car registration into the computer, 'and all of the rooms will have Nespresso machines instead of Corby trouser presses.'

'Sounds wonderful,' beams Olivia, who has packed the leopard-print mini for the dinner, which looks to be taking place in a dining room with all the charm of an office canteen.

'Now, you'll be pleased to hear that you've been upgraded to a suite.' The girl looks up brightly, smiles with perfect white teeth. 'Compliments of the manager, of course, to make up for the construction outside.'

'How lovely!' nods Nick, who has spent most of the hour-long journey wondering if the hotel will have a gym (it will not, he is beginning to realize, as he notes the peeling orange paint on the walls, and the aroma of the deep red carpet, which smells of several decades' worth of company away-day events and mid-range business conferences).

'Right,' says Olivia, as the girl hands her a key attached to a giant wooden panel bearing the cryptic words 'The C r l Th t her Su te' in faded black writing.

'The Carol Thatcher Suite,' grins the girl. 'She came and did a keynote speech at an awards ceremony we hosted here back in 1997, apparently. I think it was for the local car salesmen. Anyway, she made quite the impression and ended up having to stay over in the very room that you will be sleeping in tonight. We hope that you'll have as wonderful an evening as she did!'

'Gosh,' says Nick, raising his eyebrows in what appears to be genuine excitement. 'Aren't we lucky?'

'Unfortunately the lift is out of order right now,' continues the girl, who has stood up and is motioning to the hall behind them. 'If you take the stairs through there, go up to the first floor, take the second right, and it's just down the corridor. You can't miss it.'

'Second right, just down the corridor,' repeats Nick.

'And if you have any problems, don't hesitate to dial zero on your phone and I'll be right up with whatever you need!'

Olivia thanks the girl, and watches as Nick begins to drag her wheelie suitcase in the direction of the stairs, his own overnight bag slung casually over one shoulder. She has to admit his arms are really beginning to benefit from the regular trips to CrossFit. She watches him scamper up the stairs excitedly, feels the terrible shame of all she has kept from him over the years, of how she is potentially about to upend all the building blocks of their marriage, in the Carol Thatcher Suite, of all places. She thinks of how resentful she was of her husband up until a couple of weeks ago, how amazing their relationship has been since, and how terrible it is that she might be about to ruin it just as everything has begun to go so well. Then she shakes the thoughts away. Shame hasn't been much use to her in the past, and it certainly won't help things now.

'Sometimes life isn't all rainbows and fluffy kittens,' she says to herself under her breath, as they pass a pile of bricks in the corridor. 'And that's OK.'

'Well, here we are,' Nick says, putting the key in the lock of the room, unaware of the truth bomb she's about to drop in it. 'The big reveal.' The latch turns and the door opens on to the Carol Thatcher Suite, which is as shockingly orange as its namesake (if Olivia remembers rightly from the woman's turn on *I'm a Celebrity*). There are orange carpets, orange walls, an orange quilt thrown over the tiny double bed. There is a single dark-pine wardrobe, shoved up against a wall that hosts the aforementioned Corby trouser press, probably last used when Carol's mother was still prime minister. The bathroom is a peachy shade of pink, and not in an ironic way. In the room's favour, the windows are large, and probably once commanded wonderful views of the hotel grounds . . . back when they were actually hotel grounds, as opposed to a building site.

'Well, I think we'll be very happy here,' announces Nick, flopping down on the bed. Springs creak ominously below him, while the headboard makes a thudding noise against the wall.

Olivia goes and perches on the end of the bed, looks for the half-bottle of champagne and the box of chocolates, realizes that they must have been lost in the 'upgrade'. 'Nick, I need to talk to you,' she says suddenly, because if she doesn't get round to it now, she wonders if she ever will. 'I need to tell you something that you're probably not going to like.'

'Is it that we're spending two nights here, as opposed to just the one?' She turns around and looks at him miserably as he sits up straight, concern spreading over his lovely, kind features. 'Is it something to do with the kids?' he asks, looking worried. 'Are you ill?'

'God, no,' she replies. 'It's nothing like that. It's just, I like how we've been with each other in the last few weeks, and I think I owe you the truth about something.'

'I don't know if I can deal with much more truth, Olivia,' he grimaces. 'I'm still getting to grips with the idea of your dad in a cupboard with the magician's assistant.'

'I'm being serious, Nick.' She looks away from him, notices a signed picture of Carol Thatcher in a cheap plastic frame on the MDF desk. 'I need to explain why I've not been myself recently. Or why I've been a bit too much of myself, I should probably say.'

'OK.' He relaxes against the headboard, nods his head to let her know he is ready for whatever it is she needs to tell him.

'So it turns out that the girl I went on that night out with and took drugs with . . .'

'I'm sorry, who? When you . . . what?'

'That's not really the point of the story, Nick.' Olivia grits her teeth. 'It turns out she doesn't work for *The Morning*. She works for something called Stop the Press.'

'The pink-paint people!' He looks like a child who has got a maths question right. 'I've read about them. They could do with chucking some of that over that fucker of a boss of yours.'

'Well, that's the thing. I need to talk to you about him too.' Olivia takes off her jacket, puts it on the back of a plastic chair that sits in front of the desk. Then she removes her shoes, returns to the bed, and scooches up so that she's next to Nick, feeling the mattress springs sag beneath her increasing weight. As the bed creaks, she realizes she's never cared about the number on the scales less, hasn't even bothered to look at it for the last few weeks, and that's a small win in itself.

'So a very long time ago, like, when we had only just first started going out, something happened with Stephen.'

Nick shifts ever-so-slightly away, a centimetre that feels like a mile. 'OK,' he says, clearly not OK at all. 'Go on.'

'Do you remember when he was the news editor?' Nick nods. 'He was my boss for a bit when I was a trainee, and he used to take everyone on those big boozy nights out and I'd never go because I'd heard how raucous they got, and I knew that as a woman, it wasn't a good look to get raucous. Not if you wanted to be taken seriously.' She shakes her head at the stupidity of it all, the realization that she was fighting for an impossibility from the very beginning. 'They were every Thursday, and I actually made up a netball team so that I could get out of going to these boys' evenings that he invited everyone to. Can you believe that? I fabricated an entire sports team, a completely imaginary social life, just to avoid saying the word "no". But I'd heard about these evenings. Everyone had. The next day there was enough winking and nudging for everyone to work out that they weren't discussing the state of the nation. As a rule, we women never, ever went on them, and there were so few of us there at the time it was barely noticeable, to be honest. God knows what variety of hobbies we all claimed to be committed to so we could get out of them. I even had a kitbag I kept by my desk as a sort of prop. A fucking kitbag! I mean, talk about delusional. But one week it was absolutely pouring with rain outside, blowing a fucking gale, and Stephen cornered me before I could leave. He was all like *You can't play netball in this, come out with us all instead!* And . . . I had this moment of weakness – I think I felt special, which is ridiculous I know, and I said yes. I thought that maybe it might be a bit of fun, that perhaps I could show them all that I wasn't some dry, dull graduate with a rod stuck up her arse. To think it mattered to me that Stephen saw me as fun.'

She exhales for the first time since she's begun speaking.

'And I don't know what happened, Nick. I mean I do know what happened, but I don't know how it happened, just that it happened really quickly, and I wasn't entirely on my A-game because I'd made the mistake of having one-too-many white wine spritzers, and I'd agreed to go on to this sort of nightclub that was more of a dive bar, round the corner from the office. It's been demolished now, replaced with some swish restaurant, thank god. Anyway, my memory is kind of hazy leading up to it, which they count on, don't they?'

She looks at Nick, realizes he genuinely has no idea of the 'they' she is talking about, the ones most women have to factor into their lives at every turn. But he looks like he's listening, like he's really trying to follow what she's saying, and she loves him for it.

'I went to go to the toilet. And I saw that the disabled loo was free, so I headed in there because yay, no queuing for the ladies', and then very suddenly Stephen was there, pushing in the cubicle behind me, and it was like my brain couldn't quite catch up with what was happening. It felt like a sort of fever dream. I remember him shoving the handle up, like they ask you to do in disabled loos, and I thought, "Oh, that doesn't feel so secure, maybe someone will burst in and explain to Stephen that he shouldn't be here." As if it was all a big mistake, a misunderstanding, and someone would be along any moment to make it all better and usher him out. I remember that the cubicle was filthy, the floor was wet, and I looked at my feet, I'd changed out of my heels into those bright red Converse I used to wear all the time, fucking hell I loved those, and I remember, as he pushed me against the wall, I felt really very worried about the disgustingness of the toilet and how that disgustingness was going to be transferred to my shoes, and could I perhaps put them in the washing machine or would that cause them to fall apart? That was what was going through my brain. And then I realized his tongue was in my mouth, and his hands were down my skirt, and suddenly I felt this overwhelming nausea shoot up from my stomach. Like, one minute I was fine, the next I knew I absolutely wasn't, and my body knew what it had to do even if my brain didn't. And I threw up in the toilet next to us and he started laughing, and he said, "One of the first things you need to learn in this business is how to hold your drink. The next is not to be a prick tease." Then he left and went back out and somehow I got home to that fucking flat in High Barnet, you know the one?' She looks ahead at the door, is vaguely aware of him nodding next to her. 'And the next day I don't know how I went to work. I don't know how but I did, and when I got in there he came straight up to my desk with a cup of coffee, which he placed next to me. Nice as pie, like absolutely nothing had happened. And then he said, "No hard feelings, eh? I think that was a bit of a drunken misunderstanding, but I'm prepared to let it go if you are." He was prepared to let it go if I was! Hahahaha!' She laughs like a deranged woman, which she realizes she was, to have agreed to his terms so willingly. 'And I just nodded, mutely. And then he said that my time on news was wrapping up, that I was needed on features, and thanks for everything but now was the moment for me to move on. So I nodded, and I picked up my coffee, and my bag, and I went to the features department, and the worst thing is that I actually felt relieved, because it meant that I wasn't in trouble.'

'Trouble?' Nick sits up straight. 'Why would you be in trouble?'

'Because I thought I might have led him on, Nick.' She starts to cry. 'I thought I might have inadvertently given him some sign that he'd misconstrued as an invitation into the toilet or something. I didn't know. He was senior to me, I'd seen him bawl out grown men twice my size, he was like a fucking monster. It wasn't as if I wanted to mess with him. And I know it sounds utterly pathetic to say this now, in this post-Me Too world, but I was grateful that he had put it behind him and been professional about the whole thing, because I had basically vomited in his face.'

'That fucker is lucky that's all you did, frankly.' Nick clenches a chiselled jaw in anger. 'It's the least he deserved.'

'Well yeah, but can you just for a moment appreciate how mortifying it was to have puked on my boss. And most importantly, I was so full of shame and fear that you might see it as cheating. I know, I know, that's not what you are like, but I just felt like such a fucking hopeless tit, that I had nearly fucked up my whole life with that one night out. As soon as he handed me that coffee and moved me to features, I made a decision to behave like him and just pretend that it hadn't happened. And maybe it hadn't – I trusted myself so little that there was genuinely a part of me that questioned everything I perceived as fact. Like: "Maybe you're making this up, Olivia, to cover for the fact that you're to blame for everything." Because I'd grown up in a house where black was white and white was black and if you dared say otherwise you were treated like a lunatic. I can see that now, but I couldn't back then. Plus, it came so soon after that evening we'd had, where I'd bunked off the next day, and I was scared I was going to get found out, and I suppose I had conflated one thing with another, but that's where my brain was back then. It's where my brain's been until recently, I guess. In this sort of defensive crouch, terrified of upsetting the apple cart in any way whatsoever. And so, so fucking hard on myself. Like way harder, ironically, than anyone else could ever have been. I was always so scared of people being cross with me, but all along I was brutal to myself. I was giving myself this daily dressing-down, an almost constant monstering. Nobody could have been any harsher to me than I was to myself. But I needed that job to feel like a worthy human being. Because the uni newspaper editor had told me I was really good at journalism and good was the only thing that mattered to me as a 23-year-old. If everyone else thought I was good, then I was good, right? So I saw it as another reason to do whatever he said – it was like, the least I can give this man, this company, is my loyalty. And you know, maybe that shame might have continued to have been buried deep inside me if I hadn't ended up on that night out with Rose. It seems bonkers to say now, but she really showed me how small I'd been making myself, how narrow the margins I've been living between have been. And I told her about that moment with Stephen. I told her because it turns out her own mother had had a run-in with him too, a different kind of run-in that you can't even call a run-in because he was basically stalking her in the name of investigative reporting, and the story he did on her led to her actually taking her own life. And now I just feel fucking stupid, like fuck, had I spoken out back then, maybe this guy completely devoid of any morals wouldn't be in charge of *The Morning*.'

'Don't put that on yourself.' Nick is quiet, to the point. 'You are not responsible for the behaviour of that prick, Olivia.'

'Yeah, but I am responsible for my own behaviour. I need to be properly honest, for the first time in my life. I've always tried to be nice and sweet and caring, but actually there's nothing nice or sweet or caring about silencing yourself so that a load of wankers think you're likeable and easy. Do you know where being likeable and easy led me to? That night out with Rose, and the verge of a bloody breakdown, that's where. I need to be able to deal with the fact that sometimes, not everything is perfect. Not everything is ideal. More often than not, it's the opposite of ideal, and do you know what? That's OK. So this is me, standing before you, or sitting before you, on a creaky bed in a bright orange room named after a reality TV star from the noughties, hoping you might understand why I've been so vague and distant these last few . . .' She puts her hands up in surrender. 'Years? Decades? I'm trying to explain how my search for perfection has ironically led to me being a miserable old cow with all the wrong priorities and . . . oh god, I hate that I just called myself a miserable old cow! I'm done with being beastly to myself. Done with it! And I want you to know that I can deal with the consequences of my dishonesty. Whatever you decide going forward with our marriage, I will be able to cope with it.' Olivia stops, as Nick grabs hold of her hand in his. 'Aren't you angry?'

'Why would I be?' Nick looks at his wife, his eyebrows knitting into a concerned crease. 'You've just told me about something really shit that happened to you. Did you expect me to get up and walk out? Because if you did, then you must think pretty badly of me.'

'It's not you I think badly of, Nick, it's myself.'

'Yeah, well you should have a bit more belief in yourself because from where I'm sitting, the only person that story reflects badly on is Stephen. I wish you had told me before. We could have done something.'

'Like what?' Olivia looks out the window as she hears the sound of a drill strike up.

'We could have reported him!'

'Come on, you know that if I had raised a complaint, everybody would have questioned how I got myself into the situation with him, instead of looking at how he behaved. Even I was ashamed about it until Rose knocked some sense into me.'

'But you could have told me, Olivia.' He drops her hand and she momentarily worries that she has lost him . . . before realizing that he is only doing it so he can put his arm around her. 'I hate that you didn't think you could tell me.'

'I genuinely believed I was somehow responsible for it. I shouldn't have gone for a drink with them all, let alone several drinks. I shouldn't have gone on to that dive bar with them. I shouldn't have worn a skirt, and I shouldn't have gone to the disabled loo instead of the ladies' loos because couldn't all these things be misconstrued as come-ons? And I hate that I really believed that kind of bollocks until recently. I hate that I've felt responsible for the fucking terrible behaviour of someone like Stephen, and I hate that Stephen isn't even the only person to have made me feel that way. I hate that this shit still goes on, and I hate that I have only just properly started to realize it now, at the age of forty-four. And I hate that my sense of belief in myself is so fucking flimsy that I haven't been able to tell you this, that I am genuinely convinced that when I reveal anything about myself that isn't perfect and shiny and good, everyone around me will scarper. You'll all up sticks and abandon me at the first opportunity.'

'You know that's not what a healthy relationship is about, right?' Nick shifts round the bed so he is facing her directly. 'You know when we made those vows eight hundred years ago, we promised to stay with each other in sickness and in health, for richer and for poorer?' Olivia nods. 'I didn't say, "I promise only to love you if you are nice and polite at all times, do all the cleaning, cook all the dinners, and by the way can you make sure that you are always wearing a sexy leopard-print minidress too?" That's not what a marriage is about, Olivia. Real love is unconditional.'

Olivia shudders. 'Yes, well don't forget I grew up in a house where love was absolutely conditional, on being a good girl. On not being any trouble, and not adding to the already quite substantial pile of shit that my poor mum had to deal with. Speaking of which, I need to tell you that her new man, Clive, is the dick who felt me up on the train.'

'You're not serious?'

'I'm only serious from now on, Nick.' She lies back, stretches her legs into her husband's lap. He begins rubbing the balls of her feet, and Olivia starts talking again. 'I don't know quite what to do with the information right now, but I guess I'm going to have to figure it out. As much as she gets on my tits, she has a right to know she's going out with a sex pest.'

'Your mum's never been that great at handling reality, has she?'

'Nope. She must have had one seriously fucked-up childhood.'

'I feel really sorry for her, you know. Like, your painful obsession with perfection, you get it from her. Of course you want everything to be good, because that's all you've known: the need to make it look as if everything is tickety-fucking-boo, even when it's falling apart. She grew up with alcoholics, married one, and then she felt this desperate need to hide it from you and Lily. And then when you were unwell, she freaks out because here, again, is evidence that all is not tickety-fucking-boo. It's classic.'

'God, you're so right, I've never seen it that way before. How do you know all of this?'

'Because when you're a secondary-school teacher you have to

essentially become a psychotherapist in order to deal with thirty thirteen-year-olds and all the weird dynamics they bring with them to the classroom.'

'Wow,' says Olivia, who had until recently credited her husband with all the emotional intelligence of a fruit fly. 'I'm impressed, Nick.'

'And also, because I'm kind of outside it. Which is why I can say with some confidence that the notion that you are the difficult kid while Lily is the sweet-natured easy one is absolute bollocks.'

'Lily is pretty awesome, though. I'd move her in if I could, instead of Dad.'

'She is great, I feel blessed to have a sister-in-law I actually want to spend time with. And it's nice having her round a couple of evenings a week. The kids love it.'

'I love it. She loves it too, bizarrely. She genuinely seems to enjoy looking after them instead of simply using it as an emotional transaction.'

'Maybe we could go on some dates when she's here? And maybe we could talk about what you might want to do about *The Morning*, and working with Stephen. It'd be OK if you wanted to take some time away from it to figure out a plan, you know? We could make ends meet.'

'That's sweet, but we both know we couldn't.' Olivia feels a sickening swirling in her stomach about their finances. She hates this sensation, the one you get when you realize your wants and needs aren't compatible with your actual circumstances. 'Still, that doesn't mean we can't start rearranging the ends a bit better, so that they actually work for us.'

'Profound,' says Nick, who is still rubbing her feet, his hands warm on her skin.

'I feel like I should have probably had this conversation with you about twenty years ago.' Olivia sighs. 'It might have saved a lot of bother.'

'Yeah, but you can't figure any of this stuff out without first having to go right through it. You can lead a horse to water, but you can't make it drink. Or in the case of your dad, you can, but you get what I mean.' He stands up, goes into the bathroom where she hears some taps begin to run. Then he comes back in, sits next to her. 'I thought you'd want me to do that, given I'd just been rubbing your feet. Anyway, I guess what I'm trying to say is that love isn't about asking the impossible of each other. It is the opposite of that. There aren't clauses and caveats to love. It doesn't have a price tag on it. It's saying, "I will love you when you're being brilliant, and I will love you when you're being a dickhead, and I will love you when you make mistakes, even if you can't love yourself through those mistakes." ' He takes her face in his hands, moves closer. 'My love for you is unconditional, Olivia Greenwood. It really is. I love you when you are laughing, I love you when you are crying, I love you for your flaws and your fuck-ups as well as your innumerable plus sides. I love all of you. Not just the botoxed bits.'

She pulls back in mock horror. 'How do you know I get botox?'

'Because a few years ago your eyebrows would have raised when you asked that kind of question, but right now your face has stayed almost exactly the same. Except for the tears, which are making your mascara run down your face.' Olivia goes to wipe her cheeks, but he stops her. 'You don't need to do that. You don't need to wipe the mess off your face for me. You don't have to wipe up any mess for me. You can just be you, with mascara down your face, and I promise you, Olivia Greenwood, that I'm going nowhere.'

'Well, that's just about the nicest thing anyone has ever said to me,' she hiccups, tears starting afresh. 'Shame about the setting, eh?'

'I think the room is perfect, because with the exception of that awful signed photograph grinning at us,' and at this he gets up, and places it face down on the MDF desk, 'we're the only people in it.' He opens the wardrobe, as if to check nobody's hiding there. 'Yep, only us, though this seems to have been stashed away in here.' He pulls out a miniature bottle of Prosecco, shakes it as if he's a Formula One driver on the podium at the Monaco Grand Prix and not a teacher from Haywards Heath bunking up for a night in a cheap hotel somewhere off the A22. Then he removes the cork, unleashing the contents of the tiny bottle all over Olivia.

'Nick!' she squeals, laughing.

'Oops!' he mock apologizes. 'Now you're going to have to get out of those wet clothes and into the bath I'm running you in the 1970s en suite.'

Olivia reaches for the phone by the bed. She picks up the receiver, dials zero, waits for the girl on reception to answer. 'Oh hi,' she smiles, as Nick goes to check the temperature of the water. 'I think we're going to need a bit more of that Prosecco. And can I check that you do room service?'

28

Olivia wakes with a cracking headache and a vague memory of her husband making her come with both his tongue and the new vibrator, at the same time. A milky, subdued grey light seeps through the side of the orange curtains, giving no clue whatsoever to the time of day, only the murkiness of it. Olivia props herself up in bed, reaches for the light switch on the bedside lamp, remembers too late that it is one of those old-fashioned switches on the neck of the lamp, knocks it over trying to get at it, and then effs and blinds as she realizes she is going to have to get up and turn the overhead light on.

'Fuck,' groans Nick, as the unforgiving strip lighting roars into action. 'This is like waking up in your worst nightmare.' They both survey the room, the bright orange walls, the empty bottles of Prosecco and wine that cover the desk, the bowls of half-eaten chips stacked on a tray next to the door. With a start, Olivia notices the vibrator, flung on the floor on top of one of Nick's heated back pads, which he has started wearing to keep up with all the youngsters at CrossFit.

'Well,' she says, picking up her phone from the bedside table and getting back into bed, 'I think we might have made a mistake ordering that fifteenth bottle of wine.'

'Don't joke.' Nick pulls the covers over his face to block out the light.

'No joke is the fifteen calls from Jonathan's mother that I've managed to miss.' Olivia drops the phone on the bed and puts her head in her hands. 'Fuck, fuck, fuck, it's ten a.m. and we need to have left about half an hour ago.'

'We didn't say when we'd pick Jack up, did we?' Nick reluctantly reappears from beneath the covers.

'No, but clearly Jack has taken matters into his own hands.' Olivia picks the phone back up, begins reading the message from Jonathan's mother. '*I think it would be prudent if you came and retrieved your son as soon as possible. I'm sure it's out of character but he has been extremely rude to Jonathan and made him cry.*'

Nick snorts with laughter.

'Come on, up.' Olivia pulls the duvet off her husband fully, is reminded by the big red welts on his body that she had enjoyed a moment of biting his nipples, and giving him some love bites. 'No time for a shower, we need to go get him.'

'Would you chill out, babe? I thought we agreed on no more abandoning our own needs to meet everybody else's. The world won't end if we have a wash and delay "retrieving" our child by another twenty minutes.'

'I suppose you're right.' Olivia shrugs and heads for her wheelie suitcase, which lies flung open on the floor, easily reached by any bed bugs that might also inhabit the Carol Thatcher Suite. She gets on her knees, begins searching for the outfit she had packed for today, realizes with a resigned groan that she has forgotten to pack it. 'Well, it hardly matters how clean I am, given that I'm going to have to wear my leopard-print minidress until we get home anyway. I can hardly wear what I was in yesterday, because it's damp and smells like a bar after you sprayed that cheap Prosecco all over it.'

'May have tasted cheap,' says Nick, making his way to the

bathroom, 'but I bet you it was fucking expensive, given that they insisted on charging us fifty per cent extra just to have our dinner in the room.'

'Are we fucking mad?' Olivia elbows him aside to get to her toothbrush. 'We must have spent a fortune.'

'It was worth it, because I for one had a great time.' Nick turns on the shower, tweaks his nipples in the manner of a camp pantomime dame. 'God bless the Carol Thatcher Suite, and all who lay in her!'

The front door of Jonathan's house is flanked by beautifully clipped bay trees, the stained glass kept squeaky clean and the door knocker perfectly polished. There's one of those pretentious year-round wreaths perched on it. Olivia hoicks down the skirt of her dress, presses the Ring doorbell, and does a curtsy at the sing-song tune it plays. Then she waves at Nick, who is staying in the car because the two of them have decided – quite wisely, Olivia thinks – that the love bite on his neck is far more embarrassing than the animal-print frock that's already verging on risqué.

The door opens and Olivia is immediately confronted by the sour face of Jonathan's mother. She is wearing soft, buttery dark green yoga leggings – 'forest green' is how Olivia imagines this woman would describe the tone – teamed with a matching cashmere hoodie. Olivia thinks that Jonathan's mum should really look a bit more cheerful, since she can clearly afford athleisure wear that costs more than a year's membership at Fitness First.

'I'm Sally,' she says, handing Jack's overnight bag to Olivia as if it contains hazardous waste.

'Morning, Sally, I'm Olivia.' She holds the backpack in front of her hips, hoping it might at least disguise the sluttiness of her skirt. 'Sorry I missed your calls last night, my husband and I were having a rare evening away.'

'How lovely for you.' Sally's lip curls in distaste. 'Now you're parenting again, I take it you'll have the appropriate conversations with Jack about his behaviour?'

'Of course, Sally, of course.' Olivia will not give this woman the pleasure of a rise.

'Jack!' Sally calls into the hallway, which is decorated in huge black and white portraits of the family, clearly taken on a professional shoot. Olivia thanks the Lord that in all her people-pleasing lunacy, she never forced the Greenwoods into such a cringeworthy endeavour. 'Your mother's here.'

'Thank god!' Jack comes rushing out the door and into Olivia's arms. 'Why are you wearing that dress again, Mum?' He shakes his head in genuine bewilderment. 'It wasn't as if you had much luck the last time you wore it.'

'Lovely to see you too, Jack,' Olivia smiles. 'Say thank you to Sally for having you.'

'Thanks for letting me stay,' he huffs.

'I'm so sorry, Sally, he's clearly tired. I better be getting him home.' Olivia bundles him down the immaculate path, aware that her skirt is riding up. She lets it, reasoning that it's probably as much arse as uptight Sally will see all year.

'So what happened?' asks Olivia, as she pulls her seat belt around her.

'Nothing,' he sulks, looking out the window.

'Well, something clearly went on because I woke up to a load of missed calls from Jonathan's forest-green fairy mother.'

'It was nothing, she probably called by mistake.'

'Jack.' Olivia turns uncomfortably in the front seat so she's facing him. Some things are just more important than middle-aged lower back pain. 'I know how much it meant to you to be invited on this sleepover. I know how hard you've found it dealing with Jonathan and the other football boys. And I know how bloody awful it is when you've been looking forward to something for ages and it doesn't go to plan. A bit like how Granny and Lily must have felt when Grandad had his funny turn last weekend.'

'I didn't mean to upset him, OK? I thought I was doing the right thing.' He lowers his chin, as if he's about to cry.

'Listen, whatever happened, it's not going to change the fact that Dad and I love you, Jack.'

'That's right, kiddo,' says Nick, eyes firmly on the road. 'There's nothing that you could do that would upset me, not even if you switched allegiance to United.'

'As if,' tuts Jack. A quiet envelops the car, and Olivia allows it to. She knows, now, that you can't rush anyone into Speaking Their Truth (™). They pass two roundabouts and a junction, and are almost home when Jack starts talking.

'We'd been telling each other ghost stories, and I go to switch the light off, and he starts to cry. He says that he can't sleep without a night light on, and I say I can't sleep with one on, and then because he's sobbing so much I do what he wants and when I turn the light back on he's sucking his thumb and snuggling a BLANKET.' Jack lets out a frustrated snort. 'I mean, he's the leader of the football boys so I express my surprise that he still sucks his thumb and has a blanket, and do you know what he says?'

Olivia turns round and looks expectantly at her son.

'He says, "Actually, this isn't a blanket, this is my SHMOOSHIE."' Jack huffs. 'As if I'd done this terrible thing by calling it a blanket. As if he hadn't once tried to flush my head down the loo during a lunch break for being a wimp after the ball hit me in the face.'

'He did what?!' Nick nearly drives the car into the wrong lane in shock.

'Dad, chill out, it was ages ago, in Year Five.'

'Year Five was last year,' says Nick.

'Exactly, ages ago. Anyway, he was sobbing into his Shmooshie hysterically and obviously his mum heard him because, frankly, he was making one hell of a noise. I'm surprised you didn't hear him at your hotel.' At this, Jack widens his eyes in amazement. 'She comes in and she puts on this babyish voice, "My darling boy, whatever is the matter?" And he says that I've been scaring him with terrifying ghost stories all night, and that I'd called him a baby and laughed at him and his Shmooshie. I mean, I might have been laughing in my head, but I'd never have been so stupid as to do it to his face.'

'Jack,' Olivia winces. 'It's not OK that he tried to flush your head down the toilet, and it's also not OK to laugh at him for having a Shmooshie.'

'I told you, Mum, I didn't laugh at him to his face, just in my head! Also, his mum was totally over the top. She went off on one, and then his dad comes in and starts huffing at Jonathan for being a wuss, and then the mum and the dad are shouting at each other and Jonathan's crying and I say, "Jonathan used to bully me, you know?" It just came out of me. I don't know why I said it.'

'Maybe because it was true?' suggests Olivia.

'Yeah, well at that his mum really loses it, she says I'm rude and it shouldn't surprise her, given that I have a mum who sent such a rude message to the class WhatsApp group, and Jonathan went and slept in with his mum and the dad went to the spare room and I switched the light off and had quite a good night's kip on the trundle on the floor. It's just a shame you couldn't have come and got me a bit earlier this morning. I felt pretty lonely waiting for you to turn up.'

Olivia whimpers a bit as her heart strings are yet again pulled. 'Jack, you should have told us about what Jonathan did in Year Five.'

'What difference would it have made if I did?' Jack stares sullenly out the car window. 'It's not as if you or Dad would have been able to do anything, you're always both so busy with work or going to the gym or whatever. Plus, you'd only have made it worse. You're probably going to make it worse now, I shouldn't have said anything. I shouldn't have thought it would be a good idea to copy you.'

'Copy me?'

'Yeah, you've been happier since you started telling everyone what you think. I figured if I did the same, I'd be happier too. Maybe I'd feel like less of a freak.'

'Jack,' rasps Nick. 'You mustn't speak like that about yourself. You're not a freak, you're epic.'

'Yeah, well, I don't feel like it. Wherever I go, at school or at home, I'm the annoying kid everyone wants to go away.'

'That's not true, darling,' says Olivia. 'We don't want you to go away. WE love you. And we want you to feel able to tell us anything.'

Olivia looks down at her stupid leopard-print dress, feels in this moment the stinging hypocrisy of her endless criticism of her own parents.

'It doesn't matter, you'd just think it's stupid football stuff anyway. It's not as important as your work or your weightlifting or whatever it is you do, Dad, at that stupid gym.'

'But it does matter, Jack.' Olivia stares straight at him, even if he won't return her gaze. 'If it matters to you then it matters to us. It's not for me and Dad to decide whether something is or isn't important to you. It's just our job to support you through whatever it is you're experiencing.'

'What I'm experiencing, Mum, is how annoying you're being right now. You wouldn't understand what it's like dealing with bullies.'

'You'd be surprised, darling. I know a thing or two about people like Jonathan. And I know about *not* knowing how to deal with them. You're right to want to stand up for yourself, Jack. You've just got to go about it in a way that doesn't leave you feeling worse than before.'

Jack rolls his eyes in defensive irritation. 'Well, if you're so smart when it comes to things like this, what's the right way to stand up to someone like Jonathan?'

'You definitely don't have to go to his for a sleepover,' says Olivia, as they pull up outside the house. 'When people are horrible to you and then they're suddenly nice to you, you have every right to stay well away from them, even if it's a bit confusing because their being nice to you suddenly feels good. It's understandable that you want to carry on pleasing them, especially if they've been bullying you. But if someone has been nasty to you, it's almost always got nothing to do with you, and everything to do with them. It sounds like Jonathan has some pretty tricky stuff happening at home, so maybe he hasn't learned that it's not OK to take that out on other people. But when we are empathetic people, like you and I are, we find it hard to see that. We want to take everybody's negative energy away from them, to make them feel better – or we tell ourselves we're the reason for that negativity. But that's not our job. It's not our job at all.'

Olivia looks at Jack, sees the penny drop. As his eyes widen in a sort of wonder, she thinks for a moment that she might be beginning to understand too. That she has parented well today, and learned a little about herself, to boot.

Then he opens his mouth, and the truth comes out.

'What's Auntie Lily doing in the drive?' he says, screwing up his eyes. 'And why is she waving the mop around like that?'

29

'Sass called me last night,' explains Lily, when they get in. 'Everything's OK, she just needed a bit of help with Dad.'

'With Dad?' Olivia scrunches her nose up, pulls down her skirt for what feels like the seventy-eighth time that morning. 'What the hell?'

'Looks like you might have needed a bit of help too, Nick,' Lily says, spotting the dark purple bruise on his neck. 'Did you get into a fight with a leech?'

'Eww, Dad,' says Jack, now noticing the mark on his father. 'What happened?'

'How about we go and play a game of FIFA?' asks Nick, deftly changing the subject.

'Yes, and while you're doing that,' says Lily, turning to her sister, 'how about you come through to the kitchen with me?'

It is a command rather than a question. Olivia follows Lily into the immaculate kitchen, the only thing out of place a clear council recycling bag groaning with empty ale bottles.

'So it turns out that Dad is on the booze again in a big way.' Lily sighs. 'This is what I found in his shed. Saskia called me late last night because he was completely pissed and she didn't know what to do about it. She was really upset, Olivia, sobbing. He'd passed out in the garden in the cold with a fag in his hand, and she was terrified he was going to freeze to death.'

'Oh my god.' Olivia presses her hands to her face. Why

hadn't Saskia felt able to call her parents? 'I shouldn't have left her with him. It was so irresponsible of me, I don't know what I was thinking. Poor Saskia, I need to check on her.' She starts to make her way to the stairs, only to stop abruptly when she sees Lily shaking her head. Her sister finally props the mop against the kitchen counter and motions for Olivia to join her sitting down at the table.

'I think Dad's drinking is the least of your problems right now,' Lily says, lowering her voice and leaning in to take Olivia's hand. 'When I got here, Saskia looked a wreck. So exhausted and shaky. She'd managed to haul him on to the sofa in here where he had very charmingly thrown up, thankfully mostly over himself. Anyway, she was obsessively cleaning, I mean obsessively. Like removing-the-limescale-from-the-taps kind of obsessive. It was like she was trying to bleach away the madness of Dad. I asked her if she'd had dinner yet because she looked absolutely manic, Olivia, and she just clammed up completely, froze. She was like, "Yeah, I ate loads earlier, I'm not hungry," which was the biggest load of overcompensating bollocks I'd heard since Mum told me she was throwing me a fortieth birthday party.' She moves her chair in closer to Olivia, grips her hand a little harder. 'Listen, sis, when you're sixteen and your parents have gone away for the night you should not be choosing to polish the kitchen surfaces, do you get what I'm trying to say?' Lily rubs her eyes. 'I think Saskia is unwell. I think she might have a problem . . . you know, like the one you had when you were younger.'

Olivia gulps hard, swallowing back all her shame and the temptation to spiral into a pit of self-loathing.

'I'm sorry, can you say that again?' She shifts back in her chair, removes her hand from her sister's.

'I think Saskia is unwell,' Lily repeats.

Olivia wants this to not be true. She wants there to be some other, more benign reason for her daughter's behaviour, for the washed-out look that has been on her face for the last few weeks. But even as she acknowledges this, she feels the prickly resistance drain out of her.

As Olivia surveys the sparkling kitchen, she wonders: how had she not realized this about Saskia sooner? And yet as she catches a whiff of the beer from last night, Olivia sees how disingenuous she is being. Because she did realize it, didn't she – how could she have not? The protein bagels, the obsession with football training and the A grades – telltale traits of perfectionism. Olivia had seen them, and like her mother before her, she had chosen to gloss over them, to view them as naturally occurring parts of Saskia's personality, rather than the toxic by-product of believing that your personality alone is not enough.

'Oh my god,' whispers Olivia, placing her hand on her chest in order to try and contain the burning feeling rising there. 'Oh my god. Saskia is me, and I've become our mother.' She tries not to lose herself in the horror of her sister being able to acknowledge this thing that she could not. 'Can you believe that I actually thought the house was suddenly sparkling clean because Dad and Nick had developed a new-found respect for me after I stopped sugar-coating everything? Jesus, it didn't occur to me for one moment that I'd simply handed all my people-pleasing qualities on to poor *Saskia* instead.' Olivia shakes her head. 'How could one woman be so fucking stupid?'

'Woah, maybe go easy on yourself there, the last time I checked you had a husband slash co-parent on board for this journey. And your people pleasing isn't all horrible, you know. There's some light to that shadow side. Like . . .' She goes to think, comes up short.

'We're survivors,' says Olivia. 'Us people pleasers, we're survivors. We'll do anything to stay alive, to keep going, because we don't want to be alone. We're terrified of death, of missing out. And maybe that worked for me, in a weird way. It stopped me from taking the illness to its inevitable conclusion. I just transferred all my obsessive control over food into my obsessive control over people and making them happy. Or not making them cross. But I've just handed it all down to Saskia.' She thinks she's going to be sick, and clearly looks that way too.

'Hey, stop that. You're not solely responsible for the well-being of everyone in this house. We need to get Dad some proper help. And when I say "we", I mean "we", not just you. I've been pretty negligent on that front and left it all to you, but it's not fair, as you've got so much shit on and I'm just . . .' Lily puffs her cheeks out in frustration. 'Chakra reading.'

'I can't believe I couldn't see what was happening to Saskia.' Olivia appreciates Lily's offer to help their dad, but she can't think about him now. 'I should have been a bit more savvy, given the fact I've spent most of my adult life in seething resentment at Mum for not taking my eating disorder seriously. For not taking me seriously. Or for taking me too seriously, and dismissing me as a crazy drama queen.'

'*Psychology 101*,' Lily says. 'If we don't get therapy, we will unwittingly recreate the circumstances of our traumatic childhoods in order to try and understand why they happened. This is all textbook, frankly.'

'Have you and Nick been secretly doing psychoanalysis together behind my back?' Olivia thinks today might be the day that her horror finally manages to break through the botox and create a permanent crease on her forehead. 'Like an affair, only with conversations about Freud instead of hot sex?'

'I'm not going to dignify that with a response. Can we talk about how you direct all your negative energy towards Mum but seem to forget that you had a father who could have also noticed your eating disorder and tried to help you? A father who is currently sleeping off a huge hangover in your shed.'

'Wow, I didn't realize that my mental health was under the microscope as well as Saskia's.'

'Don't do that. I didn't traipse all the way over here on my weekend to have a fight with you.'

'Sorry.' Olivia shakes her head and hopes that in doing so she will also shake off some of the resistance she feels to her little sister, sitting here psychoanalysing her.

'I'm just trying to say that you're mega-hard on Mum but you forgive that loser a whole raft of things. Tina wasn't perfect, far from it. But for all her faults, she was actually *there* for our childhoods. She was there in the morning when we got up, she was there in the evening before we went to bed, even if she was sometimes late because of an overrunning board meeting. She was there on the weekends taking us to clubs and swimming and sleepovers. If he'd showed up more, we might have felt more loved. She wasn't drinking her time away in the pub, or running away with work, like Dad. Is it any wonder she was a bitter old cow, given the amount she had to put up with from him? And yes, she shouldn't have taken it out on you, of course, but I'm guessing that she was only doing what she learned in her own childhood, which was to blame the most spirited girl in the family for all of said family's ills.' Lily pauses, lets that sit with her sister for a while. 'And you were the most spirited girl in our family, Olivia.' She points a half-bitten fingernail at her big sister. 'You were the brave one, the one who told them the truths they couldn't face seeing themselves. Do you remember when we went on that holiday to Majorca, and they woke us up arguing because Dad had clearly been drinking? And you started yelling at them to stop? And then it was all "Olivia is making a fuss, why does she always throw tantrums", even though all you were doing was responding to their shitty behaviour? You always stood up for me, you always stood up for us, you always called out their unhealthy behaviour and they couldn't deal with it so you became the black sheep. You became the problem. But you weren't the problem – you were the solution, if only we'd seen your illness for what it was. A sort of barometer of all our dysfunctionality.'

Olivia can't believe it's taken her so long to see this: that rather than being a difficult child, she was just a lightning rod for her parents. The night out with Rose has restored her to the spirited soul she had been before she felt she had to start people pleasing. The lie isn't this new, honest version of Olivia, but the one who had existed for several decades until she accepted Rose's cannabis gummy.

'Have you heard of the fight, flight and freeze trauma responses?' Lily continues. 'They're what happens to our nervous systems when we run into a situation that is dangerous for us. They're like acute stress responses. But did you know there's a fourth one, people don't talk about quite so much?'

Olivia looks blankly at her sister.

'Fawn. That's the fourth trauma response, the one where instead of fighting or running away from the source of danger, you try to sweet-talk it.'

'Oh,' says Olivia, shifting in her seat.

'And fawn is your response, Olivia. The way you've always tried to solve the problem of our family has been to make it yours alone to nurture. But you can't make people love you by being a doormat. They just step all over you even more.'

'Yeah, I think I'm starting to believe that now. Why do you have such a good handle on it all, though?'

'I used all my savings on really great therapy and learned to set boundaries. You used yours to go to university.'

'Well, that worked out great for me, didn't it. Maybe that's what we need to do for Saskia,' says Olivia, rising from her chair. 'I need to speak to her. That's all that matters. Did she tell you anything? Did she admit to having a problem? You need to tell me what you found out.'

'Woah, slow down there, tiger!' Lily motions for Olivia to sit.

Olivia is about to open her mouth to speak, but is beaten to it by her sister, who is clearly on her own truth-telling mission.

'She didn't admit anything to me, I'm just stating what I can so obviously see. But before you go in there?' Olivia nods her head mutely at her sister. 'Please can you promise me that you will remember this one, really important thing. That however unforgiving you are of Mum? That's how unforgiving you'll always be of yourself. You hold the two of you to this utterly impossible standard of motherhood, of womanhood, one that fails to acknowledge the reality of being a human. Yes, Mum was a bit of a dick. Yes, she can still be a bit of a dick. But don't make the mistake of thinking that's *all* she is. And don't make the mistake of holding yourself entirely accountable for what Saskia is going through right now. You bear some responsibility for it, of course, but it's the responsibility of holding her through it, rather than ignoring it by pretending everything's perfect. Do not go into a shame spiral and make Saskia's problems all your fault, because you know how well that goes, right?'

Olivia nods. Lily rubs her eyes with the heels of her hands. 'We're not children any more, Olivia. We don't have to subscribe to this fairytale notion of perfection and happiness that our mum tried to push on us because that was the only survival strategy she knew. Imagine being a young woman in the sixties and seventies? We think it was all flower power and the Beatles, but they'd only just invented the bloody contraceptive pill. They'd only just been given the right to legally have an abortion. It was basically the Dark Ages. We're all really mean to Boomers. We think they've had everything handed to them on a silver platter. But fucking hell, they didn't even have period pants, Olivia.'

'Yeah, it does sound pretty bleak when you put it like that.' Olivia goes to give her sister a hug, rubs her back. 'I'm glad you're here, Lil. I'm so glad you're here.'

'I'm glad you are too,' says Nick, bowling into the kitchen, holding his phone aloft in the air. 'Because I think you're going to want to be together when you see this.'

30

A funny thing happens, as they gather round the television and watch Stephen interviewed triumphantly on a popular Sunday politics show, gloating about *The Morning*'s exposé of the sexual misconduct of various Tory politicians. Olivia understands, suddenly, what it's all been about. Every wandering hand, every uninvited kiss, every silenced complaint, every anguished rumination . . . it has all led up to this one, gobsmacking moment, where she watches her misogynist boss paint himself as some sort of feminist and saviour of women on national telly.

'Hang the fuck on,' says Lily, pointing at the picture that has flashed up on-screen.

'Well, isn't that a surprise?' Olivia tries to stop the smile from creeping on to her face, as she recognizes the Tory councillor who has just been named by Stephen.

'That's CLIVE,' nods Nick.

'Such a shame.' Olivia tries her best to be sincere.

Lily sighs. 'Poor Mum, she really does have terrible taste.'

'She really does,' says Olivia.

'Well, maybe it's better for her to find out now than any further down the line.' Nick's voice drops in genuine sympathy for Tina, and somehow, Olivia loves him even more for it.

'Quite right, babes, quite right.' Olivia nods along, tries not to appear too delighted. Just last night, she had been beating herself up for her dishonest people pleasing, the manipulative quality to her niceness. But what, exactly, was a bit of polite silence compared to some of the shit that blokes like Stephen and Clive were pulling on a daily basis? How did they find the bare-faced cheek to wander around ignoring their *actual* crimes and misdemeanours? Stephen is passing judgement on the screen before her over the group of Tory councillors for their 'deeply inappropriate' WhatsApp messages about female party members. Olivia laughs at the television, a kind of plaintive hoot at the audacity of it all. What delightful hypocrisy. What incredible chutzpah.

'We're proud of the quality of our investigative reporting on this story,' she hears Stephen say smugly to the young female reporter. 'The values of integrity and truth-telling that our journalists have displayed with this incredible bit of reportage are the same principles that have established *The Morning* over the past one hundred years – principles that we hope to take into the next one hundred years, unlike the Tory party, clearly.'

But what, really, does any of it matter when her darling daughter is upstairs, miserable and starving and alone? Olivia was damned if she was going to spend any more time feeling guilty for the decades of her life she had spent silently in submission to the patriarchal status quo. She can't go back to her life as it was before – something in her has shifted. And she was also damned if she was going to continue to allow Saskia to suffer the consequences of it.

'Let's not waste any more time on these idiots,' Olivia announces decisively, turning the television off. Then she drops the remote on the sofa, and storms upstairs to Saskia.

She finds her daughter curled up in bed, her face lit by the screen of her iPhone. As Olivia opens the door, Saskia's eyes don't divert from the device in front of her, her apparent imperviousness one of those hard-won medals of adolescence. Olivia remembers wearing it proudly when she herself was a teenager – the way she would shut down her mother for coming too close, and then be angry with her when she had the audacity to subsequently stay away. She knows she has to tread a fine line with Saskia. She knows because it was what she needed of her own mother – for Tina to listen to her rage and take it on while loving her through it regardless. To be there.

As she approaches Saskia now, Olivia has her mother's voice in her head. 'Don't make it all about you,' chastises Tina, for once actually saying something helpful. 'But remember,' cautions Rose, the other voice on her shoulder, 'that the way you handle this next conversation *will* be about you: it will be about you, and Saskia, and Tina and Lily; it will be about all the women in your family, the many generations that have come before and didn't get the support they needed, and all the ones who will come in the future but will. If *you* get this right.'

Olivia Greenwood nods at all the different women on her shoulders, the ones she doesn't want to let down. She takes a deep breath. She feels the fear, and then she does it anyway.

'I'm really sorry that you had to see Grandad like that last night,' Olivia says, sitting on the edge of her daughter's bed. 'It must have been scary.' Saskia pulls her feet up towards her chest and away from her mother, her eyes still steadfastly on the screen.

'I mean, it must be pretty disorientating generally, living in this family, with me being a bit erratic lately, and a drunk grandad living in the garden shed.' Olivia waits a moment. She's clearly not going to get anything out of Saskia that easily. 'I'm really sorry you didn't feel able to call me or Dad last night, but I'm really glad that you had Auntie Lily to phone. That's good.

I'm pleased she could help you. I'm hoping maybe we can get a bit closer as a family and I will stop being so obsessed with work and focus on what really matt—'

'Will you just stop?' Saskia drops her phone on the floor with a carpeted thud.

'I can stop, darling,' Olivia nods, compliant. 'I can do that and we can try and communica—'

'You can't, though, can you?' Saskia turns around to her mother, furious. 'You can't communicate in any mode other than high-pitched anxiety. You wang on about how awful Granny is and you think we can't hear it or understand what you're going on about but we're not stupid. And from where I'm sitting you're just as bad. You're just as controlling, and desperate to pretend that we're a nice normal family.'

'That's very perceptive of you, Sass. I wish I'd had your awareness when I was your age. It's taken me this long to even wonder what a normal family is.'

'One that doesn't go around all the time pretending that everything is perfect. One that doesn't need everything to be fucking faultless from morning until night. One that—'

'You shouldn't swear.'

'Oh my god, there you go again. Do you seriously think that your sixteen-year-old daughter doesn't swear? And calling me Sass, like we're some bestie mother-and-daughter duo with cute nicknames for each other. You have no idea about me, none at all.' Saskia sits up, puts her arms defensively around her chest. 'Honestly, how do you think it's felt to watch my mum go through some sort of breakdown? You're having a midlife crisis, fine, you're going through menopause, fine, but fucking hell, do we have to hear about it all the time? You'd think your generation invented midlife or something. Well done, you've survived a drop in oestrogen, now would you mind pulling your head out your arse and paying some attention to the rest of us?'

Olivia makes a bright 'hmmm' noise. She knows what she wants to say: that she's spent most of her life paying attention to the rest of them, that her obsession with everyone else's self-worth but her own is why she's had this little public breakdown lately . . . but she also knows that saying all of this will only make things ten times worse, and very possibly cut her off from Saskia for another sixteen years. And as she watches her daughter's face contort in loathing for her, she realizes that this is not her battle to fight. It's Saskia's.

'That's pretty bloody wise of you. You know, I'd be angry with me too if I were you. You're right that you're almost an adult, and I should start treating you like one.' Olivia shuffles up against the wall of the bed, makes herself comfortable. 'I only stopped being angry with my mum about five minutes ago, when Lily taught me a valuable lesson about love and family values. It was like being Elsa and Anna, the sisters in *Frozen*, except without the magic powers or the tragic orphaned backstory.'

Saskia unfolds her arms, looks her mother in the eye for the first time in . . . months? 'So nothing like the sisters in *Frozen*, then,' she deadpans.

'No, nothing like the sisters in *Frozen*,' nods Olivia. 'And you really don't want to hear me singing "Let It Go".'

'Not if it's anything like your Celine Dion renditions in the shower,' scoffs Saskia.

'Fair. Anyway, the point is, it's OK that you hate me right now. It's your human right to hate me right now. I am going to sit with this hatred, and hold it lovingly until it dissipates into something less hostile.'

'You could be sitting there for some time.'

'Such is my lot as your mother. Such is my lot. If I have to sit with it until you're forty-four, that's fine, I will take my parental penance. And you're right, you know.' Olivia tries to cross her legs into some iteration of a yoga pose, finds her hips too stiff for such magic. 'I have been as bad as my mother for some time now. I've been obsessed with making everything perfect and happy and I can see now that, actually, all that does is make everyone miserable and uncomfortable. You're quite right about me being obsessed with pretending that we're a normal family. It's been my life goal. Have a normal family!' Olivia raises her arms at an imaginary sign. 'But what I was trying to do was have a fantasy family that I'd maybe seen in a movie or read about in a book when I was younger. And believe it or not, I was once young. Anyway, I was trying to uphold this ideal of a family that doesn't exist and never has, despite the best efforts of the Fryers to find and perfect it. Well, here I am, a Fryer-Greenwood giving up the ghost and accepting that I already have a perfectly normal family, one that is sometimes happy, sometimes sad, and very often annoyed with each other. One that makes mistakes and gets things wrong, just as I have been doing for the last few years. I've been getting it wrong, and you know what, that's OK. That's part of being human. This is me surrendering to the wrongness which is probably, ironically, the first right thing I've done in a long time.'

'No, the first right thing you did was buy that dress.' Saskia points at the leopard-print mini, now fully ridden up around Olivia's hips, revealing a bobbly pair of 80 denier tights. 'You should wear more fun stuff like that, you look like *you* in it. Better than a boring botoxed Zara zombie.' Saskia shudders. 'Soooo middle-aged.'

'Harsh but fair. Listen, we need to talk about . . .' Olivia takes a deep breath, steadies herself for the task at hand. 'I know that

I've been in my own world lately, but believe it or not, I have been paying some attention to you. I've noticed some things about you, Saskia, that remind me a lot of myself when I was your age.'

Her daughter visibly recoils at the suggestion she might have something in common with Olivia.

'I know it's cringe when parents try and relate to their kids. I know I seem about seven hundred years old and I know you think I can't have possibly had a life outside of being your mum. But I did and . . .' Olivia rubs her eyes momentarily, knows that only wholehearted honesty is going to cut the mustard if she's going to actually connect with her daughter. 'You know at Auntie Lily's party, I mentioned that I was ill when I was seventeen? I had anorexia.' She pauses, allows her daughter to take this in. Allows *herself* to properly take it in, this reality that she has, until recently, tried to gloss over, as if it were an aberration, a bolt from the blue, a grenade she alone bore total responsibility for. 'It was really hard. They wanted me to go to hospital but Mum insisted on keeping me at home which is why I can be so down on her. We didn't really talk about mental health back then. There was a real stiff-upper-lip thing going on, and even though I like to think that I'm really enlightened on the subject I've probably carried a bit of that through with me, which is what all that perfectionism bollocks is about.'

'I thought you said we couldn't swear.'

'Yeah, well, you reminded me that sometimes we need a good swear to get the message through. Anyway, I'm telling you all of this because I want you to know that if you ever felt like you were in trouble with something, if you ever felt like you needed help, you belong to a family who would sit with you through it. Am I making sense?'

'Not really?' Saskia scrunches up her nose, but has at least moved closer to her mother. 'Or at least no more sense than you've ever really made.'

'OK, so I've noticed how much you do about the house, how you help with the tidying and the cleaning and how little I acknowledge all you do. I want to thank you for the way you've been trying to hold things together, but I also want you to know that you don't have to do what you're doing. You don't have t—'

'It's fine, Mum, it's nothing.'

'It's not nothing, Saskia. It's not nothing. You're sixteen. I know what it's like to be sixteen. And I think it would be very understandable if you had some of the same struggles I had, when I was younger. You know, with food, like with the bagels and not ever wanting to eat very much. Maybe that relationship doesn't feel so good for you, in the way it didn't feel that good for me?'

'I'm not anorexic, Mum.' Saskia has closed her eyes, turned her body away from her mother. 'If that's what you're trying to say, then you can relax.'

'But you don't have to be anorexic for me to worry about you, darling. Nobody ever has to wait until it gets that bad to ask for help. You can always get our support with stuff before it gets to that stage.'

'It's just hard, isn't it?' Saskia shrugs. 'TikTok, Snapchat, this expectation that you should be shopping in Sephora from, like, eight years old.'

'Is that a thing?'

'Mum, you know it's a thing. Don't act all shocked when you're all botoxed anyway!'

'OK, OK, that's fair.' Olivia wonders what it would feel like to live in a world where everyone just left their face well enough alone. 'Listen, I need you to know that it doesn't have to be that way. I know I'm not always the best example to you. I've been uptight and controlling and I really shouldn't be injecting things into my face. I'm not going to do that any more, I promise. But I want you to know I love you, and I'm here for you, whatever is going on with you. You don't have to be Little Miss Perfect for me. I mean, you are Little Miss Perfect to me, regardless of your school grades or the way you look or how tidy you are in the house. I want you to be you, Saskia. Not a version of you that you think everyone will love.'

'But it's easier said than done, isn't it?' Saskia stares. 'You're sitting there, forty-four years old, and only just realizing you can wear leopard print. Only just realizing that I might be unhappy. You can't just say these things suddenly, and hope that saying them will magically make them come true for me. I mean, asking me to just be me is a huge pressure in itself, right?' She shakes her head, picks at a nail.

'That's true. I mean, maybe we could go and talk to someone professional about this. Like a therapist?'

'Maybe.' Saskia exhales. 'Maybe I could do with talking to someone who's, like, neutral. But I'm figuring it out, Mum. I think that trying on all these different versions of yourself is the only way to ever work out who you actually are.'

'God, you're smart, Saskia.' Olivia goes to hug her daughter, is surprised when she lets her. And as she sits there silently in this glorious embrace, she knows there is one more version of Olivia Greenwood that she needs to try on. And thanks to her daughter, she's finally brave enough to do it.

31

Olivia Greenwood is changing. Or maybe she's just becoming more herself.

Whatever the case, she seems to have started singing out loud on the train. She's sure of it. It's the only way to explain the ability she has to spread out over an entire table without anyone daring to come near her on the morning commute. She smiles at the people bunched by the doors, who try desperately not to meet her eye. Miserable fucks, she thinks to herself, as the opening bars to 'It's All Coming Back to Me Now' strike up for the sixteenth time this journey.

It's the only song for it, frankly.

Just a few short weeks ago, this was her worst nightmare. Someone hearing her sing, let alone an entire carriage? There are so many things in Olivia Greenwood's life that until recently she hadn't allowed herself to do, like explaining to her husband how to give her an orgasm, and telling her dad to start pulling his fucking weight, and informing her boss that she's not a nodding dog he can do with as he pleases. Why wouldn't she add singing out loud on the train to that list?

As she hums along, she realizes the great mistake she's made her whole life, the thing that has led her to this moment, sitting on the train, singing Celine Dion like a madwoman: her inability to accept that life was full of problems for everyone, not just her. As a child, she had been told again and again that she only ever caused problems, and perhaps, back then, this mistaken belief had helped Olivia to survive. But now, as an adult, it is causing difficulties in its own right. Olivia's dogged conviction that she is always the problem, that she alone must come up with a solution to all of life's issues because life's issues only exist as a result of her existing . . . well, it isn't sane. It isn't normal. It is the opposite of a delusion of grandeur – a delusion of inferiority, if you will – but every bit as sick and wrong. Olivia has genuinely believed that if she wasn't such a tricky human, her parents would have been content. They would have organized birthday parties, and not shouted at her for having appendicitis. Now she not only sees what bullshit this is – but what dangerous bullshit it is. She has gone through life ignoring any truths that didn't match her childish version of reality, brushing them under the carpet and beating herself round the head with the broom when she finds there's no longer any space for them there. It's led her to some sort of breakdown, but as she stares at the backside of Battersea Power Station, she wonders if all breakdowns aren't actually more like breakthroughs.

Now, as she moves her shoulders in time to the sweeping piano keys, she knows what she has to do, in order to make everything better. Or, more pointedly, to stop trying to make everything better. As she hollers out the chorus of Celine's most important work to date, a few commuters jumping in shock at the vocal range and tone of the once mousy girl on the 8.27 to Victoria, Olivia is ready for the challenge ahead of her.

She has to face the music.

Olivia has arranged to meet her mother in the Gail's near the office. Tina had agreed on the condition it was nowhere near any of their usual Sussex haunts – right now, as she comes to terms with the fact that Clive is a sex pest, she cannot bear to be seen in polite society.

The invitation, extended shortly after that heart-to-heart with Saskia, came as a surprise to Olivia, much as it had no doubt been to Tina. But as she found herself typing out the WhatsApp, Olivia knew she couldn't even begin to help Saskia if she didn't try to heal her fractured relationship with her own mother. The conversation with Rose had reminded her, starkly, that not everybody had the opportunity to mend things with their parents. She had spent most of her adult life simmering in silent resentment at her mother for not being there in the way she needed her to be, but now she suspected that her mum had barely had the capacity to be there for herself. She had to tell Tina how she felt. She couldn't believe she was saying this, but she needed to give her mother the chance to prove her wrong.

'I could have driven you here,' announces Tina, when Olivia sits down at a table tucked in the corner of the café.

'I'm OK on the train. Used to it now. Only time I get to myself.'

'Yes, well, I know that feeling.' She pauses, fiddles with a pearl earring. 'I hope that Clive hasn't dared to show his face on the commute. Odious man.'

'No, he hasn't.' Olivia clears her throat, decides not to say anything about the incident on the train, or the message she had received a few days ago from the British Transport Police to inform her that 'after careful consideration of fresh evidence', they had decided to drop the case. 'I'm sorry that he turned out to be like that.'

'Yes, well, let the rubbish take itself out, and all that. I'm guessing you want to interview me about him for *The Morning*?'

'What?' Olivia motions to the waiter who is looking for the recipients of the giant chocolatey cappuccino and skinny latte.

'I assumed that was why you asked me here.' Tina leans

back as their drinks are placed on the table in front of them. 'To get me to give you some sort of exclusive about that tosser Clive.'

'Oh, right.' Olivia shakes her head. 'No, no, that's not why I asked you here. I don't even write articles for *The Morning* any more. I'm their Anniversary Architect.'

'Their what?'

'To be honest, Mum, your guess is as good as mine.' She sips her cappuccino, feels the caffeine light up her frontal lobe. 'But anyway, I haven't asked you here to talk about *The Morning*, or Clive. I asked you here because I feel like . . .' Olivia considers for a moment the possibility of legging it, talks herself out of it. 'I feel like we need to clear the air, Mum.'

'You don't have to do that, darling, I know how stressful it can be looking after your father.'

'Mum, this isn't about Dad. It's about us. Me and you.'

A great silence envelops them, as Olivia feels tears begin to prick at her eyes.

'Well, OK,' Tina eventually says. 'OK. That seems sensible.'

'I had a chat with Saskia the other day. I told her about being unwell when I was her age and how I didn't want that to happen to he—'

'I didn't WANT you to be ill,' Tina interrupts. 'Honestly, Olivia, do you think I wanted you to suffer?'

'No! No, that's not what I was trying to say. I was just talking to her about what it had felt like when I was a child and—'

'The thing about you, Olivia, was that you've always been so independent and headstrong. Even when you were so ill. I always knew you had the strength to pull through. You've never really needed me. You still don't need me, not like Lily does. I'm not having to fund you in your forties, thank goodness.'

'Headstrong and independent, just like you.' Olivia sits back in her chair and tries to make sense of what she has just heard.

'Maybe. Maybe we have more in common than you'd like to admit. You're always going on about how I don't love you, and the truth is that I've always felt like it's you who doesn't love me.'

'*Of course* I love you, Mum.' Olivia can feel both of their hackles rising, and knows she has to defuse the situation if either of them are going to come out of Gail's alive. 'If you'll let me finish, I'll tell you what I was actually going to say. Saskia hasn't been herself and I realized I'd been, how can I put it? Distracted. By my own stuff. And that I need to focus on the kids. She's going to have some therapy, I think it will really help. And I thought that in the spirit of getting healthier and happier, me and you could do with having a proper chat, alone, not in the loos of a restaurant during a massive family get-together.'

'I had therapy, you know.' Tina raises her mug to her lips, blows on it, then puts it back down on the table without taking a sip. 'That's why I finally had the courage to divorce your father. It was the prompt I needed after decades of enabling him, hoping that he would just get better and stop . . . stop drinking. But you can't make someone stop drinking, Olivia. They have to want to do it themselves. And I had to start focusing on myself.'

'You were always working, always busy, always chasing something else bigger and brighter than what you had.' The petulance falls out of her mouth before she's able to catch it.

'Olivia, do you really believe what you're saying? Do you really think, after going through the juggle of work and parenthood yourself, and seeing what a drunk your father is, that's what was happening?'

'I . . .' Olivia feels shame bubble inside her. 'I always felt wrong around you.'

'You were probably just picking up on how wrong I felt, but that had nothing to do with you. I was trying to be a parent and a successful businesswoman and a wife to a man I was in denial about being an alcoholic. But you weren't wrong.'

'I was, though. I was always so sensitive, so . . . I had an eating disorder, Mum. How can you say I wasn't wrong?'

'If anyone was in the wrong, I was. I'll admit, happily, that I made a whole load of mistakes when you were kids. I freaked out when I realized I'd given birth to this deeply sensitive child, because I was terrified that you'd turn out like me, like my parents. I couldn't see that your sensitivity, your empathy, that actually it was a gift, Olivia. A glorious gift. I just couldn't bear the thought of you feeling what I did. I couldn't handle it. I didn't know *how* to handle it.' She raises her hands in the air. 'Nobody ever taught me. Certainly not my mum and dad. I've told you what they were like. I suppose my way of surviving that was to try and become super-controlled. I handled your anorexia badly in part because there was no guidebook on it, but mostly because I was so caught up in how badly I had failed you as a parent. I'd tried so hard not to be like my mum and dad and I'd clearly made a mess of it. I can see now how my need to control everything had really bad effects on you. I can see how my pushing everything down was a terrible way of dealing with things because they always have to come up somewhere. But there weren't any self-help guides to explain that to me back then, and I wouldn't have had any time to read them even if there had been. Your anorexia was awful, awful. I thought I'd been terrified when you had to have your appendix out, but that was nothing. Nothing. It was like a physical pain.'

'But you didn't let me go to hospital.' Olivia clings to her cappuccino, in an attempt to stop her hands from doing their old, nervous jig . . . an impulse she suddenly realizes that she hasn't felt for some time now.

'Because it was an awful place, Olivia, not because I didn't care. I'd done my research on it, seen all these reports of teenagers who had absconded or, even worse, killed themselves on the premises. It felt safer to keep you at home. Again, I don't know if that was the right decision but it was the one I made and I can't go back now, even though I've tried to, believe me. Repeatedly, with my therapist.'

'I don't understand,' says Olivia. 'You make out that you've always cared but the last few years you've been so cold. So lacking in affection.'

'Because you've been so busy, Olivia. You have such a full life. I thought you didn't need me, that you of all people would understand that I needed to go inwards.'

'But you never once sat down and tried to explain to me what was going on with you and Dad. You could have done that, you know.'

'Maybe I could have done.' Tina finally takes a sip of her coffee. 'But when you get older you don't want to burden your children with your baggage. If you've done parenting even vaguely right, they're off living their own lives, and that's exactly as it should be. I didn't want to add to your already bursting in-tray.'

'Inbox, Mum.'

'Well, in our day it was an in-tray. Anyway, it had always been tough with your dad, but when I retired, or rather was put out to pasture, kicked out of the job I'd dedicated so much of my life to, as so often happens to women of my generation, well, it very quickly became unbearable. I couldn't watch this man I loved destroy himself in the same way my parents did. He never left the house, he'd not get up until mid-afternoon, then he'd immediately start drinking until he passed out on the sofa twelve hours later. It grinds on you. I didn't want to divorce him any more than I wanted you to be ill, but when someone has a problem and they ignore it there eventually comes a point where enough is enough. You can't tell when it's going to come but it always comes, believe me.'

'You had your own Erling Haaland moment,' says Olivia quietly.

'A whatty-whatty?'

'Oh, it's just . . . It's nothing, Mum. Carry on, I'm listening.'

'I had to put boundaries down with your father. And with you, even. I know you don't approve of how I've gone about things, but I had to stay steady. You had your own journey to go on, clearly. So I just had to carry on and focus on making the most out of my life, starting afresh, and hope that one day you might come round and let me back in. I'm sorry, Olivia, I really am.' She pauses, as Olivia nods her head. She is receiving an apology from her mother, and she needs time to let it sink in, to allow the words to really get into her bloodstream, where Olivia suspects they will have as magical an effect on her as Rose's gummy.

'But enough about me,' Tina continues. 'You were talking about getting therapy for Saskia. Is she OK, darling?'

'She's . . . she's OK, but it's tough being a teenager now, isn't it? Sometimes we all need a bit of extra support. And it was while I was talking to her that I thought we needed to have a proper chat too. Because I've sort of shut you out. Well, not sort of, I absolutely have shut you out. And I so love having Lily around. Even Dad can be OK when he's not drunk. He likes being with the kids and he's genuinely interested in what they are up to. I think he's even starting to realize how much he's messed things up. But yeah, all of that was making me think it would be good if we could, you know.' Olivia feels her fingers drumming nervously against the mug, begins clicking them to shift the energy around. 'Well, if we could spend more time together.'

'I would like that,' Tina says, putting her hand over her daughter's. Olivia feels the nervous energy in her fingers dissipate. 'You know I'm not getting back with your father, though? He needs some proper help, but you won't have any luck if you're hoping to get him out of your house and back into mine, I'm afraid.'

'Well, speaking of Dad . . . he can't continue living in our shed. He's hardly going to get well living out there with no prospect of any future ahead of him. I'm not suggesting you take him back, but given you're rattling around in that massive house . . .' She looks anxiously at her mother, finds the courage to carry on anyway. 'Maybe you could sell it, downsize? And then Dad will have some money to get his own place. We might even be able to convince him to go to rehab if we're lucky. I just can't juggle it all, Mum. It's a lot.'

'I know it is, darling.' Tina reaches across the table with her other hand, and squeezes both of Olivia's in it. 'I know it is. I'll think about the house. Maybe it's time for everyone to move on.'

To the barista, to the other coffee-drinkers, it's a simple moment, an everyday one between a mother and a daughter who happen to be passing through on their way to somewhere – something – more interesting. But to Tina and Olivia, it is a destination in itself.

32

Buoyed by getting her mother to even consider the possibility of selling up, Olivia has never felt more galvanized. For the first time, possibly ever, she is trying to be the person *she* wants to be, rather than the person everyone else wants her to be. Over the next few weeks, she sets about trying to make things right for her, Nick and the kids, rather than for anyone else. She is enthused with an energy that not even four large cappuccinos a day could give her, the energy that comes from waking up each morning and Living In Her Truth (™). She knows she has to be realistic as she does this – she can't just jack in her job, still has to plan the fucking party for Stephen because, for now, the stability of her home life is more important than seeing him get his comeuppance – but she isn't going to spend her days teetering in a terrified manner over the vast chasm that often exists between her beliefs, wants and needs, and other people's expectations of her.

So as she plans the party with Deepti, she also takes the time to mentor her, to tell her all the things she wishes someone had told her back when she was just starting out – about how to write the perfect intro, follow up a lead, and interview someone in a way that doesn't immediately make them clam up.

Olivia's even managed to get Deepti on to the Tory Pervert Project (as it's now being referred to in the office). She *may* have asked Lily to do some sneaky digging around the swanky Sussex set whose chakras she tended to, which meant Olivia was able to pass on to Deepti a few golden exclusives: namely that Clive used his tongue while saying goodbye to a woman at a charity bingo event; he was caught watching porn on his phone while he was supposed to be judging the best in show at a local village fete; and finally, that he had an affair with his secretary Barbara.

Let the rubbish take itself out, indeed.

Stephen even approached Olivia's new mentee to congratulate her on her scoops. 'Well done, Dippy,' he brayed, as she and Olivia sat in a breakout area working through last-minute party plans.

'My name's not Dippy,' said the young woman, before Olivia had had a chance to correct him. 'It's Deepti. D-E-E-P-T-I, just so we're clear.'

How proud Olivia had felt in that moment.

She is in constant contact with Rose too. Her mum has always said that there's no such thing as a coincidence, and as she and Rose WhatsApp back and forth, Olivia truly believes that it was the universe that brought them together, some sort of fate that intervened to make sure that Rose stood next to her at the bar, as opposed to some other feckless *Morning* staffer. What if they hadn't encountered one another that night? Would Olivia ever have admitted to herself, let alone anyone else, what happened with Stephen? This surprising new alliance has brought an unexpected happiness into her heart.

Best of all, Olivia has found a therapist for Saskia . . . and one for herself. She is proud of the way she has handled this: in an entirely calm and collected manner, letting Saskia know that even though shit sometimes happens, it's how you deal with it that counts. Her daughter still guards her keto bagels closely, and Olivia knows from her own experience that there is a long way to go on this one, but thank fuck they're beginning the journey now, at sixteen, instead of leaving it until Saskia is middle-aged, and forced to have a drug-induced breakdown of her own. And although that breakdown was potentially the best thing to happen to Olivia, she's going to need some help working through the fact that she'd essentially turned into her mother.

Olivia isn't living a half-life any more, and she's going to make damned sure her kids don't either.

At Gail's, Olivia orders her usual. This has become her routine – a symbolic moment, when she starts the day meeting her own needs before stepping into the office and immediately trying to meet everyone else's.

'Do you want chocolate sprinkles on the cappuccino?' parrots the boy at the till, politely, clearly new.

'As if you should even need to ask,' smiles Olivia. 'If possible, can you make it eight per cent cappuccino, ninety-two per cent chocolate sprinkles? That's just a joke,' she explains, when she sees the crestfallen look spread across the boy's face.

'I'll get this,' says a familiar voice from behind Olivia's shoulder. She turns and sees Nina, standing with a slouch. Her eyes are bloodshot, her mascara gone. 'I'll have the same as her,' Nina pouts. 'Cinnamon bun, cappuccino with extra chocolate.'

'Ninety-two per cent chocolate, eight per cent cappuccino, coming right up,' nods the boy.

Olivia steps back as Nina reaches forward to pay.

'How very kind of you,' says Olivia, in a sing-song voice.

'Uh-oh, is the old Olivia back?' Nina slaps her card down on the machine.

'The old Olivia wouldn't be here at all,' shrugs Olivia, taking her cinnamon bun from the boy and moving to the end of the counter, next to the belching coffee machine. 'The old Olivia would be at her desk, dutifully snacking on some seaweed while apologizing for existing. Good riddance to her. Anyway, what brings you to these parts? Now you're a hotshot columnist, you don't have to go out and get your own coffee.'

'What happened to turn you into such a truth-teller?' Nina says, through a mouthful of sugary bun.

'Let's say I woke up and smelt the coffee.' Olivia nods.

They are quiet for a moment as Nina chews her food.

'Well, whatever happened,' she says, coming up for breath, 'I have to admit that it's an improvement on the simpering suck-up you used to be. Your desperation to fit in used to make me and Joe cringe.' Nina wipes the flakes from her chin. 'In the spirit of honesty and all that. Though I grant you, he finds it hard to be genuinely nice to anybody.'

'Well, in the spirit of honesty, I think it used to make me cringe. It's hard work being ingratiatingly pleasant to people as they stab you in the back.'

The barista begins sprinkling chocolate on their cappuccinos. 'More please,' says Olivia, smiling. 'So much that it extinguishes the froth entirely, preferably.'

'I don't blame you for letting rip.' Nina swipes her cappuccino before the barista has the chance to turn it into a chocolate milkshake. 'They're a bunch of psychopaths. I hate them all.' Her pretty face crumples and she begins to cry.

'Do you want to sit down?'

'I thought you'd never ask.'

They take refuge tucked away in a corner of the café. 'Stephen completely humiliated me,' weeps Nina, shredding her pastry. 'Said that he couldn't bring himself to ask me to write a searing polemic about the Tory sex scandal because, and I quote, my last couple of columns have been about as insightful as the toilet paper he wipes his arse on.'

'Nina! That's awful, no wonder you're upset.'

'And then Andrew came in and said that he could print his toilet paper instead of a column by me, and it would probably get better engagement. And then Stephen said that maybe he should give my column to a proper truth-teller, and that maybe he should have promoted the mentor not the mentee.'

Nina brings her hands to her face to try to cover the shame of it showing on her cheeks, dusting herself in flakes of sugary pastry in the process.

'The thing is, Nina, I wouldn't want your column.' Olivia realizes as she says this that she really, truly means it. 'I know I've turned into a bolshie so-and-so, but there would still be a part of me that would shrivel up and die if I had to come up with an outspoken opinion each week, especially one that was needlessly mean to someone, as about ninety-nine per cent of newspaper columns are. Honestly, I couldn't deal with the stress. And anyway, you're really bloody good at what you do. Every piece you've written has been on point. Don't listen to that prick Stephen, and for god's sake, don't take it personally. You know he enjoys behaving like this? Like, he actually gets off on all the discomfort he causes in a room, all the unease that everyone is desperately, fearfully trying to suppress . . . it actually gives him joy.' She takes some of her bun, starts chewing and speaking as Nina begins to dust pastry from her cheek. 'He derives pleasure from the pain around him. Without it, he is nothing. Without it, his power vanishes. He's like me before I had my epiphany, Nina. He's entirely reliant on the people in the room to validate his existence. He would collapse into a pitiful husk without them. But at least I used to get my validation being nice to people. He just does it by being a nasty old cunt.'

An elderly woman enjoying a honey cake at the next table turns and gasps.

Olivia carries on regardless. 'He's basically like this boy who used to bully my son. He's the horrible football kid at school, forty years down the line, his Shmooshie snatched away and replaced with a news organization. I'd laugh, were it not for the fact that this kind of psychopathy basically runs the Western world, and is responsible for all of its ills.'

'His Shmooshie?' Nina sits up.

'Like his comfort blanket.' Olivia waves her hands to signal that it's not important. 'Anyway, here's the crucial part, Nina. And it's that it wouldn't be good karma for me to take your column, however satisfying it might feel, because I really, really wanted it a few weeks ago. I dreamed about it, for years! And I was totally deluded enough to believe it when Stephen manipulated me into thinking it might be mine. I was even secretly furious with you for getting it. I felt as if you'd taken it to spite me, or to prove some point about how crap my advice had been, when in actual fact, you'd taken it because you're a human being with hopes and dreams too!'

'Your advice wasn't that bad.'

'It was terrible, Nina. Terrible. I basically told you to make yourself tiny and small so as not to take up space that was meant for the big boys. Thank fuck you didn't listen to a word of it. Thank fuck you trusted yourself. I need to thank you for showing me how to put on my bloody big-girl pants.'

'No, it's me who needs to thank you, Olivia. You've been my rock these last few weeks. I don't think I would have lasted five minutes in this job if it wasn't for your support and advice and kindness.'

Olivia takes a sip of her cappuccino. She's vaguely aware that there is chocolatey froth on her nose, but finds she doesn't care, given that Nina's face is covered in sugar. Instead, she scrunches it up in a look of extreme distaste.

'Don't do that.' Olivia shakes her head. 'Do not go into fawn mode on me, not right now, Nina. We are not going to be overly grateful when someone treats us with the respect we deserve. OK?'

Nina nods. Olivia wipes the froth from her nose and licks her finger.

'Good. Stay bitchy. Stay in fight mode. We're all about to need it.'

She tilts her cup against Nina's in a toast and they stand up to leave together. She is about to start the battle of her life.

33

The suite at the Savoy feels exactly as decadent as a suite at the Savoy should. Olivia booked it especially, careful to siphon off the budget as 'entertainment' should anyone in Finance be looking too closely at the receipts. And if they do have a problem with it . . . well, Olivia is pretty sure that by the end of the night, *The Morning*'s executive team is going to be concerned with far more pressing issues than the two-bedroom suite Olivia has booked for her, Nina and Deepti to get ready in.

And Rose. Did she forget to mention Rose?

'I'm pretty impressed with your gall, Greenwood.' Rose looks around the giant living room, with its commanding views of the Thames. 'Who would have thought that the woman I went on the lash with not that long ago would be capable of this?'

'Yeah, well I had some help,' smiles Olivia, admiring herself in a long, elegant stand-alone mirror. She is wearing a floor-length ruby-red dress she purchased from Net-a-Porter with the company credit card. She doesn't allow herself to feel too guilty about this little purchase. It's all for the greater good of the institution, after all. 'Although I'm not going to lie and pretend that I'm not fucking terrified about what tonight holds.'

'All the most important things in life are terrifying,' says Rose, rummaging in her pockets. 'And bringing Stephen down will make all the anxiety worth it. I've got a few Erling Haalands if you need to take the edge off proceedings?' Rose produces a bag of gummies from the pocket of her bright blue suit.

'Absolutely not,' laughs Olivia. 'I want to remember every last bit of the evening. I want to savour it.'

'So, are we going to do this?' asks Nina, who appears from one of the bathrooms wearing a gold-sequinned minidress.

'I'm ready,' says Deepti, stepping out from a bedroom in an emerald-green gown.

'Come here.' Olivia beckons them all over to where she stands in front of the mirror. They assemble next to their leader, a shimmering collection of different women with their own strengths, flaws, talents, beauty, all united by the act of bravery that awaits them.

'Now, let's go and show those fuckers who's boss,' says Olivia, linking arms with her two colleagues. 'See you in a bit, Rose.'

'Have fun being fearless, fabulous journalists.' Rose waves them off, proudly, into the dark adventure of the night.

There is a nervous silence on the taxi ride to Oceanic House. Or maybe it's simply the quiet before the storm, a much-needed moment to gather themselves. Whatever it is, it is broken by the ringing of Olivia's phone, the dulcet tones of Celine Dion's 'Think Twice' bouncing round the car.

'Nice,' smiles Nina.

'She's my favourite,' says Olivia, uninhibited, as she answers the video call from Nick.

'Hi, babe,' he says, smiling from one of the sofas. 'We just wanted to call and wish you luck.'

'GOOD LUCK, MUM!' shouts Jack, throwing himself into the view of Nick's camera.

'Yeah, go smash it for us,' urges Saskia, pushing her head into shot. 'Also, nice dress. Can I have it when you die?'

'I'll leave instructions in my will that you should wear it to my funeral.'

'OK, kids, go and do your homework.' Nick gets up from the sofa, moves through to the kitchen. 'You OK?'

'You mean apart from the fact that I'm about to blow up my career of almost a quarter of a century? I'm fine!'

'You know that whatever happens, we'll figure it out. You let me figure out my midlife crisis, and now it's your turn to work out what makes you happy. Speaking of which, I thought I'd let you know that I've booked us a dirty weekend in an actual five-star hotel next weekend.'

Nina and Deepti try not to laugh.

'Nick, I'm with my colleagues! But cool. Can we afford it?'

'I'm seeing it as an investment. The more attention we give our marriage, the better it gets. Oh, speaking of which, your dad has gone to a meeting tonight.' He mouths 'AA' just in case this is too much truth for Nina and Deepti. 'He's promised to take the kids to school again tomorrow morning, so you can get out on another run.'

A week ago, Olivia started Couch to 5K. She wants to graduate to the local Parkrun, once she's got back into the habit of running regularly. It's a small thing, a pretty mundane thing, the type that millions of people up and down the country do each and every day. But to Olivia, these moments outside, huffing and puffing around Victoria Park in the early hours of the morning with nothing but her own thoughts for company . . . It feels like magic, to be having this time to herself that is only about her. What's even more revelatory is that for the first time in her life, she's running for the way it makes her feel, not the way it makes her look. She's running for the gains, not the losses – she wants to make her world bigger, not her waist smaller. And out there on those runs, she's had the time to appreciate how much has changed between her and Nick; how their relationship feels better than it's ever been simply because, all those weeks ago, she took a blue gummy that gave her the courage to send him a text asking him to do more with his tongue.

'Will wonders never cease?' She feels herself snap out of her reverie as the taxi draws to a halt and pulls up outside the venue. 'I better go now. Love you!'

'Love you too. You look beautiful, Olivia. Go give 'em hell, babe.'

She blows him a kiss and ends the call, zips her phone safely in her matching red clutch bag, feels a sick excitement as she steps out of the car.

Oceanic House is looking almost as fabulous as Olivia, Nina and Deepti. It should be, given that the Anniversary Architect and her team have, on the say-so of their boss Stephen, spent a lot of money creating the kind of party that will have him go down in legend. The entrance to the building has been fitted with a blue carpet, the same cerulean tone as *The Morning*'s logo, while fantastical sculptures made from turquoise balloons frame all the doorways. Searchlights scan the building, while men dressed in naval uniform line the halls, guiding guests in the right direction to the lifts that will take them directly to the penthouse apartment hosting the party. Olivia sends Deepti and Nina up but remains at the entrance to greet Stephen. She doesn't want to miss a moment of his arrival.

Deepti has done a stellar job in gathering the great and the good of British society to witness *The Morning*'s big night. There are politicians, there are cabinet ministers, and there is even a rumour that the prime minister will try and make an appearance at some point during the evening. Stars of stage and screen sweep down the blue carpet, posing for *The Morning*'s photographers. Olivia spots a string quartet playing to people as they arrive and thinks to herself, 'What a nice touch.' But she won't be able to start enjoying herself until Stephen is actually here.

Like all the most awful megalomaniacs, he arrives only when he is sure that everyone else has got there first. There will be no greeting guests on arrival for Stephen, no lowering himself to the level of someone who has to stand and wait around for other people. Joanna, his PA, scurries behind him, the nervous energy coming off her in waves which Olivia does her best to shield herself from. She cannot afford to falter now. Not when she has come this far, and she is so close to finally, really making a difference.

'Liv!' Stephen comes at her with his arms open, his suit and shirt perfectly starched. 'I know it's not the done thing to compliment a woman any more, but if I may be so bold, you are looking rather fabulous this evening.'

Olivia projects a rictus grin on to her face, reminds herself that she won't have to keep up appearances for much longer. 'That's very kind of you, Stephen,' she says, curtsying for effect. 'I can't wait for you to see what we've put together upstairs. Can I escort you up?' She smiles, tries not to flinch as he slips his arm through hers.

'I love the uniforms, Liv,' Stephen says, noticing the staff dressed up in early-twentieth-century attire. 'Is there some sort of sailing theme going on? Oceanic House? Men who look like they're on the deck of the *Titanic* . . .' He guffaws, his pomposity erupting from his hideous, twisted gob.

'Well, funny you should mention the *Titanic*,' says Olivia, carefully guiding him into a lift. 'Turns out that Oceanic House was originally the London headquarters of the White Star Line.

It was from this very building that the company sold people tickets for the *Titanic*.'

The lift door closes on the two of them.

'Gosh, how fascinating.' Stephen looks up at the bright lights of the floor display. 'Well, let's hope, for your sake, Liv, that this party has a better ending than the *Titanic* did.' He pauses, waits for her to protest.

'Oh, I'm certain that it will.' She continues to smile tightly.

'Also, I'm glad you've finally come round to the idea of me calling you by a pet name.' Another guffaw, another moment to remind herself that, soon, this will all be done. 'Next week, we need a proper chat about you taking over from—' The door pings open as they reach their floor. 'Nina!'

She stands there, welcoming Stephen with a glass of fresh champagne and a smile as fake as her new hair extensions (also paid for on the company credit card). 'Everyone's waiting for you, boss,' she purrs.

Olivia declines any champagne. It's not just that she wants to be fully present for what is about to happen. It's that she realizes, with a start, that she doesn't need it. She can do this, all by herself. Booze has always been her go-to for Dutch courage, but in the last few weeks, she has learned how to be genuinely brave.

Smugness rolls off Stephen in waves, his whole demeanour projecting the attitude of a person who believes he has everything – and everyone – in his control. They step out of the lift and into the packed party, Olivia guiding Stephen past MPs eager to chat and women in more White Star Line uniforms bearing trays full of canapés and drinks. 'So I hope you don't mind, but I asked the organizers to create a sort of stage area,' Olivia says, motioning to a purpose-built platform at the back of the grand room, complete with a lectern, microphone and large screen behind it. 'It's the perfect position for your speech, and after that I've got a little surprise for you. A special video we've made to honour you.'

Olivia watches as the most satisfied of smiles spreads across Stephen's face. He is delighted. 'Well, if you insist, Liv.'

'I do, I do,' she says, scanning the crowd near the platform for Rose's bright blue suit so she can motion to her secret sidekick that they're ready.

'Do you think I should freshen up first?' he asks, putting a hand through his oily dark hair. 'Don't want to disappoint my public.'

'I think you look perfect, Stephen,' Olivia lies. 'No time like the present, I'd say. You don't want everyone too drunk to appreciate what you have to say.'

'You're right,' he nods, his hand on the small of her back sending ripples of revulsion through her. 'What would I do without you, hmm? I always knew you were the woman for the job.'

Olivia bites her tongue.

As Stephen walks towards the stage, Olivia feels a tap on her shoulder. She spins to see Deepti standing alongside a tall man in a suit.

'Surprise!' Deepti says. 'I thought you'd like to meet the guest of honour!'

'Oh, wow,' says Olivia, staring at Erling Haaland. 'My son is not going to believe I met you!'

The young footballer shakes her hand, just as Stephen reaches the stage and starts tapping the microphone vigorously.

'Is this thing on?' He laughs hollowly, surveying the room.

'Hi, everyone. If I could just have your attention for a few moments.' He pauses as the guests turn to the stage. Behind Stephen the screen flickers to life, the bright blue logo of *The Morning* casting a light on his starched suit. 'So, as the editor of this esteemed organ, I just wanted to say a few words to thank you all for coming tonight to celebrate our hundredth birthday. I know, I know, we look much younger than that!' He pauses again, as a smattering of polite laughter bubbles up from the crowd. Olivia smiles at the Norwegian Goliath standing next to her, who gives her an awkward shrug in return. 'So yes, I know you're all here to have fun, but I just wanted to take a moment to do a bit of serious reflection, about the important work this news organization has carried out in the one hundred years it has been going. I've only been editor for a relatively short portion of those hundred years, of course, but it's an absolute honour to take it into the next one hundred. Especially with a story as important as the one we recently broke, about the sexual predators existing in plain sight in the Tory party.'

He pauses once more as people in the crowd murmur their approval.

'My promise to you tonight is that I will continue to uphold those values, and *The Morning* will continue to be a paper of integrity, whatever the next one hundred years hold. So if you will join me in raising a glass . . . to *The Morning*!'

'*The Morning*,' repeat the crowd, with all the enthusiasm of a group of people who have come to sample the free champagne, rather than be lectured by a smug middle-aged man.

Stephen turns to look at the screen behind him just as the masthead of *The Morning* flickers, switching to a static image of Olivia, sitting at the grand oak table in his office. Stephen lets out a small laugh and leans into the microphone. 'I believe that we are now going to watch a little video that my dear colleagues have made to mark this momentous occasion.'

In the back of the room, Rose clicks a button, and the static image of Olivia begins to move.

34

They had made the video when Stephen was away in the Maldives with his family, a couple of weeks before the party. It was one of the many lavish holidays that Rose, and Stop the Press, had discovered were claimed improperly as expenses, not to mention the designer clothes he had bought for his wife or the fizzy-water tap that had been installed in his home, put down as 'entertainment'. These discoveries gave them the hard evidence, and the confidence, to take Stephen out with a bang. They could have simply reported him to the chief executive and the other powers that be, but Stephen had told Olivia to make the party a night that nobody would forget, after all.

And it wasn't the only evidence of impropriety that Rose had gathered about Stephen. In the last couple of weeks, STP had spoken to numerous women who had, like Olivia, found themselves on the wrong end of his advances: young reporters and PRs and up-and-coming starlets who had been too scared to say anything lest he turn the might of *The Morning* against them. But there was strength in numbers, and many of them had agreed to take part in this video, to tell their stories.

Right at this moment, their voices were being projected loud and clear into the ears of the hundreds of guests in the room, all of the women's faces, except for Olivia's, blurred for anonymity. Rose had stayed up late to edit the video for maximum impact, and was uploading it to social media at the same time.

The room is silent but for the women's voices – even Stephen is horror-struck, staring at the screen like he truly can't believe what's happening. The final words are Olivia's.

'If journalism is all about reporting the truth, and holding power to account, then *The Morning* has failed, at least for the time that Stephen has been editor. Thanks to the vital testimony gathered in this video by Stop the Press, we can ensure that the next generation of journalists at this organization are able to work frankly, fearlessly, and most of all, with complete freedom.'

As the video ends, Rose steps on to the stage and approaches Stephen from behind, a pot of bright pink paint swinging in her wake. Several things happen at once, and Olivia is glad, later, that there are enough people in the room to capture it from every angle on their smartphones.

He turns just before Rose empties the contents over his head.

'You bitch!' he snarls. He swings for her, almost knocking her on to the floor, as a load of horrified guests rush the stage to pull him off. Joe and Erling Haaland form an unlikely pincer movement, the footballer grabbing Stephen around the neck, covering himself in pink paint, as Joe throws himself in front of Rose. The crowd are whooping and cheering at the show they didn't expect but are very much enjoying.

Rose nonchalantly dusts down her bright blue trousers while tutting at the pathetic specimen in front of her. A group of security guards have clambered on to the stage, pinning Stephen to the floor as he tries to wipe the neon paint from his eyes. One of them checks on Rose in a very serious, officious manner – but, given he's an undercover STP reporter, Olivia's not worried.

Now is her moment.

'You all right there, boss?' she says, walking up to the stage, and standing over the sprawled figure on the floor.

'Olivia!' he rages.

'Good of you to finally call me by my actual name, you ocean-going arsehole.'

Stephen starts to scramble towards her, but is held back by the security guard.

'You're fired, Liv!' Stephen spits at her.

Olivia throws her head back laughing. 'Good. I reckon the same goes for you too.'

She watches as a group of security guards drag her bright pink tormentor towards the fire exit. She knows that they won't want to cover the lifts or the lobby in paint, but thinks it's a shame that he won't be dragged out along the blue carpet, in front of all the waiting photographers. As he flails around, she realizes she is shivering. Shaking, but strong, simultaneously. She's expelled the toxin that was poisoning her life, and as she sees him carried off, she understands that her body is thanking her for it.

It's then that Olivia feels her son's favourite football player pat her on the arm. 'What an absolute prick that man is,' says Haaland, with all the powerful, brilliant simplicity of a striker directing the ball into the back of the net. There is pink paint in his white hair, but it only improves him. 'How brave of you. If there's anything I can ever do to help, please let me know.'

'Well, actually,' says Olivia Greenwood, as frank, fearless and fabulous as ever, 'there is just one little thing . . .'

Epilogue

Olivia Greenwood is looking at the sky. It's been threatening to rain all day, the weather on this late-autumn afternoon in Manchester typically northern, and Olivia thinks it would be a shame if the clouds were to open on to the twenty-two young men running around the pitch in front of them. Not that Olivia has to worry, sheltered in the comfort of the directors' box at the Etihad stadium. She's just finished a two-course champagne lunch, and later, at half-time, there will be dessert.

Saskia can't believe the heated seats, the royal-blue blankets that they have been given to put over their legs should the temperature feel too cool. Jack is still banging on about the butter, embossed with the emblem of Manchester City, while Nick is merely impressed by the fact that Noel Gallagher is sitting two rows behind them, not in front. Tina doesn't much care for football, but she supposes that if she has to go to a game, it might as well be here in a directors' box, where she has every chance of meeting a handsome young man. It's just a shame that, currently, the man sitting next to her is her ex-husband, who is neither handsome nor young. She comforts herself with the fact that he is at least sober.

Olivia negotiated a six-figure pay-off from *The Morning*. She says 'negotiated'; it was offered willingly to her by the paper's mortified HR executives, keen to do whatever she wanted in order to make the whole thing go away. Olivia was almost disappointed by the speed at which they capitulated to her demands and met her needs. She had hoped for a bit of a fight, another chance to show them her grit. But Clare, her lawyer, had been realistic about what taking them to court would entail, and Olivia couldn't face having any more of her precious time and energy wasted. She'd done what she needed to: found her voice, helped other women find theirs, and then held Stephen to account.

Nina has left *The Morning* too, moving to edit a glossy magazine with offices on Bond Street. Deepti has been made a permanent research assistant on the news desk, and even got a byline recently. The last Olivia heard, Stephen was the subject of a widespread internal investigation at *The Morning*, sacked and unemployable, and his wife had walked out and taken what was left of his assets in the process.

Olivia looks out over the stadium and thinks life is good. She still stays in touch with Rose. They meet for coffee from time to time, and the younger woman updates Olivia on the ins and outs of the newspaper industry, all the big projects they are working on at Stop the Press. Olivia is barely interested in journalism any more, planning to spend the next year footloose and fancy-free, focusing on her family and herself. She's signed up to a local choir, having begged for a place when she discovered they were currently working on a medley of Celine Dion's greatest hits. She just needs a bit of time to work out what it is she wants to do with her life, as opposed to what she thinks she should do. The package Clare secured for her has made that possible, and she and Nick can just about make ends meet for a while. She looks over at him, and he's already looking at her, beaming.

Erling Haaland is running down the centre of the pitch below her, the ball at his mercy, the defenders from Manchester United powerless in his wake. He skips by them and boots the ball past the goalkeeper's head and into the back of the net.

As everyone around her jumps for joy, Olivia looks up at the blue sky, at the white wisps scudding across the face of the sun, and her vision.

She feels a warmth rise inside her. She lets the clouds be.

Acknowledgements

People Pleaser is a work of fiction, but like most works of fiction it is undeniably based on elements of my own personality. So in the spirit of someone who is terrified of upsetting people, I present to you a list of all the wonderful humans who helped make this book possible.

First, step forward Harriet Bourton, editor-extraordinaire and remarkable human. I knew the moment we met that you were the woman I wanted to spend the rest of my writing life with, and this experience has made me feel like the luckiest author alive. Thank you for your notes, your patience, your encouragement . . . you probably don't know it, but you're the chief of the Women Rising project that has taken place in my head these last two years.

To my agent, Nelle Andrew, for being my book mum, even though you're way younger than me. You've taught me everything I know about boundaries and believing in myself.

To my actual mum, for showing me the power of words (and mascara).

To everyone at Viking for making this such a ride: Rosey Battle, Natalie Wall, Sarah-Jane Forder, Rose Poole, Kayla Fuller, Juliet Dudley, Chloe Davies. How lucky am I to work with the best girl gang on the block?

To Becca Barr and Katie Unger: thank you for keeping me sane.

Barbara, for bashing most of the people pleasing out of me.

To Celia Duncan, Catherine Hardy and Olivia Dean: thank you for making my world of journalism nothing like Olivia's at *The Morning*! It's an absolute joy to work with you.

ACKNOWLEDGEMENTS

To Emma Reed Turrell for her brilliant book *Please Yourself*, which helped me get (even) more into the mind of a chronic people pleaser.

Kate Bull, Ruth Jones, Tara Dodson, Danielle Crombie, Camilla Davis, Polly Wilson, Sam Jones, Beth Holmes, for your help and support through everything.

Kit de Waal, for your brilliant advice on first drafts. Diana Evans, Amelia Warner, Deborah Joseph, Claire Shanahan and Annabelle Wright for letting me be part of the best book club there ever was while I wrote this novel. So much glorious inspiration.

Arsenal, just in case anyone mistakenly thought I support Man City.

Dad, Naomi, Rufus, Allie . . . see you at 7 p.m. on FaceTime.

Harry and Edie, for always cleaning up and letting me wear your Crocs.

Lastly, to my darling Laura Cole. For bringing Alex into our lives. And for showing me what it is to be brave and extraordinary. I love you more than you can ever know.